ROLL FOR INITIATIVE

ROLL FOR INITIATIVE

JAIME FORMATO

RP|KIDS

PHILADELPHIA

Running Press Kids
Hachette Book Group
1290 Avenue of the Americas, New York, NY 10104
www.runningpress.com/rpkids | @RP_Kids

Printed in the United States of America

First Edition: September 2022

Published by Running Press Kids, an imprint of Perseus Books, LLC,
a subsidiary of Hachette Book Group, Inc. The Running Press Kids name
and logo are trademarks of the Hachette Book Group.

The Hachette Speakers Bureau provides a wide range of authors for speaking events.
To find out more, go to www.hachettespeakersbureau.com or call (866) 376-6591.

The publisher is not responsible for websites (or their content)
that are not owned by the publisher.

Print book cover and interior design by
Marissa Raybuck.

Library of Congress Cataloging-in-Publication Data has been applied for.

ISBNs: 978-0-7624-8106-4 (hardcover), 978-0-7624-8108-8 (ebook)

LSC-C

Printing 1, 2022

**FOR MOONDUST, QUADE,
LUFNAR, WILSON, AND FAFNIR**

CHAPTER 1

I AM NEVER GOING TO MAKE IT HOME.

Nope. Instead, I'll be here, cowering at the back of this overcrowded bus ramp, squeaking nervous inquiries and fluttering my arms like a lost baby penguin, until there's no one left to ignore me. The sun will go down, and I will drop to the sidewalk in exhaustion and pass the lonely night on a bed of cement and dirt-hardened gum chunks.

Mom won't even notice my empty room. She'll creep in late from work, careful not to wake me as she scuttles past my door in the darkness, then sleep like the snoring dead until morning.

Devin most certainly will not notice my absence, as he is 2,500 miles away, living it up in California, giving exactly zero hecks about the safety and well-being of his poor, small sister back in Florida.

Or the fact that my current predicament is all *his* fault.

I should be halfway home by now, riding shotgun and enjoying the sweet AC of his pickup. *Not* contemplating the eight sprawling bus lines outside school like I'm searching for an escape route out of the Endless Catacombs.

A hard nudge to the shoulder sends me flying nose-first into the backpack of the eighth grader in front of me. I jump back, mortified. The nudger, an extra-tall boy in head-to-toe camo, mumbles a weak "Excuse me." Without a backward glance, he slides into the line on my right. Normally, I would feel a little more offended, but right now all I can do is admire his superior intellect.

He knows what bus to get on.

The girl attached to the backpack I bumped into has now turned and is looking at me, all like *Ex–CUSE me?* so I join the club and mutter a pitiful "excuse me" of my own. She tosses her long blond hair, then gives a little shrug, like she wasn't just staring daggers at me, and slides into the line on my left.

Which creeping blob of noise and indifference to choose? My hesitation has put me dead last no matter which line I pick. By the time I'm close enough to catch a glimpse of the driver (who I can only pray is the same as this morning's), the other buses will be closing up and driving away. No margin of error here.

My face is an embarrassment fire, dripping with sweat and over-heated-toddler vibes, but I can't waste this interaction. In this swirling hot mess of preset friend groups, post-bell teachers, and noise-blocking earbuds, I finally have someone's attention. Too bad I had to faceplant into her to get it.

"Hey!" It comes out too loud, and the way she wrinkled her nose tells me I shouldn't have grabbed her arm. "Do you know what bus I ride?"

The nose wrinkle deepens, and her eyebrows furrow in solidarity. "How would I know what bus *you* ride?"

Um. Good question. Why would a disgustingly normal and intim-idatingly self-assured eighth-grade girl know some strange little sixth grader's bus number? "Good point." I let out a ditzy giggle, even though I know it's more pathetic than cute, then try again. "Do you know which one goes to Bridlewood Apartments?"

She shakes her head, and tears prickle the back of my eyes.

No.

Anything but that.

I'd rather sew my eyes shut than cry at school. Where'd those even come from, anyway? Embarrassment? Stress? Fear that I'll miss my bus, and Mom'll have to leave work to come get me?

Fear that I *won't* miss my bus, and I'll have to spend the rest of the day alone?

"Are you gonna cry?" I shake my head frantically as the girl's face softens. She puts her hand on my shoulder and bends down until our eyes are level, just like my kindergarten teacher used to do. My stringy brown hair, damp with sweat, falls into my eyes. She tucks it back behind my ear and speaks softly. "OK. We'll figure this out. Did you ride the bus this morning?"

"Mm-hm."

"OK, so, what number was on the side?"

"I don't know." I was so worried about where I was going to sit *inside* the bus that I paid absolutely no attention to the outside this morning. It was big, it was yellow, it pulled up to the stop—that was enough for me.

"Didn't your mommy tell you?"

My . . . MOMMY?!

Welp, it's official. I will relive this conversation, writhing in shame, every time I wake up in the middle of the night, for as long as I live.

I shake my head and pray for an earthquake.

My new nanny grabs my pale scrawny hand in her tanned capable one, gives it a light squeeze, and proceeds to drag me through the crowd. "Do any of y'all live at Bridlewood?" she hollers, cupping her mouth like a megaphone with her free hand. "Who's goin' to Bridlewood?"

She drags me from line to line, hollering about *Bridlewood* and *Who's gonna help this lost kid?* Amused looks run over me like spiders and snickers ring in my ears.

"Whatcha got there, Bree? A lost puppy?" some brilliant up-and-coming comedian calls out.

"Shut up, Greg. Can't you see she's upset?" She drops my hand for a moment, just long enough to tuck in the tag on my shirt, then pulls me onward, ignoring my mumbled protests.

Wow. This girl is really kind. And helpful. And well-meaning.

I've never wanted to send someone to the depths of the Dismal Caverns more.

Right when I'm about to supernova from embarrassment, a friendly voice cuts through the crowd. "Hey! I live at Bridlewood. What's up?" says a girl as she hurries toward us. Her dark-brown corkscrew curls are tinged with gold, bouncing as she walks. Her skin is a light brown, and she has kind eyes, plus a smile that's made of sunshine. She peers around my helper, directing that smile my way, and suddenly I've never wanted to *be* at the depths of the Dismal Caverns more.

It's Lucy. The very last person I want to see me in this predicament. She lives in my apartment complex and I've been trying to figure out a way to talk to her for the past two weeks, and this . . . was not how I saw our first meeting going. The thing is, I really want to be friends with Lucy. Like, really bad. I never made any close friends in elementary school, but I had this idea over the summer that sixth grade would be my year. You know, to get out there and hunt me down a BFF.

The first day of school, halfway through health-and-fitness class, it became obvious that she was the perfect candidate. She wore an Animal Crossing T-shirt, had Marvel pins all up and down her backpack straps, and every time the teacher looked the other way, she snuck a peek at the graphic novel hidden under her desk. She seemed so cool—*and nice.* The kid next to her dropped a pencil, and she picked it up right away for him. Another kid sneezed, and she handed her a tissue from the little pack she had stashed in her backpack.

The problem is, I was never one of those kids who could just go up to someone at recess, and be all like "Wanna play?" I was the one digging around in the sand, peeking at people out of the corner of my eye, wishing they'd come up and ask *me* to play. Ask *me* to be friends.

Well, Lucy was coming up to me, all right, but not to be friends. Nope, she's just here to witness my failure.

"Everything OK?" Lucy asks me.

"She's a little confused," Supernanny Bree informs her. "Wasn't sure what line to get in."

"Oh…yeah, it's this one. I saw her this morning."

The conversation takes place literally over my head, like a daycare drop-off.

"Perfect." She passes off my hand. "Y'all can buddy up."

"I think I've got it now." Cringing, I reclaim my hand and step into line. "Thanks." My palm is hot and sweaty, and I can feel tears lurking in the corners of my eyes. I swing my backpack around onto my hip and rummage through it, searching for something to do with my hands and face. I shuffle my binder to the back, smooth the bent corner of my sketchbook, and pull out Devin's copy of *A Wizard of Earthsea*.

"You don't usually ride the bus, huh?" Lucy asks, still smiling.

"No," I answer, unable to even *think* about smiling.

In fact, until this day, I'd never ridden the bus except for field trips. Devin walked me to my first day of kindergarten and drove me home my last day of elementary. Even when he was super-busy getting ready for college, he still got up and took me every day for the first two weeks.

But now, I'm on my own.

CHAPTER 2

I PERCH ON THE EDGE OF THE BUS SEAT, MAKING MYSELF TINY and pretending to read. Every time the bus hits a pothole (which is, like, every four seconds), every muscle in my body stiffens and I bear down hard on the seat. There's no way I'm going to let myself go airborne and risk shoulder-bumping, hand-grazing, or thigh-touching the sweaty football guy sitting next to me in this assigned seat.

By the time we pull into Bridlewood, my foot and half my butt are asleep. I shuffle off the bus and slowly climb the steps to my apartment. As I'm lumbering up like a tired old crone, Lucy takes the stairs two at a time and easily beats me to the top.

"Hey." She lays a hand on my arm.

Is she going to hold my hand and guide me home?

Terrified by this thought, I force out a whispered "Hey" in return.

"I'm Lucy, by the way."

"I know. I mean, I'm Riley," I say, trying not to grimace as pins and needles erupt with each step, washing away the numbness in my foot.

"It's 2012."

"Huh?"

"The bus number. It's 2012. I forgot to tell you, and I'm not sure you looked."

She's right. I absolutely didn't look. Even after this afternoon's disaster, I forgot. But how does she know that?

Because it's obvious I'm an idiot, of course. "Thanks."

"I ride the bus every day, so let me know if you need anything." She stands there a minute, fiddling with the collection of superhero pins on her backpack straps, smiling at me.

What does she want me to say? Am I supposed to make a list of things I need right here on the spot?

OK, Lucy, I need a glass of water, a shower, a new mode of transportation, a locker that's not barricaded by eighth graders, someone to sit with at lunch, something to do on the weekends . . . I don't know, girl, this list could get long. You sure you want to start this?

"Thanks," I repeat, unsure of what else to actually say.

"No problem." She flashes me another smile, which I struggle to return.

"I better go inside now."

"Oh, yeah. Sure." She kind of shrugs and waves all at once, then darts down the stairs.

Ugh.

▲ ▼ ▲ ▼ ▲

"It's *not* that big a deal," Devin says, confidently clueless.

"Um, yes, it is," I snap into the phone. I called Devin the second I got in, certain he'd understand. But here he is, not understanding. "The girl literally held my hand and paraded me around the school, like, 'Who can help this poor lost child?' Everybody stared at me. Or laughed at me. Or laughed and stared at me. One guy called me a puppy! Then, *then*, Lucy, the supercool one I told you about, took my hand and was all like, '*I* can help this poor lost child.'"

"That was nice."

"No, that was humiliating. I may have literally died from embarrassment. For all you know, you're talking to my ghost right now." I collapse onto the couch, mummifying myself in my Pusheen blankie. Devin gave it to me for Christmas, and I love it, but lately I've noticed its fleecy plushiness isn't quite as cozy as it once was.

"Seriously," Devin continued. "I am telling you, as your brother and your friend, this is not a big deal. No one will even remember it tomorrow."

"I will. And the next day and the day after that and the day after that, so on, forever. Why didn't anybody tell me my bus number, anyway?"

"I told you before I left on Friday afternoon," Devin says. "And I texted Mom last night to remind her."

To be honest, I don't remember much that he said on Friday. Just goodbye. "Mom didn't tell me," I huff.

"She was at work when I texted, so she might have forgotten. Or she thought you'd look before you got on at the stop this morning. Don't go fussing at her about it, OK?"

"Of course not. But you know, if she'd gotten me a phone like I asked, you could have texted *me*. I don't know why she won't."

Devin sighs. "You know why. It's not a *won't*. It's a *can't*."

"You're right. You're right. I'm being a jerk." Without warning, my eyes fill up. I blink hard, but a big, fat tear escapes and rolls down my cheek anyway. "It's just . . . I don't like middle school any better than I liked elementary, and I wish you were here."

"I know, but think: when I graduate and get my big job designing games for EA, I can buy you all the phones you want."

I let out a big gusty sigh of my own directly into my sad little land-line phone, hopefully blasting his ear with my misery.

"I'll be home for winter break before you know it. We'll start a new game."

"Oh yeah, Dungeon Master? Which one?" We'd finished the Ghosts of Saltmarsh campaign right before he left, so now my poor elf sorceress was in limbo until Devin got back. It'd be months before we'd play another game of Dungeons & Dragons. Months and months of stone-cold sucky reality.

"Hmmm . . . not sure. You pick."

"OK."

"I gotta head out. I've got Orientation in a few. Call you tomorrow, OK?"

"OK," I repeat, this time in a small, extra-sad voice. Maybe if I sniffle he'll stay on the phone.

"Hey, don't forget, we're going to Winter-Con. Just four short months!"

Sniffle success! Devin can never resist sad-Riley.

"Yeah? Really?" I ask, even though I already know the answer. We've been talking it about since last year, when he and his girlfriend, Evie, let me tag along. Every winter, the Natural 20 (best comic-book store, ever, by the way) puts on a huge event for gamers and cosplayers. It. Is. *Amazing*. And at least Devin will be home for that.

"Of course. Maybe this year we'll even dress up. Evie's got some ideas."

"Like what?"

"Like, I'll tell you later. I really have to go, Ri-Fi." He busts out my old nickname, and I know I'm through. "I love you. Try to have fun, OK? I'll call you tomorrow. Later, sis!"

Then click.

The sniffle, which was not a fake sniffle by the way, threatens to grow into a sob. I swallow it down and slam the phone back on the receiver.

I still can't believe he left me.

But he did, and here I am. On literally opposite side of the country, pining away in crummy old Florida, while he's out there, having a grand old time in California. I guess I'd better get used to isolation and loneliness.

The hours stretch out before me, four and a half of them, to be exact. Hours with no one to talk to but myself, and I've been trying not to do that lately. Instead I roam the apartment, assessing the situation. Snacks are limited—three baby carrots, a half-ripe banana, and the crumb-filled corner of a Ruffles bag. Without cable, afternoon TV for wallowing is even more limited—little-kid cartoons or sad middle-aged talk shows.

Homework is, as always, homework. Yeah, going to take a pass on that one. It's not like Devin's here, breathing down my neck, making sure each and every problem is completed with a freshly sharpened pencil and 100 percent accuracy. So, I step over my backpack and head to the Almost Office.

The Almost Office is really just the corner of our living room with a small white desk wedged between our faded green couch and a slightly tilted bookshelf. There are way too many books on it, and we all know it could collapse at any second; however, we also know that moving those books could cause the collapse, so we just leave it be, overstocked and wonky. A rolling chair surrounded by worn tracks in the carpet sits in front of Devin's first computer, a mechanical fossil on the verge of collapse. I drop into the chair and jam my finger into the power button. It glows blue, but the monitor stays black, so I spin a few waiting spins in the chair.

Right on the verge of dizziness, my feet slam on the carpet brakes. I stop, eye-to-eye, with the kitty-cat calendar tacked to the wall on my right. Devin's neat, black-inked writing fills the squares, mapping out the entire month. August 2: Back-to-School Shopping. August 11: Riley Back to School. August 20: Devin & Riley Movie @ 7:00. August 22: Devin to UCA. I have a dentist appointment the twenty-seventh, the electricity bill's due the twenty-eighth, and Mom works, like, every day. I flip through the months, past the tubby gray cat staring at a plate of doughnuts, a black cat playing in leaves, and an orange tabby parading around in turkey feathers. The reminders fade, and by the time I hit December, a fluffy white Persian under the Christmas tree, there's only one. And it's in bright-red ink.

December 6: Devin comes home.

I let the pages fall. Rows of empty boxes flutter down like the world's saddest flip-o-rama, and my chest gets that weird feeling I hate. It's the crushing thing that makes me feel like my ribs have twisted and broken, folding into a flattened heart-and-bone sandwich. Then fat tears spring to my eyes, and this time I let them go. They're hot and stinging and determined to all come out at once, accompanied by throat-splitting sobs and unbeautiful snotting. I cry until it gets old. Which, to be honest, is a lot sooner than I expected.

Turns out a good cry isn't as satisfying when no one's around to hand you tissues and bring you chocolate. Using my palms as Kleenex, I wipe my face as I flip through the calendar again. I take another look at that red ink, at December 6.

It only takes four flips. Once the kitties are done swimming, eating doughnuts, playing in the leaves, and posing with turkey feathers, we'll be ready for that Christmas tree. And Devin.

Only four kitty-cats to go.

I can do this.

Probably.

Maybe.

Minutes later, after some whirring and blinking, the computer finally boots. The background image is a picture of me and Devin outside the movies the Wednesday before he left. He has a big ol' grin on his face, but I am quite obviously fake-smiling. He must have snuck it on there to be sweet, but, really, that's the last thing I want to see right now.

I right-click and reset the background to my original picture. It's a huge red dragon annihilating a village with white-hot fire. Villagers are running from their little thatched huts in terror, and the dragon's grinning like *What's up? Y'all like my breath?*

I sit back and admire the image. Much better, and definitely more suited to my mood. I just love me a good dragon adventure. Not that I've ever actually gotten to have one, outside of books and movies. That's my one and only issue with Dungeons & Dragons. There aren't enough dragons. I mean, there's dungeons for days, and I've fought pirates, ogres, trolls, gnolls, necromancers, animated skeletons, and even flesh jellies (ew), but Devin's never let me go head-to-head with an *actual* dragon. He says they're way too over-powered for Arwenna, my beautiful but low-level elf sorceress. Supposedly, he didn't down his first adult white dragon until he was a level 8, so Arwenna's level-3 magic missiles would be like gnats bouncing off a dragon's scaly hide. But maybe, just *maybe*, he says, I'll be ready to fight a green dragon by the time I'm level 5.

Hmph. Like I would even try magic missiles on a dragon. I'm pretty sure I could come up with a better plan than that, a smart, sneaky trap-like one. *Like, come on and have some faith in your sister, Devin.*

Oh, and how am I supposed to even reach level 5? Now that Devin's off in California 92 percent of the year, I'll probably be thirty years old before I get anywhere near that sad-sack little greenie. Arwenna's going to be stuck, just like me, spinning her wheels until he gets back. It's not like I have any friends to play with.

At least I get to pick our next campaign. If I've got to wait four months to play, it better be good. I hit the Google and search up *Dungeons & Dragons campaigns that actually have dragons.* Then, I promptly realize that yes, Devin is correct. The vast majority of these dragons will eat me for lunch and leave me with nothing but a tear-stained character sheet to bury.

But dragons are so cool.

I scroll through a bit more, in awe of all the different dragon types and imagining how awesome it would be to face one when it hits me. Maybe I don't wanna *fight* a dragon. Maybe I wanna *be* a dragon.

I'm going to write a campaign and I'm going be the Dungeon Master this time.

The *Dragon Master* Dungeon Master.

▲　▼　▲　▼　▲

"Riley, did you eat?" Mom taps me on the shoulder, knocking me out of my deep communion with Microsoft Word. "And did you finish your homework? It's getting late."

"Sorry! Not yet. I was just finishing up this, uh, paper." I pull away from my campaign and jump to my feet, blocking the screen of definitely-not-homework with my body. The chair shoots out and slams into her kneecaps.

She yelps in pain, bending down and rubbing her legs through her work khakis, which causes some of her thin dark hair to slip out of her ponytail and shade her face. I lean forward, trying to get a read on her aggravation level. She straightens, pushes her hair back, and smiles. It's a small smile, but it lights up her pale face and tired brown eyes. Good, she's not mad.

"Why didn't you eat?" she asks. "Did you have a hard time with the microwave?"

Did I have a what with the what?

Does *everybody* think I'm helpless? It's not only the girl at school; even my own mother doesn't believe I'm capable of pushing a button.

"I meant to call," she says, biting her lip and then sucking in a breath. "I should've called. It's your first day on your own. I can't believe I didn't check on you. I *should've* checked on you, but Brian didn't show *again*, and I had to take over his lane, so I never got a break and—"

"Mom. Chill. Devin called and checked on me or whatever. And I know how to use the microwave. I just forgot. *To* use it," I clarify, "not *how* to use it."

17

Just like I forgot to even start my homework because I was busy creating a brand-new dragon-filled world. One which I very badly wanted to get back to. I peek over my shoulder at the keyboard, trying desperately to remember what I was going to type before I got interrupted and interrogated about dinner. Mom follows my eyes to the monitor.

"Are you about done?" she asks. "Devin always had you tackle it first thing when you got home."

"Yeah, pretty much." For tonight, anyway, it seems. Mom's not moving until I eat something, and I never did manage to squeeze in any actual homework. I lean over, save, and close out. "So, you gonna teach me to use that newfangled kitchen device? What was that you called it? A mi-cro-something-or-other?"

She laughs and yanks her cashier's vest and navy-blue polo over her head in one swift motion, revealing her Black Widow tank top underneath. "That's better," she says, tossing her work shirt on the couch. She crooks her arm and offers it to me. "Now, if you'll follow me, ma'am, I will make you a genuine gourmet Hot Pocket in that newfangled device of which you speak."

"Oooooh, can I push the Start button?" I ask, taking her arm.

"Whoa, there, kid. Let's not get ahead of ourselves."

CHAPTER 3

MR. CAMERON AND HIS BUSHY BROWN MUSTACHE FILL THE doorway, blocking my escape from math class. Together, they glance through the stack of papers one more time. "I don't see your homework, Riley."

"Really?" My eyes widen with surprise. Not in surprise because he doesn't see my homework (obviously, because I didn't do it), but in surprise that he checked for it immediately, like this was some kind of pre-algebraic emergency.

"My procedure is that students place it in the bin on the way *into* class," he says, pointing with a flourish to the blue basket on his desk labeled "Homework." *Thanks for the visual, buddy.*

"Sorry, I'll remember that next time." I go to sidestep him, but he slides to the right, barring the path once again.

"I'll make an exception," he says, exhaling deeply, "*this time.*"

Oh, I see—he's doing me a giant, inconvenient favor. Then, I realize he is holding out his hand.

"Oh. . ." He's going to make me say it, isn't he? "I didn't do it."

His mustache quivers in annoyance as he sucks in a breath. "Unacceptable. This is an honors class, Riley. You have to keep up."

A wave of burning red crashes over my face, and my mouth goes dry. I fiddle with my thumbnail, picking at the cuticle and resisting the urge to bite it. What's he looking for here? Is there some secret password I'm missing? Something that will get him to move and let me leave this fresh heck and move on to the old heck of bus-riding? "Um, sorry? I . . ."

I have no idea how to finish that sentence.

A small sigh of annoyance hits the back of my neck. I peek over my shoulder to catch a glimpse of the sigher; a petite Black girl, struggling under the weight of her overstuffed backpack. It's Jen, master of math and organization. A girl, who within the first two days of school, had cemented herself as Mr. Cameron's favorite for her "problem-solving abilities" and "excellent class participation." A girl who seemed so nice and down-to-earth, it was impossible to resent her teacher's-pet status. A girl whose homework had been promptly and procedurally placed in the proper basket before class even began.

20

A girl whose bad luck (aka me) has unfairly trapped her here, post-bell, at Mr. Cameron's interrogation station. I bite my lip, a hot flush creeping over my face.

Jen rubs her chin thoughtfully, taking in the situation. Her deep-brown eyes look from me to Mr. Cameron then back to me. She gives me a tiny smirk of a smile and a *Can you believe this guy?* shrug, causing her long box braids to slip over her shoulder.

"Why didn't you do your homework, Riley?" Mr. Cameron persists.

Jen's silver-sandaled foot taps in frustration, but her smile widens encouragingly. Which is nice, because at least now I know she's not aggravated at me, but not nice because it makes me feel like a sad, ruffled duckling who lost her mama. "I'm sure there's a good reason, right?" She talks fast, but her voice is kind. "Like, you didn't understand it? Or you left your book in your locker? Maybe you didn't have any graph paper?"

Good idea! Excellent problem-solving, Jen. You're my favorite math student now too. I turn back to Mr. Cameron and blurt out, "I didn't have any graph paper!"

Jen steps between us and gives my arm a friendly squeeze. "We can take care of that." She whips a neat stack of grid paper out of her backpack and presses it into my hands. "Now you do. She'll do it tonight, Mr. Cameron. Now, may we *please* go? My mom will worry if I'm late."

"My procedure is that late work is half-credit." He says it all grumpy, but at least he moves.

We book it out of the classroom before he can change his mind. "Thanks," I mumble, about 70 percent humiliated and 30 percent elated to be free.

"No problem!" Jen calls over her shoulder as she takes off down the hall, her long braids bouncing behind her.

I carefully slide the paper into a folder in my backpack. What a score! This was exactly what I needed to sketch the map for my campaign. I mean, do my math homework.

Because I had to stop to talk to Mr. Cameron, I'm all red-faced and out of breath, and, of course, the absolute last one on the bus. I run up the steps, and Lucy smiles at me from her seat as I make my way down the aisle. I kind of wish she wouldn't. She's got to be like, *Oh, that poor kid. She just can't figure it out.*

I should march over there and explain like, *Excuse me, Perfect Girl. Contrary to what you may be thinking, I was not lost. As a matter of fact, I knew exactly where I was going today. But then I was held hostage by my math teacher, which made me unable to get where I was going in a timely fashion. Thank you for your concern.*

Of course, I don't though. Instead, I give a her a small smile back, drop into my assigned seat, and pull out my math homework. Maybe I can get most of it done by the time I get home.

▲ ▼ ▲ ▼ ▲

"Devin, you can't go." My grip on the phone tightens, as if that'll keep him on the line. "You haven't checked my homework yet."

"Riley, I can't check your homework. I can't even see it." There's an impatient edge to his voice, which I do not appreciate.

"I'll turn on the computer and download the video-chat thing."

"No way. That'll take until midnight to load, and I have to—"

"Fine. I'll read the equation to you, and I'll tell you what my graph looks like."

"Riley, I have to g—"

"But Mr. Cameron's scary!"

Devin laughs. "Mr. Procedures, you mean. He's not so bad once you get used to him."

"Yeah, whatever. You're just saying that because you were his favorite." Devin's every teacher's favorite. At the senior assembly, his AP Physics teacher literally cried while giving him his award.

"I'm sure it's fine," he says, impatience creeping back into his voice. "For real, I have to go. Professor Duncan's meet-and-greet starts in half an hour, and I am not about to be late. Do you know what a big deal she is?"

"Hmm . . ." Of course I know. She's the super-mega genius who's worked on all the games and done all the things, and Devin was so pumped to get into her stupid program that he abandoned his one and only sister. "Which one is she again?"

"Girl, stop. I'm hanging up."

"But my—"

"—Your homework is fine. Download the thing later, and we'll go over everything this weekend."

"I—"

"Love you, Ri-Fi. Bye!"

I start to tell him I love him, too, but he's already gone.

I decide to go ahead and get the video-chat app now, just in case he changes his mind and calls me back. The computer whirs like a dying helicopter, giving everything it's got to complete the download. I don't even want to attempt to open Word right now—that'll just crash the whole thing. It's fine, though, I know my world by heart. Or I'm making it up by heart anyway.

My math homework, complete and ready for the bin of procedures, goes into my backpack and then out comes the rest of the graph paper. I smooth it out on the coffee table, rummage around for a ruler and a mechanical pencil, then tell myself the story.

The campaign begins at the edge on an enchanted forest. Devin, aka Daventry the Paladin, explores the area, looking for adventure. A flash of silver darts across the sky. It catches the sun's rays and releases them in a blaze of light and, for a moment, Daventry is blinded. His vision clears, and the mysterious silver streak is gone.

Ancient trees, the size of giants with gnarled and knotted trunks, stand like sentinels along the forest's edge for miles in either direction. The only break is the entrance, which is a dirt path, canopied by the entwined, moss-dripping branches of the two largest trees on either side. The path is littered by untouched leaves, and the only tracks are those of foxes and deer.

Daventry stands at the edge of the path. Does he choose to enter?

I pick up my pencil and get to work. There's got to be somewhere for him to enter, if he does choose to enter (and he'd better enter). At the bottom of the paper, I sketch the trees, filling in all the spaces from left to right, except for two squares in the middle.

Using the ruler, I draw the path. I make it so every square counts for about five feet, which'll be good to know when I'm checking his spell radius or how far he can shoot his magic. Devin's so picky about that stuff. When I'm playing Arwenna, if I am, like, one measly square out of range, he will not let me fire my magic missiles.

I want him to get lost, so before blocking off the area for the dragon's lair in the top-right corner, I plan out an intricate maze of twists and turns. I'm laid out on the carpet, nibbling on my graphite-smudged eraser, when the key clicks in the lock. I slide my map into my backpack and hustle off to the kitchen.

I can't have Mom genuinely thinking I don't know how to use the microwave again.

▲ ▼ ▲ ▼ ▲

"Everyone, please pass your poster to the front of the room." Mrs. Lane, the health-and-fitness teacher, gives an excited clap and smiles like a silver-haired fairy godmother, eager to bestow good grades upon us all. "I can't wait to see what you've come up with for Spirit Week! It starts next Monday, you know, and these are going to look fantastic gracing the halls of Franklin Middle School. Our football team is going to get such a boost for next Friday's game!"

Hm. Yes. Well.

The thing is, while I am one hundred percent prepared for math today, I am zero percent prepared for health and fitness. I completely blanked on the Spirit Week project. Why even give homework in this class? What educational value could possibly be gained by making a poster to boost the football players? Like, drawing the thing isn't going to actually make *me* any more fit. And I'm pretty sure the football dude who sits next to me on the bus gives zero hecks about any stupid thing I'd make.

Ugh. This is why I need Devin, he's like a personal assistant, tutor, and snack genius all rolled into one.

I slink down in my seat, letting my thin brown hair fall into my face. The girl behind me leans over my shoulder and drops a heavily markered paper onto my desk. "Our team is the coolest!" proclaim three cockeyed penguins floating on an iceberg. I mean, I guess it makes sense. Penguins are the pinnacle of coolness, so they would be the experts, but still . . . why penguins? Our mascot is a tiger. I shrug and snatch the paper, chucking it forward fast so no one'll notice I didn't add mine.

A little *too* fast.

I overshoot and the paper flutters to the floor. Mrs. Lane bustles over and picks it up, beaming at the penguins. "Adorable. Great slogan. So much school spirit!" Then her beam dims in concern. She peers at the floor around her. "Oh no! Riley, where's your poster?"

Oh, come on.

Doesn't she want to, you know, start teaching or something? And can somebody tell me why my homework is top priority for every teacher at this school? Oh, and why is Lucy turned around in her seat giving me sympathetic looks?

I do *not* need sympathy.

"Um. I have to get it. I'll pass it up in a minute."

I pull my backpack into my lap and search desperately for something, anything that resembles a Go-Team-Go poster. All I've got is my map, and while it kills me to give it up, it would literally kill me to sit here any longer with Mrs. Lane staring at me. The longer she stares at me, the more other people stare at me to see what all the staring is about. Any more eyes on me, and I'll burst into flames.

Or worse, cry.

"Hold on, I have to write my name on it." I grab a pencil and hunch over the paper, racking my brain for a catchy slogan that has something, anything to do with my map. I'll never be able to compete with those cool and spirited penguins, but I've got to come up with *something*. The twists and turns on the map mirror my thoughts like a maze, which at first, is incredibly stressful, but then . . . stress gives way to inspiration.

"OUR TEAM IS A-MAZE-ING," I scribble across the top, then shove the paper into Mrs. Lane's wrinkled hand.

"I knew Devin's sister would never forget her homework," she gushes.

Seriously? The whole school system is full of devoted Devin lovers, which makes it a pain to follow him. My fourth-grade teacher actually called me by his name half the time, despite the fact that I'm a girl and my desk tag said R-I-L-E-Y.

"This is interesting." Mrs. Lane's gush quickly fizzles to a meh when she sees my paper (another common teacher reaction). She cocks her silvery head thoughtfully, turning it every which way, trying to make sense of it and failing. She shrugs and slides it to the bottom of the stack. Can't say that I blame her. That thing looks bonkers, especially since I hadn't finished all the awesome parts yet, but at least it's *something*. Something that is none of Lucy's business, by the way.

I watch as she cranes her head to peek at my hot mess of a paper as Mrs. Lane click-clacks in her little heels back to her desk. Her eyes narrow thoughtfully, and she swivels my way again. Lucy tilts her head toward the stack of papers, sending her golden-brown curls bouncing. *What was that?* she mouths.

A flush creeps up my neck, over my face, and all the way up to my ears. *Nothing,* I mouth back, blinking hard. I turn away and stare down at my desk, ducking behind my hair again. I tell myself it's not that big a deal and to blow it off. Devin says I worry about stuff that nobody else cares about or will even remember in a day. I'm sure he's right. Nobody's going to remember what my homework looked like or the fact that

I turned twelve shades of purple and nearly crumbled when nice old Mrs. Lane asked me for it.

But I *will* and I *care*. I hate looking dumb. I hate feeling dumb. Especially in front of the one person at school I thought might be nice enough to be my friend. Of course, Devin would say this is a small thing, and I get that it's ridiculous, but it's the small and ridiculous things that keep me up at night and remind me that I'm weird. And alone.

Plus, I really want my map back.

▲ ▼ ▲ ▼ ▲

I'm the first one off the bus, practically running down the steps. All I want is to get home, lock myself in, and call Devin. But as I sprint toward my apartment, I get the feeling Lucy's following me. Which is ridiculous—why would she follow me?

I reach the stairs to my apartment and glance over my shoulder and there she is, cutting across the parking lot with a determined face. I take the stairs two at a time, unlock and relock my door in record time. The knocks are soft but still jolt me halfway out of my skin. I hold my breath and peer through the peephole.

Yep, Lucy followed me. Louder knocks rattle the door, and I jump back. I let out my breath, taking another deep one to settle my nerves. What do I do?

The knocks upgrade to an aggravated pounding, and Lucy shouts. "Oh my God, Riley. I know you're there. I saw you go in." Another rapid-fire knock. "Can you open the door for, like, five seconds so I can ask you something?" She sounds completely exasperated, but also a little sad.

OK, fine. I pull open the door a tiny crack, and before I can say a word, Lucy busts it open and barges on in asking, "Did I do something to you?"

"What?" I don't know what I thought she was going to say, but that definitely wasn't it.

"Are you mad at me?"

"Huh?" Confusion smothers my brain, overpowering my ability to speak in more than one-syllable sentences.

"Oh, come on." Lucy paces my living room, her backpack bouncing with each wild wave of her arms. "You know what I'm talking about. Every time I try to talk to you or even dare to glance your way, you look like you swallowed a bug. You weren't even gonna open the door when I knocked. Why do you hate me?"

OK, now I feel like I really *did* swallow a bug. I've never picked a fight with anybody in my life, and I've definitely never been mad at Lucy, but here she is stomping around the apartment like I owe her an explanation or an apology or something.

Wait . . .

A shiny glowworm of a thought creeps through my brain fog. Maybe Lucy wasn't being fake-nice all those times she smiled at me or offered to help. Maybe she was being nice-nice, and I was the one being a jerk.

She's standing there, hands on her hips like she's mad, but her eyes are a little watery too. I for-real hurt her feelings. And she *barged into my home* to tell me off about it.

Lucy is so cool.

"I'm sorry," I blurt out. "I thought you were only being nice to me because you thought I was weird."

Lucy laughs, disengaging her hands from her hips. "Of course I was being nice to you because you're weird."

"Um, thanks?"

"I *like* weird. Well, your kind of weird anyway. The kind of weird that'll turn a freakin' labyrinth in to the health teacher."

OK, I'll admit it. That was a pretty strange thing to do. I can't help but laugh. "Do you think our team will win now?"

She giggles. "Oh, for sure. And it'll be your poster that gives them the spirit and strength they need to do so."

"Glad to be of service," I say with a slight bow.

"Yeah, go Tigers and all that. But seriously, what was it really for?" She slips off her shoes and takes a flying leap onto the corner of the couch. She pats the cushion next to her and strikes a listening pose, sitting super-straight with her fist to her chin, eyes wide. "Do tell."

I sit on the patted cushion, debating how much to tell her. I decide to go for it and explain about the campaign. She did say she liked weird and she did just use the word "labyrinth" in day-to-day conversation, so she might get it. The second I open my mouth, though, the phone rings.

Devin.

I could let it go to voicemail, but then he'll think I've been kidnapped, or bus-left, or bus-wrecked, or any one of a million dramatic and deathly possibilities.

"I have to get that. It'll only take a second." I run for the kitchen and grab the phone. "Hey, Devin. I'm fine. I made it home in one piece! Call you later?"

"Whoa! I got a few minutes. You want some help with your math homework? We can do a video-chat."

"That's OK. I'm actually talking to a girl from school right now—"

"Oh! Say no more." I can practically hear his grin through the phone. "Talk to you later."

"Wait. How was the thing with Professor Duncan?"

"Amazing! She's incredible, like I knew she'd be. But I'll tell you about all that later. Go talk to your friend."

CHAPTER 4

LUCY'S BOUNCING UP AND DOWN ON THE COUCH CUSHION, slapping an impatient rhythm on her thighs. "Oh, good!" She launches herself off the couch, grabs my hand, and drags me toward the door. "I wanna talk about the labyrinth, but we gotta go to my place first. The Tag Team's about to do the trade-off, and I gotta be present and accounted for. *Or else.*"

She pauses and turns, just long enough to bug out her eyes and run a finger across her neck, dagger-style.

"Um, OK. Sounds serious," I say, baffled. I don't know what or who the Tag Team is, but if Lucy wants to yank me away from this lonely apartment and over to her place to talk about my labyrinth, who am I to argue? She pulls me out, orders me to lock up, then hauls me off toward her building.

"I'm here, Dad!" Lucy announces as she flings open the door.

"About time!" he grumbles, but his face is all lit up. He has dark-brown skin, short black hair, and one of the nicest smiles I've ever seen. It reminds me a lot of Lucy's. He crosses the room in about three steps and gathers her up in a tight hug. I feel a little awkward just standing there, but it's really, really nice.

He puts Lucy down and clips his nurse's ID to the front of his blue scrubs. He grabs his keys off the counter, muttering good-naturedly. "Now, if I could just find that worthless brother of mine. . ."

"Who are you calling worthless?" says a twentysomething-ish guy bearing a strong resemblance to Lucy's dad. He walks in behind us, dropping his Computer Center name tag on the counter while pulling his shoulder-length microlocs out of a ponytail and slipping off his shoes. "Your daddy is so mean," he says, shooting Lucy a grin. She grins back, then rolls her eyes as he holds out his hand, and Lucy's dad gives it a slap.

"You're in. I'll be home at eleven."

"Is that why you call them the Tag Team?" I whisper to Lucy.

"That's what they call *themselves*," she whispers back with an affectionate eye-roll. "They do this literally every time they trade off Lucy-care duties. You'd think it'd be old by now, but no."

I giggle, and Lucy's dad and uncle turn my way.

"I'm Anthony," her dad says, taking my right hand.

"I'm Jay," her uncle says, taking my left hand.

"Riley." I giggle, shaking both of their hands at the same time.

"All right." Lucy pulls me away by the elbow. "Now that that's all sorted out, we're gonna go to my room. For girl talk. Lots and lots of girl talk. Like, the girliest girl talk two girls ever talked."

She shoots the guys a wicked grin, and they squeal in mock horror as we retreat to her room. A room that is, in fact, the polar opposite of mine. Everything's brand-new, from her sun-and-moon comforter to her matching white nightstand, dresser, and bookshelf. The books on the shelves are lined up evenly, arranged by color in the world's most orderly and educational rainbow. She hangs her backpack on the silver "L" hook by the door and gestures toward her bed.

I sit on the edge, not daring to disturb the artistic arrangement of blue and yellow fringed pillows. I don't even know if I should be allowed on her bed. Mine hasn't been made since Devin left, and the nubbly sheets smell more like feet than Gain.

"Your room is so nice," I say. "Really clean."

"Really, *really* clean. Like, inhumanly clean. So clean it makes my eyes itch." Lucy laughs, then lowers her voice secretively. "You wanna know something? This morning, as an experiment, I pulled that book out an inch further than the others. One measly inch." Lucy points to a dark-blue Chronicles of Narnia anthology, located directly after the greens in the bookbow. "Now look at it."

My eyes follow her finger. "Right back in line."

"I know, right? Dad must have done it when I was at school. It's a little weird." She shrugs. "I guess I'll get used to it."

"You're not used to your dad yet?" *That* was a little weird. I mean, I'm not used to my dad, either, but it's not like I live with him. We don't even live in the same state.

"I just moved in with him last month." Lucy leans across the bed and starts digging around in the drawer of her nightstand, knocking over the silver-framed photo on top. "They thought it'd be better. Mom's been real busy with work and stuff, you know? That's her." She picks up the photo and holds it out to give me a better look. Her mom's pretty and blond, with white skin and a sprinkle of light-brown freckles across her nose. She's sitting at a restaurant, a Coke in one hand and chopsticks in the other, smiling into the camera. "She took me to Ming Tree the night before I moved. Anyway, it's whatever." She gently places the picture back on the nightstand, then pulls a pack of gum out of the drawer. "You want some gum?"

"Sure," I say, glad to have something to do with my mouth besides asking awkward questions.

Lucy jams a piece into her mouth and tosses the pillow pyramid to the floor, then stretches out on the bed with her hands behind her head. "OK, so are you going to tell me about this map or not? I've been waiting for, like, hours."

You don't have ask me twice. I tell her all about the origins of my map, but that's not all. I get way too excited and tumble down the

36

nerd rabbit hole, with a deep-dive rambling explanation of my own D&D origins.

"So, you guys played actual campaigns, like with dice and spells and battles and everything?" Lucy asks when I finally pause for breath. She's sitting up straight now, hugging a star-shaped pillow to her chest.

"Yeah, Devin was always the Dungeon Master, that's the person who organizes and narrates everything, and they control all the monsters and non-playable characters. So, like, he'd describe the world and set up the story, then I'd make all the decision about what *I* wanted to do. Whatever I did or said, he'd have to react to that."

"I know what the DM does." Lucy rolls her eyes, but she's grinning. "You know how many hours I've spent online watching D&D Twitch streams?"

"Um, no." I grin back. "As a matter of fact, I don't."

"A million, OK? I just never get to play because everybody I know is boring. Who's your character?"

"Arwenna. She's an elf sorceress; level three. She's not super powerful or anything yet," I say modestly.

"It's still cool. At least you're not level negative zero, like me. I don't even have a character." Lucy lets out a huffy little sigh, arms crossed.

"What would you be?" I look her over, trying to guess. Probably a druid or a wizard or maybe a bard.

"Hmmm . . ." She fiddles with her gum, stretching it between her mouth and fingers. "I think I wanna crack some skulls."

I snort-laugh. "Like a fighter or a barbarian?"

"Yep. A barbarian." She drops the gum back into her mouth and chomps it fiercely. "A big, scary one."

Totally not what I was expecting, but maybe I should have after the way she busted into my apartment. "All right, I can see that. What race? Like, an elf? A dwarf? Dragonborn?"

"Nah, human."

What? Why? I don't get people that roll humans. Like, you can be whatever you want—why pick *human*? "Really?"

"Yeah, like me, but bigger and stronger. A fierce human woman, questing through a magical world. What's wrong with that?"

Well, when you put it that way, nothing. "OK, so a big, scary human barbarian—"

"With a mysterious past."

"Naturally."

"And an axe."

"A great-axe, even."

"*And* a dagger. That I keep in my boot." She sits up even straighter, ticking her list off on her fingers. Her brown eyes are wide and sparkling with character love. "And studded leather armor. And short black hair that's shaved on one side. And a battle scar that runs from my temple to my cheek, from an old wound that narrowly missed my steely gray eyes. Oh, and my name's Octavia."

By the time she finishes, I'm sitting up straighter than a polearm, grinning so wide it hurts. "She's perfect!" I squeal.

"Yeah, it's too bad she'll never get to play." Lucy pushes out her bottom lip and looks down at her comforter sadly, tracing a crescent moon with her finger. "'Cause, you know, I don't even have a character sheet, or dice, or a Dungeon Master to guide me—"

"I have character sheets! And dice! I could be a Dungeon Master and guide you!"

"*No!*" She slaps her hands to her cheeks in mock surprise, then drops them into her lap and leans in seriously. "Can I go in the enchanted forest? I want to find that silver flash."

Suddenly, mixed feelings battle it out in my chest. The joy hits first, a warm, sunshiny feeling of friendship, camaraderie, and exclamation points. All like, *Yay! This is going to be so fun!* and *Whoa! She really believes I can run a campaign all by myself!!!* Then the oozing shadows of doubt bubble up, grabbing that glow in a stranglehold, extinguishing all but the slightest speck and replacing my exclamation points with sad question marks. All like, *Is it OK to take the campaign I was making for Devin and play it with someone else? Is that weird? Even if it is OK, what if I do a terrible job and she never wants to play again? What if it makes no sense? What if she does something and I don't know how to respond? What if it's boring?*

What if she figures out I'm *boring?*

"It's fine if you don't want to." Lucy shrugs, picking at a remnant of blue polish on her thumbnail. I can't see her eyes, but all the excitement's left her voice. I think I might have waited too long to answer and hurt her feelings.

Maybe this is why I don't have any friends—a perfectly nice girl comes along and what do I do? First, I freeze her out, then when she gives me another chance, I choke on hesitation and make her feel bad.

"No!" I say, a little too loud, and she jumps. "I do want to! Like, a lot. I'm just not quite done with the campaign, and I have to start over on my map. Obviously. I think I can be ready by Sunday—that'll give me all day Saturday to finish up. I can come over tomorrow, though, and we can make your character sheet."

I mentally cross my fingers and make a wish that I haven't ruined everything.

"Oh! I get it." She grins and rubs her hands together. "Should I get cupcakes?"

"Cupcakes?"

"Yeah, since it's Octavia's birthday tomorrow!"

I giggle. That is one of the nerdiest things I've heard in my life—and I've heard some nerdy stuff. It's also brilliant.

"Yes, yes. A thousand times yes," I say. "Please. Get the cupcakes."

"This is going to be so fun!" Lucy squeals. Her hands are clenched in excited little fists and her eyes are shining. She's all eagerness and high expectations, which is awesome but terrifying, because if it's not fun, she's going to be so let down. And it'll be all my fault. I have to nail this.

CHAPTER 5

I SHOULD PROBABLY CLEAN MY ROOM. MAYBE NOT RIGHT NOW or anything, but sometime. I almost missed the bus this morning hunting down my left sneaker, and now my spare set of dice has gone MIA.

My personal favorites and Arwenna's go-tos are easy to find. The green dice with the golden numbers are right where I left them on my dresser, nestled safe and sound in their velvety black pouch, between my dragon figurine and an amethyst geode. You know, so they could get charged up on magic for Arwenna between games. Obviously, I don't *really* believe that. Although ever since I started keeping them there, I've rolled a lot more crits and a lot fewer ones . . . What I really need, though, are my other ones. I want to give Lucy a set, but I also want to give her a choice. Dice are kind of personal, and it's important to have the right ones.

Plus, it's extra-important that everything goes right today, down to the details. Lucy thinks I've got this, and while that's nice and all, I'm freaking out and definitely a little bit sweaty because I've never actually created a character. Devin did all the work with mine and all I did was roll the dice. I take a deep breath because it'll all be OK though. He's supposed to call in a few minutes, and he's gonna have to break it down for me then. There's a little notepad and a pencil all ready to go by the phone, and I can even call him from Lucy's house if we get stuck.

But first, where are the heckin' dice? I can see them so clearly in my mind so why can't I see them in my apartment? One set is red with orange numbering, and the other is blue with silvery flecks. The red set might be good because they're all *rawr* and barbarianish *or* Lucy might like the other ones because I noticed a lot of blue and silver stuff going on in her room. Oh man, her room. Too bad her dad didn't come over to *my* place while I was at school. He'd have a field day in here.

I'm wriggling over a pile of dirty clothes in an attempt to squeeze my head under the bed when the phone rings. I hop up, only slightly grazing my forehead on the bed frame, and run to the kitchen to answer it.

"Do you know where my dice are? The blue and red ones?"

"Well, hello to you too." Devin laughs.

"Hello," I say politely, then ask again. "My dice? The blue and red ones?"

"Why would I know where your dice are?"

42

"Because you know where everything is. Think. *Think*." I glance at the clock on the stove. I'm supposed to be at Lucy's at four, which gives me exactly forty minutes to find the dice, grab my character sheet, and get Devin to explain the intricate workings of character creation.

He mumbles for a minute, and then I hear a finger snap through the phone. I *knew* he knew where they were. "All right. Look behind the computer monitor for the red ones. They should still be in their plastic box. Check your second drawer for the blue ones—pretty sure they were there last time I put your shirts away. But they're all over the place."

"Hold on." I drop the phone, leaving it dangling on its cord and run to the Almost Office. Red dice behind the monitor? Check. I sprint to my room and yank open Drawer Number 2. The blue dice skitter around the near empty drawer. I shoved them in my pockets, making a mental note to remind Mom to do some laundry.

I dash back to kitchen and grab the phone. "Got 'em!"

"Uhhh . . . you're welcome."

"Thanks," I say. I pause and wait for him to ask what the dice are for.

"Oh, hey! I never got to tell you about the thing with Dr. Duncan!"

Instead of inquiring about my dice and afternoon plans, he launches into a giddy account of not only how amazing the meet-and-greet was, but how incredibly cool *everything* is there—the campus, the professors, the clubs, the weather, the whole entire hecking state of California. *I get it. I get it. West Coast rules; East Coast drools.*

How can he be so completely oblivious to the fact that I'm still a little (OK, a lot) salty about him picking California over me? Not to mention that nowhere in any of his excited ramblings does he mention missing me. He is not the eensiest bit homesick, and he doesn't even have the decency to pretend to be. It is a job to keep myself from sighing heavily, making snarky comments, or yawning into the receiver.

Devin's midway through a sermon on the deliciousness of In-N-Out Burger (which sounds an awful lot like every other burger place in the country, except it's a *California* burger place and so automatically superior) when an alarm beeps and cuts him off. "Oh, hey. I've got to run down to financial aid to sign some papers, so I'm going to let you go."

"Oh."

"I know, I'm really sorry. And I've got training for my work-study program at the library tomorrow. I have to start this weekend, so I'm not one hundred percent sure I'll be able to do the whole math thing."

Really? A five-minute phone monologue about how great his new life is and he's out?

I need him.

I don't know what I'm doing. I don't know why I told Lucy I'd help her make her character. I'm not a Dungeon Master; I've barely mastered the school bus. Every time I think about running this campaign on Sunday, I break out in a cold sweat and I taste a little vomit in my mouth. Plus, I was counting on being able to talk to him Saturday, not for math, but for a crash course in DMing.

"OK, but, um, I'm supposed to Dungeon Master a campaign for Lucy soon. Can you read what I've got and tell me if it's any good?"

"Riley, I'm so busy right now."

"When you get a chance? Please?"

"Fine," he says. "Email it to me. I'll read over it and give you some pointers. *When I get a chance.* Don't forget, though, there's tons of free campaigns online. You can download one of those. I'll send you some links."

"Yeah," I say, but I don't really want to do that. I already promised Lucy the Enchanted-Forest-Bonkers-Map campaign. "I'll email mine tonight."

"Oh, and I also wanted to remind you," the epic blow-off continues. "Next week my classes start for real, so I won't be here when you get home. Are you going to be all right with that?"

I don't really have a choice, do I? He's already not *here* when I get home, and he sure didn't bother to consult me before he ran off across the country. Why ask now?

"It's fine," I say, because there's nothing else to say. He hangs up in a burst of excitement, leaving me with my hands tingling with nervous energy, crawling up my arms and settling in my chest. How do you even begin to make a character? I toy briefly with the idea of faking a stomachache until Devin remembers he has a sister and is available to help out.

But who knows when that will be?

I look around the empty apartment. It's so quiet, it makes my ears ring. There's no way I'm spending my afternoon locked in this chamber of solitude.

With a huff, I snatch my pencil and notepad off the table and march over to the Almost Office. While the computer boots, I grab the *Player's Handbook* off the bookshelf and flip through wildly. I've got about twenty minutes to figure this out. The second the monitor's blackness is replaced by my fierce dragon background, I search *D&D Character Creation*.

Who needs Devin the Deserter? I've got Google.

▲   ▼   ▲   ▼   ▲

Lucy's dad opens the door wide and gestures for me to come in. "Riley, right? Come on in. I'm tapping out." He leans over the couch and slaps hands with his brother. "You're in."

Lucy tosses Uncle Jay the remote and jumps off the couch to grab my arm. "What'd I tell you?" she whispers. "Every. Single. Time. I'm surprised they don't do it when one of them has to go the bathroom."

Giggling, I follow her to her room.

"Love you, Luce!" her dad calls.

"Love you too!" Lucy blows him a kiss from her doorway.

"More girl talk?" Uncle Jay asks, flipping through channels.

"Yep!" She shoots me a grin, then hollers, "So keep out, dude!" as she slowly and dramatically closes her door.

I love that creating a raging, scarred barbarian with a mysterious past is Lucy's idea of girl talk.

She takes a flying leap onto the bed, sending the museum-worthy display of celestial pillows tumbling. "You ready?"

"Yes!" I say, but then my nerves get the better of me. I drop my eyes down to the *Player's Handbook* in my sweaty grip, studying the cover like I've never seen it before. After a painfully awkward pause, I decide it'd be way easier to be up-front than try to fake expert DM status. "I mean, kinda. I should tell you I've never actually made a character sheet before. My brother made the one for Arwenna. All I did was wait around on the couch and roll the dice when he told me to. I *thought* he'd help us out today, but apparently he's too busy or something. I Googled it, though, and I have the *Handbook* and stuff, so . . ."

"So, we'll figure it out. I have the Google too." She points to a slim blue laptop on her desk.

The stress ball in my stomach unwinds and melts away, and a goofy smile creeps across my face. "Awesome." Still grinning like a fool, I dig around in my backpack and pull out the dice. "First things first. Which ones do you want?"

She looks them over carefully, then pulls the twenty-sided die from each set. "Octavia's leaning towards the red ones, but I need to be sure." She cups her hands around them and directs them to "Fight it out, little dudes." After a violent shaking, she sends them clattering across the nightstand.

Red, 17.

Blue, 4

"Red!" We shout in unison.

"Sorry, bluebies," I say, tossing them into my backpack. "Better luck next time." I hand her the case with the rest of the reds. "Count them out and make sure they're all there. There should be seven: a four-sided, a six-sided, an eight-sided, two ten-sided dice, a twelve-sided, and well, you already know you have the d20."

"All here!"

"Good. Put them all back except for the d6."

"Aw . . . that's the boring one. It looks like a Monopoly die."

"That Monopoly die is about to determine your stats, so you'd better be a little nicer to it."

Lucy puckers up and kisses the offended die. "I'm sorry, baby. You know Mama didn't mean it."

Laughing, I unpack the rest of my stuff. "Devin took the printer, so I couldn't print off a character sheet—"

"One step ahead of you, kid," Lucy skips over to her desk and grabs a handful of papers. "I already downloaded an official 5e character sheet and printed it off. And a backup in case we messed up. And a backup for the backup in case we messed that up."

"Nice," I say. "Although there is such a thing as erasers, you know."

"Oh no." Lucy shakes her head. "My girl's character sheet is going to be gorgeous and smudge-free."

"Gotcha. OK, so." I grab a pencil and one of Lucy's character sheets. Time to get down to business. "We know you're a human. We know you're a barbarian. By the way, that means you'll get to roll a d12 when you attack."

"Yes!"

"Now we need to pick your special skills.

"Athletics and Intimidations," she says promptly, making what I can only guess is her intimidating face.

"That was fast." I'd put a sticky note on the "Barbarian" page in the *Player Handbook* and was prepared to read them all to her.

"Like I said, girl, I have the Google." She picks up her die and bounces it around in her hands. "Can I roll now?"

"Yeah. We need to get your scores for your different abilities. It says you can use this preset of numbers, but . . ."

"That's no fun! I roll it four times and add to get the total number, right?"

"Yep, but you get to drop the lowest score. So, really, you're only adding three numbers, and the totals will end up anywhere between three and eighteen, depending on your luck. Oh, and you have to do that six times, since there's six categories: Strength, Dexterity, Constitution, Intelligence, Wisdom, and Charisma," I list them off, barely looking at the handbook. Maybe I'm not so terrible at this. "I'll write down the numbers to keep track, and then when you're done you can figure out where you want to put them."

"Here . . . we . . . GO!" The die rattles between her palms and she sends it flying. It bounces off the bed, skitters across the floor, and retreats deep beneath her dresser. She immediately dives after it, screaming, "Athletics Check!"

"That's the problem with barbarians," I say, laughing. "They don't know their own Strength."

"I got you, you little rascal!" She springs to her feet, holding the die in one hand and waggling a stern finger at it with the other. "Don't you run off again."

Both the die and Lucy behave themselves for the rest of the rolls, and we're able to get her numbers. The totals for each category are: 14, 11, 15, 17, 9, and 7. Now, she has to pick which number goes where.

"That seven, though." I giggle.

"Um, yeah." She shakes her head at the red die lying innocently on the nightstand. "Looks like I'm gonna be a little ditzy."

"You're putting it in Intelligence, then?"

"Yup, and put that seventeen in Strength."

"You'll definitely be able to wreck some face with that." I write the numbers down carefully, then we divide up the rest of her stats, get her a great-axe, some armor, and a traveler's pack full of rations and supplies, and then she is good to go.

I hand Lucy her character sheet. "I know you said Octavia has a mysterious past, but if you want, you can write her backstory. It's kind of fun and helps you get to know your character. You don't have to show me, though. It's not like homework or anything. It could just be for you."

"Cool." She smiles down at her paper thoughtfully, then grabs a red folder and a black Sharpie from her desk drawer. She slips the paper in, careful not to crease any corners, and writes "Octavia" in huge bubble l etters across the front. She slides it into the red section on her shelf, then arranges her dice in a neat little row in front. Highest numbers up, of course.

She gives a little double thumbs-up, more to herself than me. "Be right back!" she shouts, then runs out of the room. Then I hear her say, from down the hall, "Uncle Jay! We're ready!"

A few minutes later she prances back in, carrying a plate with two chocolate cupcakes topped with mountains of red frosting. A silvery candle rises out of each, tiny flames dancing as she walks. Uncle Jay lurks in the hallway, fingers crossed, murmuring. "Please don't set your room on fire. Please don't set your room on fire."

She rolls her eyes and kicks the door shut behind her. "Now it's time to sing."

"For real?"

"Yes, for real. Like I said, it's Octavia's birthday, and I'll be danged if I let it go uncelebrated. We will sing. We will blow out these candles. We will eat cake." Without waiting for a response, she counts down. "One, two, three. SING!"

She bursts into song, and I have no choice but to join in. Quietly at first. Like, really quietly because I've got the voice of a high-strung Chihuahua, but by the time we hit *Happy birthday, dear Octavia*, we are both shout-singing to the worst of our abilities.

The door creaks open. Uncle Jay pokes his head in, hollers "Blow out the candles, already!" then pokes his head back out.

"Make a wish," Lucy says.

"But it's your character."

"Yeah, but you helped bring her to life, so we both get wishes." Lucy closes her eyes, and her lips mouth some words I can't quite make out.

In that moment, two wishes bubble up in my mind. One is that Lucy and I will become best friends and stay that way—no splitting up, nobody moving away. The other is that Devin will quit California and come home. I hesitate, because you're only supposed to get one wish per candle, but it's really hard to choose.

Then Lucy opens her eyes and blows out the tiny flame, so I do too. Even though I never decided on my wish.

CHAPTER 6

"WHAT THE HECK ARE YOU DOING?" MOM GLANCES FROM the extra-sharp scissors in my right hand to the old science fair back-board in my left. Loose markers, construction paper, and glue sticks are spread out on the kitchen table, surrounding my *Player's Handbook* and *Monster Manual*. A group of tiny plastic kobolds frolic around my open binder (aka the Binder of Adventure) as a silver dragon figure holds down the pages. Nothing *weird*.

And nothing I want to drop everything to explain. I'm kind of in a hurry.

The thing is, while I'd spent every spare moment this week getting ready for today's game, there weren't as many spare moments as usual.

I'm not complaining—I love going to Lucy's, and I love that she keeps inviting me. But it did put a cramp in my productivity, and by Sunday I'm a little strapped for time. I've got about half an hour to put this thing together before I'll need to clean up and set up.

That is why I'm spending my Sunday morning sitting on the kitchen floor, desperately trying to saw a giant piece of scientific cardboard in half. "I'm making a Dungeon Master screen," I mutter, bearing down hard on the scissors.

"A what?"

"A Dungeon Master screen," I repeat slowly, resisting the urge to roll my eyes. How can this woman have lived with me and Devin this long and not know what I'm doing? "You know, to hide all the DM's secret information, so you don't give anything away. And so you can roll for the monster without anybody seeing."

"You can't just tell people not to peek?"

"I have the full map, my notes, the stats for my monsters, plus, again, my rolls. It'd be impossible not to 'peek.' You know Devin always had a screen."

"He did." She smiles at me and takes the scissors. "You hold, I'll cut."

Mom expertly cuts the cardboard, leaving me with a perfectly sized screen to decorate.

"Thanks." I grab brown and green construction paper from the table and start snipping trees. The plan is to make the screen look like the enchanted forest.

"You're welcome," Mom says. "Now, your turn. I need you to do something for me. Well, for us, actually, your stuff's pretty rank too."

"What?" I curve the scissors in a smooth line, and branches rise from a twisted paper trunk.

"I need you to do the laundry."

"*What?* No!" My beautiful tree flutters from my hands and rests sadly against the cracked linoleum.

Timber!

Where did this come from all of a sudden? I've never done laundry in my life. We don't even own a washing machine. All we have is the apartment laundry room—a dark, creepy cavernous place with flickering, moth-filled fluorescent lights and a mysterious odor that's a cross between swamp water, dead flowers, and Tide. I went down there *once* for, like, five seconds to take Devin a pair of jeans that had missed the basket, and that was enough laundry room for me. "I can't do the laundry!"

"Sure you can. What you *can't* do is go to school tomorrow smelling like a sasquatch. Have you noticed your drawers are empty?" She points at my shirt. "Pretty sure you wore that yesterday."

"I thought you were going to wash stuff today."

"Welp, so did I. You know, I was really looking forward to tackling Stank Mountain on my day off." She shakes her head and gestures down at her cashier's vest, which I'd somehow missed. "But now, I don't even have a day off. I got called in."

"I'm supposed to game with Lucy. This is going to take forever."

Mom shrugs, but her eyes are sympathetic. "I know, but I can't let you go to school nekkid, and the laundry room will be locked up when I get home, so . . ."

"I don't even know how." It comes out so whiny, it makes me cringe, but I push forward anyway. "How about I stay home from school tomorrow, and we can do it together?"

"How about no?"

"I guess I can throw it in and go back and get it later," I mumble.

"No, ma'am. You can't leave clothes unattended."

"Why? Are the laundry police gonna get me?" I pick up a green piece of paper and rage-snip a leaf.

"There is a very clearly posted sign that says 'Do Not Leave Clothes Unattended.'" Mom takes my scissors and my paper. "And I don't want Ms. Hannigan throwing our stuff all over that nasty floor again to make room for hers. She's worse than the laundry police. Now, I gotta go. Love you."

She kisses me on the forehead and hustles on out the door.

Before I have time to properly seethe, the phone rings. "Hey, do you need me to bring anything?" Lucy asks.

"You got a washing machine lying around anywhere?"

Confused silence, and then, "Uh, is that, like, code for something?"

"No, I literally need a washing machine." I launch into a rant about the ruination of today's plans.

"OK, but," Lucy jumps in, the second I pause for breath. "Hear me out. Why don't we play in the laundry room? There's a big table in the back for folding clothes. We can use that. It'd be perfect, actually."

"Play *in* the laundry room?"

"Yeah, it'll really put the 'dungeon' in Dungeons & Dragons." She laughs, then lets out a shuddery breath. "That place is kinda spooky, you know?"

"What if somebody comes in?"

"I don't know. Who cares? They're just gonna be sitting there, looking at their phones anyway. The folding table's way back behind the dryers. Nobody ever sits there."

"Except the spiders."

"And the cockroaches."

"And now, us, apparently." I start to sigh but end up giggling instead. "All right. Fine. I'll meet you there at one."

"I'll bring the bug killer. My dad just bought a can of Raid— it should come in handy."

We hang up and I rush around the house, gathering up all the dirty clothes and towels. Before I leave, I drag the heavy laundry bag over to the computer for one last email-check before I go. I type in my password, click Sign In, close my eyes, and cross my fingers.

Please, please, please let there be an email from Devin.

Preferably one that not only tells me my campaign is awesome but provides step-by-step instructions on How to Be the Best Dungeon Master Ever.

Because right now, I have no idea if it's any good.

I have no idea if *I'll* be any good.

I open my eyes, uncross my fingers, and check the screen. No new emails.

Welp, here goes nothing.

▲ ▼ ▲ ▼ ▲

Lucy gives me the run-down of her laundry system and, in under ten minutes, everything's separated and into the machines on the proper setting, with the precise amount of soap necessary.

"That was awesome. Thank you," I say, my voice wobbly with nerves. We're almost past the row of dingy, rust-tinged dryers, and soon our game will begin.

"No problem," Lucy says, oblivious to my internal freak-out. "I did the laundry at my mom's all the time." She shrugs, then widens her eyes at our "gaming table." "Whoa, OK. A little scarier than I thought."

The overhead light flickers ominously as my eyes track from the web-filled corners to the fuzzy little lint bunnies blowing around the grimy floor. A thick tablecloth of dust coats our playing area, and the thumping dryers pump a steady stream of humidity into the already-sweltering room. It looks like my brain feels.

An itchy sweat breaks out on my forehead.

I drop my gaming screen and dig through my backpack for the Clorox wipes.

"Good thinking," Lucy says approvingly. "Now, look what I have." She pulls a small electric fan out of her Undertale tote bag, followed by a couple half-frozen water bottles, and a Party-size bag of Doritos.

And the Raid. Really glad she wasn't kidding about the Raid.

Once the area is clean(ish), I settle in behind my Dungeon Master screen. The wall of whirring dryers provides a welcome barricade, hiding us from view and muffling our voices. Still, I begin softly, my heart fluttering in nervous pulses that fly up and crack my voice.

You are on the verge of an enchanted forest. You've left your old life behind and are in search of new adventures.

"That's right, I am!" Lucy/Octavia shoots me a grin and jumps to her feet. Raising her fists dramatically, she strikes a triumphant pose.

She is so goofy. And so nice. She acts like every nerdy thing I say is cool and never makes me feel stupid. I stifle a giggle and continue, trading my nerves for determination. I'm going to give her an adventure to remember.

A flash of silver darts across the sky. It catches the sun's rays and sends out a blaze of light, and for a moment you're blinded.

Lucy drops back into her seat, blinking.

When your vision clears, the mysterious silver streak is gone.

She tilts her head thoughtfully, then asks, "Which way did it go? What do I see now that my vision's clear?"

Ancient trees, the size of giants with gnarled and knotted trunks, stand like sentinels along the forest's edge for miles in either direction. The only break is the entrance, a dirt path, which is canopied by the entwined, moss-dripping branches of the two largest trees nearby. The path is littered by untouched leaves, and the only tracks are those of foxes and deer. There is no sign of the flash.

Lucy leans forward, listening intently.

You stand at the edge of the path. Do you choose to enter?

"Of course. I bust on into that for—Wait! I wanna do a Perception Check! What if there's something pacing around off to the side that wants to eat me? Or a band of trolls planning an ambush? I'm not trying to get killed off here."

Like I would kill her off two seconds into the game, that's so messed up, but I don't say that to her. It's good she's thinking. "All right, roll your d20."

She selects her twenty-sided die, holds it to her ear like she's listening intently, and rolls.

"A twenty!" We both shriek in unison.

"I'm not sure if that's a good sign, or if that means I wasted my good roll," Lucy giggles.

"Guess we'll find out," I say, secretly racking my brain for a response to this epic Perception Check.

"So what do I hear?"

You hear the flutter of a crow's wings, the chitter of a squirrel that's dropped its acorn, and the heartbeat of an abnormally large cockroach.

"Like that one right there?" She points over my shoulder to a small, shadowy figure skittering across the wall.

I glance back. "Precisely."

"Is it armed?"

"You do not hear the clink of any weaponry."

"How close is it to the path?"

I gesture from the wall to the table. "About that close."

She slowly wraps her fingers around the Raid can. "Does it have any weaknesses?"

"You can't *hear* weaknesses," I say, laughing.

"But I rolled a twenty!" She sticks her pointer fingers behind her ears and pushes them out and forward. "I hear ALL!"

Devin would be losing his snap by now, telling me to stop asking random questions and get serious.

I think it's hilarious, though. And I'm not even nervous anymore.

▲ ▼ ▲ ▼ ▲

The gnoll towers over you, his hyenalike features twisted into a menacing sneer. His yellow mane is dirty and matted against his mottled gray-green skin, and sharp claws curve around the handle of the spear. He brandishes the razor-sharp point in the air, then points it at your chest. The smell of rancid meat and dried sweat fills your nose, nearly making you gag.

"Yikes." Lucy wrinkles her nose. "Can I talk to him?"

"Do you want to talk him?"

"Sure. I'll talk to him."

"Do you speak gnoll?"

She checks her character sheet. "No, just Common and Dwarven."

"Well, you can try." I give a little shrug. "Maybe he speaks Common, you never know. It's up to you."

"OK, so." Lucy bites her lip, twirling the curl that's slipped past her ear.

"So?"

"So." Lucy drops the curl and sits up straight. "So, I look up into his big, stupid face and I say, 'What do *YOU* want?' Oh, and I put my hand on the hilt of my axe. Threateningly."

"Nice."

The gnoll looks you over with narrowed eyes, then he shakes his head and bares his teeth. He doesn't understand you, and he doesn't want to. He points to your traveling pack with his huge, filthy paw, then back at himself.

62

"He's mugging me."

"Pretty much."

"Well, then." Lucy blows out a breath and rubs her hands together. "I'm going to kick his butt."

"You choose to attack?"

"Yeah. This guy is going down."

"It's on, then. Grab your d20 and roll for initiative." A nerdy thrill shivers up my spine. I never got to say that part before—that was always Devin's gig. Before any fight, everyone has to roll to find out the order of attack, so the initiative order can make a big difference in the outcome of a battle.

Lucy rolls a 2 to my 10, which means my gnoll gets the jump on the attack.

"All right, Octavia," I say, rattling the die between my palms. "Let's see what you're made of."

"Bring it, Stanky."

I drop the dice behind my screen. A 15. Just enough to pierce Octavia's armor. "It's a hit." I grin at Lucy over the cardboard.

"I don't believe you."

Well, color me shocked. "What do you mean you don't believe me?"

"Hiding behind your curtain over there, like you're the Wizard of Oz or something. I don't know if I buy it."

"I rolled a fifteen."

"Prove it."

"Oh, my lord, are you serious?" I stare at her, eyes wide. She stares back, eyes wider. "You're serious." I can't believe it. I never questioned Devin like this. He would have exerted his DM authority and put the whole game on time-out. But, I'm not Devin. I pick up the die and raise it slowly so she can see I'm not turning it, then I shove my big, fat 15 in her disbelieving little face. "Happy?"

"Mm-hm." She smirks and gives a tiny nod. "I mean, not happy that I'm gonna get poked with a spear, but happy to have such a kind and trustworthy DM. You passed the test."

"I'm rolling my d8." I get to my feet to better prepare for my roll. "You better hope I don't roll the full eight, because that's, like, half your health."

"Oooh, she's a feisty DM, she is." Lucy giggles, and I chuck my d8 across the table for all to see.

It's a 1.

Lucy cracks up. "You better sharpen that spear, dude. It's got nothing on my axe."

She's right, of course, and the gnoll is easily vanquished. Which, by the way, was totally the plan. The real reason I rolled behind the screen was so that I could fudge the numbers in case I accidentally killed her. *Not* so I could cheat. Anyway, Octavia loots the gnoll's body and finds two coppers and a lump of green cheese.

"I'm gonna decline the cheese," Lucy says.

"Solid choice."

You make your way deeper into the forest and come upon a small pond. The water is crystal blue and sparkling. Suddenly—

"SUDDENLY YOU'RE UNDER ATTACK!" A husky voice bellows from the other side of the dryers. A fresh-smelling shower of blue-and-green packets rains down on our heads. One hits my screen and sends it tumbling, and another one hits me square in the nose. It bounces off and falls into my open palm.

I gaze down in confusion at the very strange, very unexpected missile. "Is someone throwing Tide Pods at us?!" Mom was right—you really can't leave your stuff unattended down here.

"It is I! The Tide Queen! Water Elemental and Mistress of Cleanliness." Perched atop a nearby dryer is a tall girl with hair the color of pumpkin pie and a face full of glee and freckles. She's wearing an

oversized tie-dye shirt, ripped jeans, and mismatched socks (one Pikachu, one plain black) peeking out of the dirtiest old pair of Converse I've ever seen. There's a wicked gleam in her blue eyes as, one by one, she chucks another round of Tide Pods at us. "Pew! Pew!

It's really, really weird. So weird that I'm frozen in place, allowing myself to be pelted with laundry detergent. But not Lucy.

"What the heck?" She giggles and scoops up an armful of Tide Pods and hurls them back. "Surrender, Tide Queen!"

"Never!" The girl crosses her eyes and grimaces, then lets out an evil cackle. "Your base belongs to us!"

My snort-laugh echoes through the room. I shrug and lob the packet in my hands toward the girl. It hits her square in the chest, and she clutches her "wound" dramatically. "My heart . . ." she wheezes, collapsing on the lid of the dryer before sliding to the floor.

"No, no, Tide Queen. Get up and rise again. That floor is a next-level dungeon." Lucy pulls her to her feet, then she says, "I know you. You ride our bus. Were you spying on us?"

"Only for, like, an hour." The girl grins. "Ms. Hannigan thinks you're summoning demons, by the way. Oh, and your clothes beeped forever ago."

"The clothes!" I slap my forehead. I'd completely forgotten they existed.

"Come on, I'll help you move them over," she says. "Don't worry, I won't look at your underwear or anything."

▲ ▼ ▲ ▼ ▲

Her name is Hannah. She has four-year-old twin brothers who are absolute chaos monsters, so she hides in the laundry room to get away from them. She likes dogs, but she's not allowed to get one. She thinks fish are boring, but she has three of them. She used to play Fortnite until she got tired of it, and now she doesn't know what to play. Regular

Skittles taste like gnome barf (which is bad), but Sour Skittles taste like dragon scales (which is . . . good?). She likes reading, but only comic books, not school stuff. She hates math anywhere. She's in sixth grade, like us, but she's not in any of our classes. She does have our same lunch period, though.

I find all this out in the time it takes to move the clothes from the washer to the dryer.

"Can I pick a guy?" Hannah asks as she takes the quarters from my hand, slides them into the machine, and pushes Start.

"Pick a guy?"

"Yeah, for your game. I wanna pick a guy."

Devin. Would. *Die.* Character creation to him is a sacred act, a commitment, something not to be taken lightly. And this girl here is talking about I wanna pick a guy like she's choosing between Mario and Luigi.

I love her.

"OK, well, the thing is, you can't *pick* a guy—"

She lets out a disappointed *Oh*, and her face falls.

"Wait, let me finish. You have to *make one*, but we can help you."

"We're experts now," Lucy chimes in.

"Well, kinda experts," I correct her. "Newish experts. Newish enthusiasts, let's say."

Hannah grins, finger guns brandished. "Let's do it!"

A loud siren goes off, wailing from Lucy's back pocket, and we all jump. With a grimace, Lucy pulls out a phone in a sparkly blue case and swipes impatiently with her thumb. "Sorry. That's my alarm." She sticks her tongue out at her phone. "I have to go. It's Sunday dinner, which is apparently a thing now. My dad orders one of those meal-prep boxes, like in the commercials of happy families cooking, and then we become a happy family cooking."

"Sounds nice." My dad wouldn't make me a bologna sandwich if I were starving in the desert. Honestly, he wouldn't even know I was in the desert.

After a moment, her scowl softens. "OK, fine. I guess it is. At least he cares if I eat dinner or not." It's like she read my mind.

"Hannah Grace McMillan!" A woman's voice booms down the sidewalk, right by the laundry-room door. "Where you at?"

Hannah puts a finger to her lips, giggling silently.

A stomping shadow passes the door muttering something about disappearing daughters.

"I better go," Hannah says. "I'm supposed to watch the twins so my parents can go to the store."

"Why didn't you say something?" I ask.

She gives me a look like *Duh*, "This is my secret hiding spot."

"Ahhhhh."

"But I still want to make a guy."

"Sure, how about tomorrow?" I ask, glancing at Lucy for confirmation. "After school?"

She nods. "Yeah, that'll work. I'll bring the cupcakes."

"You the official cupcake girl now?" I ask.

Lucy salutes. "Ready for duty."

"What are the cupcakes for?" Hannah asks.

"You'll see. After school." Lucy snaps her fingers. "Oh, hey! Speaking of school, it's Spirit Week."

"Oooh, I wonder if Mrs. Lane hung up my poster yet," I say.

"Your very *interesting* poster." Lucy elbows me in the side. "I sure hope so. Anyway, did you see the thing about the school spirit dress-up days?"

"Yeah," Hannah says. "Like, every day has some corny theme."

"Exactly," Lucy says. "And I get that they're corny, but do people actually do them? Like, if I don't dress up, am I going to be the only one that doesn't? Or if I *do* dress up, am I going to be the only one that *does* and look like a sixth-grade noob?"

These are very good questions. Questions that it never occurred to me to ask, but now fill me with great anxiety. If Devin were here, I could run upstairs and ask him. Problem solved. But now . . . I'm on my own.

Lucy's phone rings and interrupts my pondering. She answers it with a quick "I'm alive. I'll be up in two seconds," then jams the phone back into her pocket with a groan. "I really gotta go, but seriously what do I do?"

"What's tomorrow's thing again?" Hannah asks.

"It's 'Let's Team Up!' so you're supposed to dress, like, identical to somebody." She cringes, and a flush creeps over her cheeks. "Not that I go around memorizing school spirit posters or anything. It's just that I never middle-schooled before and—"

69

"I get it," I cut her off. She does *not* need to explain that to me.

"Me too." Hannah says. "I've been thinking about it all weekend. I don't have anybody to dress like, even if I wanted to. What if I'm the only girl in the cafeteria in a lonely just-me outfit?"

That surprises me. I didn't expect the Tide Queen to worry about what random people in the cafeteria thought about her.

"Hannah Grace!" The exasperated motherly voice returns.

Think fast, Riley.

"OK, I've got an idea," I say. "Why don't the three of us dress the same, but wear something totally basic. So, like, if nobody is team twinning, it'll just look like a kooky coincidence. But if they *are*. . ."

"Then we've got it covered!" Lucy claps her hands.

"Genius!" Hannah shouts directly into my left ear, and now I may never hear the same again. "What do we wear?"

"Jeans and a black T-shirt?" I take a step back out of shouting range, in case Hannah likes the idea.

"Perfect!" she hollers.

Lucy nods. "Got it. All right, I'm gonna go before Dad sends a search party after me. Tomorrow! Jeans, black shirt, character creation, cupcakes!"

She bolts out the door, with Hannah right on her heels. Mom won't be home for a while, and the clothes aren't dry yet. I pick up the rest of the rogue Tide Pods, then settle back down at the table and work on the next part of my campaign.

CHAPTER 7

THE PHONE RINGS, SURPRISING PART OF A CHERRY POP-TART out of my mouth. It is especially surprising when I pick up and it's Devin. "Are you OK?" I ask. "Isn't it, like, four in the morning there?"

"It's 4:02 to be exact." He lets out a gusty yawn. "I felt bad I didn't get to talk to you this weekend, and I wanted to check on you. I know Mondays suck."

I brush the crumbs off my black T-shirt and smile. "This one's not so bad."

"Really? Great!" He sounds surprised and a hint relieved.

"Yeah. I'm OK, but the bus'll be here in a minute. You want me to get Mom or you want to go back to sleep?"

"Back to sleep!"

"All right. Love you."

"Love you, Ri-Fi. Email me later."

I hang up, and OK, I admit it, that was nice. Maybe the Devin the Deserter thing was a bit harsh. I mean, he would at least know if I were starving in the desert—and he would definitely make me a bologna sandwich.

Feeling all warm and toasty inside, I grab my backpack and hustle off to the bus. Lucy's already on, deep in conversation with the driver, when I get there. He scratches his white beard thoughtfully, and his deep-blue eyes, framed by crow's feet, twinkle. I'd never noticed how Santalike Mr. Al was until now.

"Imagine if it was your grandchildren." Lucy gestures toward the photos on the dashboard. "You'd want them to be able to sit with their friends, wouldn't you? It's such a long drive, and it gets so lonely when you don't vibe with your seatmates." She opens her eyes wide and pushes out her bottom lip slightly. "We wouldn't be any trouble. We'd talk real quietly. Right, twin?" She pulls me up the steps.

"Uhh, yep."

The bus driver shakes his head, but he's smiling. "Fine. Y'all can sit together. You just tell that redheaded one to keep it to a dull roar."

After a couple minor seating-chart adjustments, I'm free from smelly seat-hogging football boys. "I figured our party should sit together," Lucy says, waving Hannah over to our new spot.

"Nice," Hannah says approvingly. "That one girl I was sitting with hates me. Says I keep bumping her leg, but how do we know she's not the one bumping *my* leg?"

"Right?" I take another look around the bus, and whisper. "Hey! It looks like a lot of kids are matching. Even the eighth graders."

Once we reach the school, we see even more friends teaming up to show their school spirit by way of matching garb. The bus ramp is crowded with selfie-taking twins. We squeeze past two girls in yellow rompers with newly dyed purple hair and a trio of guys in neon-orange hoodies. Lucy pulls out her phone and beckons us closer. "Squeeze in, my triplets."

We lean in, smiling, and she snaps a couple of pics. "I'll email them to you later," she says, smiling down at her phone. She slides it into her backpack and turns her smile on us. "See you at lunch? I couldn't find you on Friday, Riley, so I figure we can meet over by the stage and then try and find a decent spot."

I don't tell her the reason that she didn't see me at lunch is because I haven't set foot in the cafeteria since the first day of school. I had no one to sit with, no idea where even to sit, so I just wandered around with my tray until the bell rang. It was a nightmare, one I was not eager to repeat, so I've been hiding out in the media center ever since. Grinning, I nod way too hard. "Definitely! Our party should sit together."

▲　▼　▲　▼　▲

After school, Hannah sprawls across Lucy's bed, flipping through my *Player's Handbook*, each page flip a rejection. "Nope. Nope. Uh-uh. Not it. Boring." Then, suddenly Hannah stops and points, tapping the page roughly with her index finger. "This one! That's me!"

I peek over her shoulder. "A half-orc?"

"Yes!" She sits up straight, grinning. "Listen to this. It says they have towering builds, prominent teeth, and dark vision. Like, they can see sixty feet in the dark. That'd be pretty handy, huh? Oh, and it also says that battle scars are tokens of pride. Look!" She points to the tiniest silvery scar on the edge of her left eyebrow. One that I had not noticed and probably never would have noticed if she hadn't thrust her face about an inch from mine. "In first grade, I got in a little disagreement with Jonas Waltermon on the playground about who would win in a fight between John Cena and the Rock. Ladies, let me tell you, this child got so beat down by my powerful arguments that he picked up a literal rock and threw it at my head."

"For real?" Giggling, Lucy takes the book and reads over the Half-Orc pages.

"Yep. He was all, like, 'If you love the Rock so much, have one.'" She rolls her eyes. "Nice comeback, turd."

"All right, battle scar achieved," I say.

"Look," Lucy adds. "It says here they laugh loudly and heartily. That's one hundred percent you."

"Totally," Hannah agrees. "Except I don't want to be gray. I want to be green. Like Shrek."

I take the book from Lucy and scan the page doubtfully, "It says they have 'grayish pigmentation.'"

"So?"

"So, I don't think you can be green."

"Isn't Shrek an ogre?" Lucy asks. "He's not an orc."

"I didn't say I wanted to *be* Shrek." Hannah shakes her head at us fools. "I said I wanted to be green *like* Shrek. But an orc. Half-orc. Whatever."

"Yeah, but . . ." I flip through the pages one more time. "The rule-book says they're gray."

Hannah crosses her arms. "You're telling me that you can be an elf, I can be an orc, Lucy can carry a fifty-pound axe and fight hyena-headed monsters, and we can drink magical potions to heal all our boo-boos, but I can't be green? I don't get it."

Jeez, when you put it that way, I don't get it either. "OK, you can be green." But I can never tell Devin about this deviation from the rule-book. His rule-following, by-the-book heart couldn't take it. "What do you want your name to be? Princess Fiona?"

"Don't be ridiculous." She tosses her hair and gives us a prim look. "My name is Buffy."

"Buffy?" Lucy and I bust out laughing.

"Buffy Van Orckingham, if you please."

"All right, Buffy Van Orckingham, what's your class?"

"I wanna be a bow-and-arrow guy."

"A ranger it is." I toss her my blue set of dice. "Now, let's roll for your stats."

Not surprisingly, Hannah's rolls are chaotic and filled with enthusiasm and half our time is spent chasing down the wild dice. Eventually, though, we get her totals and set up her abilities. Also, not surprisingly, Hannah is high on charisma. Once Buffy's character is officially created, Lucy hollers for her dad. He hustles in with a plate of cupcakes, three birthday candles, and a lighter.

"You summoned the fire lord?" he asks. He flicks the lighter dramatically and a tiny flame appears.

"You know what to do," Lucy tells him with a grin.

With a flourish, he lights the candles and hands us each a cupcake. Lucy waves him away and he hustles back on out, but we all know he'll linger in the hall to make sure we don't burn the place down. Once the room is clear, we burst into song.

Happy birthday, Buffy Van Orckingham . . .

Happy birthday to you!

I miss my wish window again, wavering between bringing Devin home and the permanence of my party. A tiny sliver of smoke snakes up from Hannah's and Lucy's silvery candles, while mine melts under a sputtering flame. I blow it out before it gets weird and pull the candle from its bed of pink frosting. You'd think Lucy's dad worked at the bakery instead of the hospital, the way he keeps conjuring up cupcakes while she's at school.

"Now that Buffy's officially born," Lucy asks between mouthfuls, "when do y'all want to play?"

"When do you want?" I've got all the time in the world. "The next part's all planned out, and Octavia can run into Buffy at the pond."

"That's right she can." Hannah grins, then frowns. "But I'm on twin patrol tomorrow. And the next day. And the next day. Dad doesn't get off work until five, and Mom has to go in at four. Boo."

"That's OK," I say, hiding my disappointment.

"You can totally come by and hang out, though. Like, seriously come by." She clasps her hands pleadingly. "Hang out. Save me. We'd outnumber them."

"That could be fun," Lucy agrees.

"Probably not," Hannah says, then gives us a look. "Sorry, just keeping it real."

Laughing, I ask, "So do battle with the twin chaos monsters during the week, then play Friday?"

"I'm going to my mom's Friday," Lucy says, glancing quickly at the picture on her nightstand with a smile. "How about Saturday?"

"Perfect!" I shout before anyone can change their minds, and Hannah nods her agreement.

"Oh, and while we're getting ourselves organized, my dear party members," Lucy says. "Tomorrow is 'Put a Lid on the Competition' day, so we're supposed to wear hats." She jumps up and disappears into her closet. After rummaging around for a few minutes, she reemerges with a Viking-style helmet, complete with horns, and pops it onto her head. "I got this baby right here from my Halloween costume last year. What do you think?"

Hannah bellows out a *Yaaaaaaaaaaaas queen!* and I give her a thumbs-up. "Octavia would approve."

"All right, what y'all got?"

"I have a wizard hat." Actually, it's Devin's hat, but he left it, so finders keepers. "One of those pointy black velvet ones with gold stars all over it."

"Nice." Lucy gives an approving nod. "Buffy?"

"Hmm." Hannah rubs her chin thoughtfully. "One of my brothers has a Robin Hood hat. That'd be good for a bow-and-arrow guy."

"Isn't he, like, four?" Lucy asks. "That hat'll be tiny."

"Exactly." With a click of her tongue, Hannah shoots a finger gun her way. "Half-orcs have big heads. Do you know how hard it is for Buffy to find a decent hat that fits? Don't judge."

Lucy holds up her hands. "I wouldn't dare. So, everybody in? Character hats tomorrow?"

Hannah can't decide between thumbs-up and finger guns. Her hands are all over the place as she shouts out her "Yes!" I decide on a plain ol' thumbs-up and a smile.

"I'm gonna need an axe for Friday, though," Lucy says, rubbing her chin.

"What happens on Friday that requires axes?" I ask.

"It's 'Dress Like a Superhero' day. You know, because 'Our team is super!' or so they say." Lucy rolls her eyes and giggles. "So I'm thinking we should dress like our characters. They're kind of like superheroes—they have powers, anyway. That's enough for me."

"Holy yes!" Hannah springs to her feet and jumps on the bed. I grip the comforter to keep from flying off onto the floor.

"Shoes off the bed, Buffy." Lucy points at her sternly. "Were you raised in a barn?"

"Buffy was raised by wolves, thank you very much." She bares her teeth and snarls, but drops back down onto her butt.

Giggling, I turn to Lucy. "You think we should dress up?"

"Yeah," Lucy says. "Wednesday and Thursday are kinda boring. Like, weird socks for 'Sock It to the Opponent' day and then it's just 'School Colors' day—"

"You'd be a great cruise director," Hannah says. "You for-real have the whole itinerary memorized."

Lucy rolls her eyes and continues. "Anyway, since the next two days are super-easy, we'll have plenty of time to make our costumes for Friday. Riley, you can be your elf-sorceress chick you told me about."

Hannah rubs her hands together gleefully. "And I can be green."

▲ ▼ ▲ ▼ ▲

"Try him again."

Mom mutters something under her breath, something that sounds an awful lot like a cuss. We've been holed up in her bedroom for over an hour, trying to put together my Arwenna costume, and it looks like somebody's getting cranky.

"What was that?" I cup my ear and lean toward her, all innocence.

Crouched at my feet, like a wicked old gnome, she glares up at me. "None of your beeswax," she snarks, violently stapling the hem of her old and my new blue skirt.

"Look out!" I jump back. The fabric swirls around my legs, its softness marred by the scritch-scratch of rogue staples. "You almost got my ankle."

"I did not." Mom groans her way to her feet and chucks the stapler onto her bed. "And just so you know, I'm perfectly capable of helping you with your costume. Devin's not the world's foremost authority on sorceresses and their garb."

"You sure about that?" I ask, raising a doubtful eyebrow, which is one of Devin's signature moves. "I'm pretty sure he is. Even if he's not, I'm one hundred percent sure he would have used a needle and thread to fix my hem, not the stapler."

Mom rolls her eyes. "Fine, I'll try him again. You're welcome for *my* skirt, by the way." She whips her phone out of her back pocket and punches in the number. Of course, it goes to voicemail. Mom hangs up and tosses her phone onto the bed. It bounces off the stapler, which she grabs and brandishes triumphantly over her head. "Hah!" She clicks it menacingly, sending a shower of silver staples to the floor. "Looks like you're stuck with me and my stapler."

I sigh. "But I want it to be right."

"It will be. We can do this," Mom's voice softens. "Just tell me what you want."

"I don't know. That's why I wanted to call Devin."

"You don't know what you want? Arwenna's *your* character, right?"

"Yeah, I guess."

"You guess?"

"I mean, of course, she is."

"Alrighty then." Mom smiles. "What shall we conjure up for her?"

▲ ▼ ▲ ▼ ▲

Hannah slams her tray down on our lunch table, a ferocious scowl on her newly green face. A strand of red hair falls forward, sticking to the thick emerald coating on her cheek. She daintily extricates the hair, careful not to smear the makeup, and tucks it into her new archer's cap. This one *almost* fits. She found it at the dollar store, then snipped holes in it and rubbed dirt on it to look like she'd "been in battle." Her outfit's an oversized black pillowcase with jagged arm and head holes snipped into it, over a pair of faded black leggings. Cardboard arrows are wedged into the frayed rope that serves as her belt.

"Why're you looking like that?" Lucy asks, digging around her lunch bag.

"People keep calling me She-Hulk." The scowl deepens, leaving forehead lines in her makeup.

"She-Hulk is cool," I say, popping a tater-tot into my mouth.

"I'm *not* She-Hulk." She crushes a ketchup packet between her fingers, sending a blood-red squirt over her hot dog. "I'm Buffy Van Orckingham."

"Yeah, but how are they supposed to know that?" Lucy pulls out a turkey sandwich and takes a huge bite. "You got to admit, she's kind of . . . new."

"Fine. Maybe they've never heard of Buffy. But seriously, She-Hulk doesn't even use arrows." Hannah whips out her cardboard versions and waves them at us. "That's Hawkeye."

"You'll have to introduce yourself." I grin, knowing there's nothing Hannah'd love more than to share her magnificent half-orc with the world.

She winks and shrugs. "No worries. I have, and I will continue to. By the time the last bell rings, rest assured these miserable peasants will never forget the likes of me."

"I'm sure I won't," Lucy says.

"Where's your axe?" Hannah asks.

Lucy rolls her eyes, drawing attention to the angry red "scar" created from red lip liner that runs from her right temple to her left cheek. "Mrs. Williams took it. Said it wasn't school-appropriate. Kind of threw off my look." She gestures down at the silvery plastic breastplate, also courtesy of the dollar store, layered over her gray T-shirt. Her ripped jeans are tucked into fur-lined boots, and her dice pouch dangles from her brown leather belt. This morning, a plastic toy axe was hanging from it as well.

"You still look cool," I say. "And your hair is fierce."

"It oughtta be. Dad and I were up at five thirty this morning creating this masterpiece." She pats her hair, which is pulled up and back in a complicated series of ladder braids leading to a waterfall cascade of curls down the nape of her neck.

"Who are you supposed to be?" Math Class Jen stands over me, her lunch tray balanced against her hip. Nestled between her spork and her milk is a thin wooden wand. She's wearing a yellow Hexside sweatshirt, like from *The Owl House,* over a pair of black leggings. Looks like she put her own spin on superhero day too.

"I'm a sorceress," I say.

"I get that," she says. "But, like, which one? I don't recognize your outfit."

"Oh." Most people were good with sorceress. Nobody actually grilled me on which specific one. I look down at my costume, trying to think of the best way to explain. I'd ended up cutting out a bunch of stars and moons from an old white sheet and stapled them all over Mom's skirt. While I was doing that, she busted out her silver-sequined tank top from college days and layered it over one of my blue tees. My favorite part, though, was the glitter hairspray and silvery lip gloss Mom surprised me with this morning. We were never able to get the Devin seal of approval, but I was happy with how Arwenna turned out.

I open my mouth to say *Oh, just a sorceress*, when Hannah answers for me. "She's Arwenna, an elf sorceress from Dungeons & Dragons land and she can shoot magic missiles from her fingers up to thirty feet." She sticks out a hand for Jen to shake. "Buffy Van Orckingham, at your service. Half-orc ranger, soon to be conqueror of the enchanted forest."

"Girl, we are not trying to *conquer* an entire forest. We're trying to find that silver flash," Lucy reminds her, then turns to Jen. She leans forward, elbows resting on her knees, and fake spits. "I'm Octavia, skull-cracker extraordinaire, but that's all you'll find out about me."

"She's got a mysterious past." Hannah snort-laughs.

"Wait. What?" Jen gracefully slides her tray onto the table and pulls up a chair. "Back up and explain."

Over the next fifteen minutes, we give Jen a crash course in D&D. She takes it all in, listening carefully and reining us back in with questions when we get too wild or veer off topic. When the bell rings signaling the end of lunch, we all look at her expectantly.

"What do you think?" I ask. "Would you ever want to, you know, play?"

"It's all that fantasy stuff you said *plus* math?" she asks.

"Yeah, I guess you could put it that way," I say.

She crushes her empty milk carton with a grin. "Well, then. Looks like it's time to upgrade my training wand. I am *so* in."

CHAPTER 8

AFTER SCHOOL, THE FIRST THING I DO IS OPEN UP MY EMAIL.
Today was awesome, and I've got to tell Devin all about it. Even more
awesome, though, is that Devin finally wrote me back.

Hey, Ri-Fi!

*Wanted to let you know I haven't forgotten about your campaign. Things
are super-busy here, but I promise I'll read it over soon and give you some
notes as soon as I get a minute.*

*Your pictures are awesome! I love that you all went as your characters!!!
That had to be so fun.*

Finally! The Devin Seal of Approval. Of course, I have been spam-
ming his inbox with pics of my costume all afternoon, plus Mom texted

him a bunch this morning. Either way, it's about time he got back to me. Smiling, I read on.

Just a thought—Arwenna's a wood elf, so I'm not sure about the silver and glitter. Next time, you might want to use more browns and greens. Make it more foresty, you know? Here's a couple links you should check out, so you can see what I mean.

Happy Friday! Chat more this weekend.

Oh. My smile fades, and I glance down at my split ends, silver sparkles still glittering against the brown. That's right, what was I thinking?

Yeah . . . that was Mom's idea. I type back, then head off to shower.

Shower-fresh but not quite glitter-free, I sprawl out on the couch, rereading my campaign for, like, the millionth time. I really wish Devin had read it. There have to be parts that are all wrong or cringey, but no matter how many times I flip through the pages, I have no idea what needs fixing. With a huff, I snap the binder shut and jump to my feet. Clutching it to my chest, I pace the living room, trying to get a handle on my thoughts, but all I do is anxiety-spiral. The thing is, it's not just Lucy anymore, it's a whole group, and I don't know Jen that well yet. What if she thinks the campaign's dumb and the laundry room's disgusting? Hannah and Lucy made a big deal about our secret D&D lair, and I worry she's got the wrong idea. Like, maybe she's not expecting to spend her Saturday afternoon surrounded by dust, lint, cobwebs, and creepy-crawlies. Even I'm not particularly looking forward to that part.

I toss the Binder of Adventure onto the coffee table. I've read the stupid thing so many times, it doesn't even look like words anymore, but the laundry-room situation is definitely something I can improve. I gather up our bucket of cleaning supplies and a sturdy pair of rubber gloves, then head on down to the laundry room.

The machines are still and quiet. Not surprising, since no one wants to spend their Friday night hanging out in a dungeon—I'm the only one desperate enough for that.

Just past the wall of dryers, I stop short. I'm not alone.

Lucy is sitting at the folding table, head in her hands, sniffling softly.

I take a step back, then forward, then back again, uncertain. What is she doing here? She's supposed to be out having fun with her mom, not crying in the laundry room. I don't want to get all up in her business, but she looks like she might need someone all up in her business. A little sob escapes her throat, and she rubs her eyes roughly with her palms.

That decides it.

"Hey," I say softly, putting the bucket down.

Lucy sucks in a breath and looks up with startled, watery eyes. She pulls a tissue from her pocket and wipes her reddened nose, mumbling something that sounds like a groan and "hi" got mashed together.

I pull up a folding chair next to her. "What's wrong?"

"Nothing." She gives me the world's tiniest smile. "I'm fine."

I smile the world's most awkward smile and rack my brain for the right thing to say. "Is your mom OK?"

"My mother is fine." Lucy's face hardens, and I cringe.

Welp, that was definitely the wrong thing to say.

"Completely and totally fine."

"Oh. That's good," I say faintly. I pick at the cuticle around my thumb, eyes focused on the dry, cracked skin. Looking at Lucy makes me feel like crying, but I don't know why.

Lucy sniffles.

We sit there, sad, silent blobs of mosquito food. The sunset orange peeping through the doorway fades to a deep purple, leaving the fluorescents in charge. Crickets start their twilight chirping, chanting something that sounds an awful lot like *Talk now. Talk now. Talk now.*

Lucy doesn't seem to hear them, though. She has stopped crying, but everything about her silhouette is hard and pointy, from the jut of her chin to her tightly crossed arms. For a minute, I see Octavia, the tough-as-nails fighter with the mysterious past, and I realize that Lucy's never really been one for backstory, in or out of the game.

She's still here, though, so she must need to talk. She just might not want to go first.

"My dad might be fine too," I blurt out.

"Might be?"

"Yeah." My voice is high-pitched and wobbly. Still staring down at my hands, I pick a little too hard and the skin by my nail cracks. The little sliver of blood is gross, so I shove my hand in my pocket. "Or he might not be. He might have a cold. He might have a broken arm. For all I know, he's been swallowed up by quicksand or mauled by bugbears today." I shake my head, swallowing a sigh. "Hard to say, really."

Lucy's tense self-hug loosens a tiny bit. "Where is he?"

"Nevada." Almost all the way across the country, but not quite.

"Doing what?"

I shrug. "Managing some restaurant. He got a transfer about the same time he transferred families. I'm pre-fresh-start Florida fam, so I don't get a lot of updates."

"Oh." She reaches over and gives my arm a little squeeze. "I'm sorry."

"It's whatever. He's been gone since right before I started kinder-garten, so it's old news." I give her a little smile to show her *I'm* fine. "Your stuff seems like new news."

"Kinda." She sighs. "But not really. Mom's always done her own thing, but since she got this last boyfriend she's just, like, gone-gone."

"Is that why you moved in with your dad?"

"Yeah. He's been trying to get me for a while, I guess. She used to fight him on it, but now . . . she had no problem booting me out. She tries to act like it's 'cause her work schedule's all busy, but that's not what changed. What's changed is what's important to her."

"I'm sure you're important to her."

"Not important *enough*." She raises a hand and cuts me off before I can protest. "She ditched me tonight because her boyfriend bought movie tickets. Like movies don't play all day every day. She could've gone tomorrow, or Sunday, or next week, but *his* tickets were for tonight, so . . . ." She pauses, blinking back a fresh round of tears. "She didn't even ask if I wanted to go."

Anger blooms in my chest, and I bite my tongue to keep from saying anything else. You're not supposed to talk bad about people's mamas, but it's kind of hard when they make your best friend cry. "I'm really sorry. I get it, though."

"I'm glad." Her eyes widen and she grabs my arm. "That sounded terrible. I didn't mean it like that. I'm not glad your dad's a butt-munch, it's just nice to have someone understand. It stresses my dad out because he wants to fix everything for me—"

"But he's not the one who can."

"Exactly. Whenever I get sad, he gets sad, and then I feel bad for making him sad. Then he feels bad for making me feel bad, so he starts acting weird-fake-happy, humming and doing bizarre little dances. Then I start acting weird-fake-happy, giggling at nothing and cracking jokes that make no sense. Then Uncle Jay runs and hides in his room."

"Yikes."

"Yikes is right." She laughs, a soft, sad little ghost of a laugh. "It's downright unnatural. I couldn't do it tonight, so I came down here."

"I'm glad," I say. "Not glad that you had a bad night, of course, but glad you came down here."

"Me too."

"You can talk to me about it, whenever you want," I say, remembering the million and one times Devin listened to me complain about our dad. "I'll always understand, and you'll never have to act weird-fake-happy."

"Thanks." She exhales loudly, shaking out her hands like she's shaking off all the feels. "What're you doing down here anyway, you creeper?"

"Ooooh, big Friday plans," I say, picking up the bucket. "I was gonna clean this dungeon for tomorrow's game."

"For real? You are the bestest DM ever!" She gives me a quick, tight squeeze before grabbing a sponge. "Let me help you. Together, we will conquer this harsh terrain."

▲ ▼ ▲ ▼ ▲

The next morning, in the newly scrubbed laundry room, we all gather ready to play. Jen stands against the backdrop of whirring driers, a slim gray binder cradled between her left hip and arm, and with her right hand, she pushes back her hair. Silver threads are wrapped around her long box braids in a crisscross pattern, matching her dangling silver star earrings, and she's wearing gray ankle boots with a crisp white dress that makes me really, *really* glad we washed the chairs.

From our seats at the now-gleaming folding table, we look up at her like students while she clears her throat like a teacher. She opens her binder to the first sheet-protected page and reads, "My character's name is Lovelace. I am an elf, from deep in an ancient woodland. My family has lived there in peace and harmony for thousands of years, and my parents are considered the leaders of our village. They are six hundred years old and very wise. They are also very traditional, dislike humans, and prefer to stay deep in the forest. Their only interests seem to be art, music, poetry, and elf history. Which is fine, but I . . ." Jen looks up at us, pressing a hand to her chest. "I prefer adventure. At the tender age of one hundred and one, I decided to venture out into the world and test my wizardry skills while learning all I can. And so, I bid my parents farewell, left the safety of my village, and I am now ready to begin the ultimate journey of exploration and discovery."

She closes the binder with a satisfying snap, and we all burst out in applause. Seriously, that is quite a backstory. I was about to jump out of my seat and go running down the road myself, looking for an "ultimate journey of exploration and discovery."

"Oh, wait," Jen says, flipping the binder back open. "I drew a picture too." She holds up the second page, which is also in a sheet protector, and it is lovely. She's drawn an elven woman that looks like her, but older, in a long white dress and a silver circlet resting on her long black hair. Jen's blended her color pencils to create the deep brown of her own skin tone, and the points of Lovelace's elven ears are to die for. Tiny gray-slippered feet peek out from beneath the skirt, and she's surrounded by multicolored stars and swirls.

"You drew that?!" Hannah jumps up and grabs the picture for a better look. "Will you help me draw Buffy sometime? Please? I'll pay you! That's a lie, I won't pay you. But I'll give you a cookie or something."

"You like it?" Jen asks.

"It's amazing," Lucy tells her. "Octavia would like one too."

"You're a really good artist," I say, my mind completely blown. "Like, really good." There was a lot more going on in Jen's head than numbers and overachieving. "Until now, I thought you were made of math."

Jen laughs. "I am made of math, and don't you forget it. But I'm made of art too." She rubs her chin thoughtfully. "And tacos—lots and lots of tacos."

After placing our orders for Jen originals, we get down to the business of rolling Lovelace's stats. Jen, always prepared, pulls a silvery set out of the pencil pouch clipped in the front of her binder. She's super-into this part, adding up her rolls before I even get the numbers written down. She chooses her spells and cantrips, and then we're ready to play.

Almost.

"Before we begin," I tell her, "there is one more order of business to attend to."

"Yep." Lucy nods, then pulls out her phone to send a quick text. "A very serious initiation ritual."

"Very serious," Hannah says, making her most serious face, which is not very serious at all.

"Wait . . . what?!" Jen wrinkles her eyebrows suspiciously. "Who were you texting? Don't tell me I have to drink pig's blood or sign away my soul or something."

"Now you've spoiled the surprise." Lucy tsks, hands on her hips.

"Shhh, not so loud." I put a finger to my lips. "Ms. Hannigan's over there doing a load of whites, and she already thinks we're summoning demons. We don't want her complaining to management."

Hannah holds her hand to her ear, sticking out her pinky and thumb like a phone. "Excuse me, management?" she says in a prissy, old-lady voice. "We've got a situation. I'm gonna need you to call in an exorcist for the laundry room."

Lucy grabs the hand-phone and shouts into her thumb. "While you're at it, get the AC guy!"

Giggling, Jen asks, "OK, but seriously, what is it?"

Lucy picks up the paper bag next to her chair and pulls out a box of pink-and-white cupcakes. She pops open the container, passes them out, and slides a candle into each. Right on cue, Lucy's dad strolls up, a small pack of matches in his hand.

"My father doesn't trust me with fire," Lucy informs us with an affectionate eye-roll. "But he's the cupcake guy, so I have to humor him."

"Pretend I'm not even here." He leans forward to light the candles, dropping a kiss on top of her head.

Once the candles are lit, Hannah, Lucy, and I burst into song.

Happy birthday to you.

Happy birthday to you.

Happy birthday, dear Lovelace.

Happy birthday to you!

"Make a wish, Jen!" I say. Smiling, I watch my friends blow out their candles, one by one.

Lovelace, the wizard, made of magic, math, art, and tacos.

Buffy, the ranger, confidently strolling through life, shooting little arrows of fun at everyone she meets.

Octavia, the fighter with the huge heart and brave spirit.

Where would I be right now if Lucy hadn't banged on my door that day, demanding to be let in? I'd be alone, missing all this. I'm really glad she's a fighter. My heart swells, and I blow out my flickering candle.

I wish this party will stay together forever.

▲ ▼ ▲ ▼ ▲

"Can I drink the pond water?" Hannah asks.

"Do you want to drink the pond water?" I ask.

"I don't know." She scratches her head thoughtfully. "I mean, you said it was clear and beautiful. If it was good, then I could fill up my waterskin."

"What if it's a magic pond?" Lucy asks. "Like, maybe the water heals you. It *is* an enchanted forest, right?"

"It could be poison, though," Jen says. "Or it could do something to you, like, turn you into a frog or something."

"Or put you to sleep for a hundred years," Hannah says.

"Yeah, or maybe it could shrink you," Lucy adds.

"What if there's a monster in it?" Hannah asks, eyes wide. "Like, you lean over to get a drink and it gobbles you right up."

OMG.

We have literally been at this dang pond, which is the same pond Hannah attacked us at last week, for half an hour. For the record, Lucy's right, and the pond water heals up any hit points, but from the looks of things, they will never discover that fact because they're so busy describing all the things that the pond *might* do to them. I lean back in my chair, shaking my head at this nonsense. When I originally made it, I expected Lucy to go up to it, take a drink, get healed, then grab some for the road. I did *not* expect to spend half the game examining it. I've got to get them back on track.

I open my mouth to make a tiny suggestion, but Hannah cuts me off. "I'm shooting an arrow into the water. In case of monsters."

"Um, OK," I say.

You pull your bow from your shoulder and shoot an arrow into the pond.

As it pierces the surface, it sends out a small series of ripples. A startled frog jumps from a nearby lily pad onto the grass.

"I pet the frog," Hannah announces.

The frog beats a splashy retreat to the pond.

"Poor froggy." Jen laughs. "OK, I want to do Detect Magic."

"On the frog?" I ask.

"*No!* On the pond, silly."

Oh, thank goodness. Now we're getting somewhere.

You detect a strong aura of magic emanating from the pond.

"But what kind of magic," Jen murmurs.

"I'll bet it's good," Lucy says. "That frog's perfectly fine, right?"

I nod. Good thinking!

"I'm going for it," she says. "I scoop a little bit up in my hand and drink it."

The water is cool and delicious, and it sends a pleasant tingle through you. You regain the four hit points that were lost in the battle with the gnoll. You are now at full health.

"Yes!" Lucy cheers. "I knew it! All right, y'all, get your waterskins!"

Finally! They fill their waterskins, and the party makes its way through the forest and, after fighting off a particularly nasty pack of bandits, they find themselves at the mouth of a large cave. Hannah's about to perform a Listen Check when Jen's phone dings.

"Nooooooo," she wails, checking her texts. "How is it four forty already? I was supposed to be out front ten minutes ago." She hops up and quickly shoves her binder, dice, and water bottle into her bag.

"I guess we'd better camp," Lucy says. "Maybe not by this cave, though. We don't know *what* is living in there."

"Yeah," Hannah agrees. "We can go back to where we took out those bandits; that area's clear."

"Sounds like a plan." Jen gives us a tight smile and nods. "Sorry, ladies, but I've got to run. Mom is not big on tardiness. She thinks it's rude."

"Play tomorrow?" I ask, half walking, half chasing her to the door.

"I'm not sure." Jen grimaces. "I think I have to study."

Hannah wrinkles her nose like she caught a waft of a terrible smell. "Studying? What kind of evil sorcery is that?"

"Not just any studious sorcery; my mom calls it a Study Boost. I have to prep for the whole week. After I finish my homework, I've got to go over everything from last week. If there's a test coming up, I have to make note cards and study for that. Then I have to fill in my agenda book with all the due dates and other important stuff."

"My brother used to do that," I say. He used to also try to make *me* do it, which did not go over well. "Except he called it his Intelligence Buff."

"I like that. Makes it sound less dismal. But yeah, I don't know if I can come tomorrow. I might be too busy, what'd you call it? *Buffing my intelligence.* My mom's seriously strict about school stuff." The corners of her mouth turn down, and her shoulders slump with them. "You can go on without me."

"No way," I say. We follow her out onto the sidewalk, trying to match her stride. "We'll only play if you can."

"You don't have to do that." She catches sight of her mom's car parked in front of the building and gives a quick wave before turning back to us. "But I'll try. I'll do my best begging, and I'll call you later. But for real, I better run."

"We'll never desert you, Lovelace!" Hannah hollers at Jen's back.

CHAPTER 9

A FEW HOURS LATER, JEN CALLS. "WHAT'D SHE SAY?" I ASK, crossing my fingers that all her best begging was effective.

"She said yes." Jen's voice is a whisper.

"Yes!" I shout back into the phone.

"But if she asks . . ." Her voice drops to something below a whisper and barely above silence.

"What?" I smash my ear against the phone. Now would be a great time for a Listen Check.

"If she asks, tell her I'm way ahead on my STEM Club project, OK?" she says, just loud enough to be heard.

Um, OK. Not really sure why Jen's mom would ever feel the need to talk to me about a random STEM Club project, but sure. "Of course."

"I mean, it's not like I don't have plenty of time. The STEM Bowl competition's not for another three weeks. I can totally get it done."

"Totally," I whisper back. Wait, why am *I* whispering? Nobody's even at my house. But it feels kind of weird to talk normal to someone who's not, so I go with it.

"It's not like it's a grade or anything. It's just a competition. No big deal."

"With my mom, there's no such thing as *just* a competition, and *everything* is a big deal." She sighs. "So, if it comes up, tell her I got this?"

"Of course," I promise. "I'm pretty sure you do, anyway."

"Wait," she says, full voice. "What do you mean *pretty* sure?"

"I mean, I *know* you've got it."

"That's better." She laughs. "See you tomorrow!"

▲ ▼ ▲ ▼ ▲

The party leans in, all eyes on me. They've been slowly and carefully making their way through the cave, checking for traps and listening for monsters, and now that they've reached the end, the tension is high.

You reach the end of the cave, and there, cowering behind a pile of bones mixed with treasure, is a small silver dragon, no larger than a wolf. Its scales shimmer in the dim torchlight, reflecting the colors of fire. A heavy chain, bolted to the wall, is wrapped around its hind legs. The dragon flutters its wings but is unable to raise itself more than a few inches from the ground.

"That has to be the silver flash," Lucy says.

The others nod in agreement.

"Poor thing," Hannah says. "Should we talk to it?"

"You can try," I say.

"I'll start by introducing myself and the rest of the party, so it knows we're not dangerous."

You hear the dragon's voice, not with your ears but with your mind. "I am Moondust," it says. The voice is tiny and feminine, with a slight tremble.

"Awwww," Lucy says. "I ask her what happened—why is she trapped?"

"While you do that, I'll keep an eye on the mouth of the cave," Jen says quickly. "Just in case."

"Good thinking. We don't want to be caught flat-footed," Lucy says. "OK, *now* I ask Moondust what's going on."

Moondust tells you the tale of how she was captured by a corrupted red dragon named Scorchtongue. It overpowered her mother, slashing her with its sharp claws and breathing fire over her wounds. It then gathered Moondust up in her talons and brought her to this cave before returning to steal the rest of her family's treasure.

"Was that you I saw flying at the edge of the forest?" Lucy asks.

Moondust shakes her head, but her sapphire eyes widen hopefully. "I've been trapped here for months. But . . . perhaps it was my mother! Could she have survived?"

"Oh, I hope so!" Hannah says.

Just then, the earth begins to rumble and shake. Moondust squeals in alarm, "She's back! Run!"

"No way!" Lucy shouts.

Lovelace sees it first. A hulking red beast fills the mouth of the cave, blocking any exit. Her scales are worn and battle-hardened, lacking the shine of Moondust's, and ridged scars crisscross her garnet wings like spiderwebs. Steaming saliva drips from her long, yellowed fangs and sizzles on the dirt floor.

"Oh no," Jen says, chewing her lip.

Oh no is right. Normally, a red dragon is a little (OK, a lot) over-powered for level-1 characters, and *I've* certainly never gotten to fight one. But when I started the campaign, I had Devin's character in mind. I guess I could have changed it, but dragons are cool, so why would I? Instead, I leveled Scorchtongue down to match my party.

I know they can do this.

"I'm going to take my great-axe and smash Moondust's chain," Lucy says. "Maybe she can help us fight."

"Hmmm," I say, rubbing my chin. "It's a pretty thick chain, it's holding a dragon, you know. You're going to have to roll a Strength Check." At least a 14 if she wants to free that dragon.

"Fair enough." Lucy grabs her d20, cups it in her palms, and whispers, "Come on little buddy. You can do this." For a ridiculously long time, she rattles it around in her hands.

"OMG, will you roll already?" Hannah hollers. "The suspense is killing me! And poor Moondust. Free her, will ya?"

"For Moondust!" Lucy shouts, letting the die fly. It hits the table, bounces twice, and lands on 15.

"You got it," I say. "But just barely."

"Yes!" the girls shout in unison. Stifling a giggle, I continue.

You bring your axe heavily down upon the chain. It cracks and Moondust is free. She flaps her wings gratefully, then readies herself to fight. Scorchtongue advances on the party.

"You're going down, Scorchtongue!" Hannah shouts.

"We'll see." I shoot her a wicked grin. "Everybody, grab your d20s and roll for initiative."

Hannah immediately snatches up her blue die, rears back, and throws. The die goes sailing over the table and skitters across the floor. "Whoops!" She catapults out of her chair and runs to scoop it up. On her way back to her seat, she drops it gently on the table. "Oh, look, a twenty!" she says with a smirk. "Guess I'm going first."

Laughing, the rest of us roll. Not surprisingly, although maybe not 100 percent legally, Hannah has the first attack. I roll a less-than-impressive 2 and Scorchtongue is last.

Hannah finds that hilarious, giggling as she rolls to pierce my armor. I lowered the armor class of my dragon, so the party could actually stand a chance, and her roll is successful.

"Told ya you were going down," she gloats. "With great strength and coordination, I pull out my longbow, notch my arrow, and . . . shoot!" She rolls her d8, hitting me for 5 damage.

I clutch my chest dramatically. "Nice one, but Scorchtongue's not going down that easily." I turn to Jen. "Lovelace, you're up, if you dare."

"Oh, I dare all right," she says with a menacing grin. "Let's see if my magic can pierce that scaly hide."

The battle rages on as the party works together to defeat Scorch-tongue and free Moondust. They even get the baby dragon in on the the action, directing Moondust to use her sharp talons on Scorchtongue's soft belly, but it's Octavia's great-axe that delivers the final blow.

With a groan and a stream-filled sigh, Scorchtongue falls to the cold, hard ground in defeat. Her wicked red eyes close, never to open again. As you look upon the downed dragon, the ground shakes behind you beneath the weight of heavy footsteps.

"Seriously?" Lucy shrieks. "What now?"

You turn and see an enormous dragon, silvery blue with eyes the color of sapphires. Eyes that are much kinder than Scorchtongue's malevolent gaze. With a joyful roar, Moondust runs to the dragon, rubbing against her in a scaly caress.

"It's her mom, isn't it?" Jen asks.

I nod.

In your mind, you hear a soft, musical voice. It says only two words, "Thank you," before Moondust and her mother turn and exit the cave.

"Welp, bye," Hannah says, waving. "Do we get treasure now?"

"Yes, you get treasure now."

Scorchtongue had been defeated, and Moondust joyfully reunited with her mother, who *was* alive and searching for her, and now the party was dividing up the loot they'd found among the bones in the cave. I was a little nervous about that part. Devin never got back to me on my campaign, so I'm not sure I did it right. But I'd chosen the treasures carefully, picking items that would be perfect for their characters, and they seemed happy.

"The silver Arrow of Returning is mine," Hannah says. "It's, like, the boomerang of arrows."

Jen nods. "Of course, you're the only one that can use it. Lucy, you should take the chainmail. It'll add to your armor to give you some extra protection while you're tanking."

"And make me look good doing it." Lucy fluffs her hair. "You're getting the ruby Ring of Wisdom?"

"Affirmative. A girl can *always* use more wisdom. Oh, and there's fifteen gold, you said?"

I nod.

"That's five gold apiece. Ladies, we are rich!"

The campaign was over. Well, not really. That's the great thing about D&D; there's always a new adventure.

"What are you staring off into space about?" Hannah snaps her fingers in my face. "There's not, like, some secret plot twist or booby trap coming, is there?"

"No!" Although that'd be kind of funny. "I was thinking about how great you all did."

"Awww, thanks, Mom." Lucy leans in her chair to side-hug me.

"So, next Saturday?" Jen asks, rummaging around in her bag. She pulls out a sunshine-yellow planner with the words "Make Things Happen" glittering in gold across the front. She pulls a dark-green gel pen from behind her ear, ready to schedule. "What's next?"

Oh my God. I have no idea.

I've been so busy trying to finish up this campaign, I haven't even thought about what comes next.

"You know what'd be cool?" Lucy asks. "A swamp campaign, like the Everglades but magical. You could have, like, mutated alligators and giant mosquitos and weird snake monsters."

A swamp campaign? That sounds a little bit icky and whole lot awesome, but how to go about it? Why would the party be hitting up the swamp? Who would the final boss be? What would that map even look like?

Lucy studies my face, then lowers her eyes. "You don't like it."

"No!" I say quickly. I've really got to start paying attention to what my face is doing. Apparently, it's not always doing what my brain is. "It's an awesome idea! I was just trying to figure out how to start it."

"Well, like, what if as the party's leaving the forest, they're approached by an incredibly stressed-out-looking woman? Tearfully, she tells the group that *something* is leaving the nearby swamp at night and dragging people from the village. Last night, it got her husband. She doesn't know what to do and is there any way this fine group of warriors would help out a poor, helpless village?" Then she shoots me a sharp look. "Why are you grinning like that, Riley?"

A grin, that's good. My face is now in alignment with my brain. "I love it. Like, *love it* love it."

"Yeah?"

"Totally."

"Perfect. Now, get crackin', DM." She grins at me. "I can't wait for next Saturday!"

"Me neither!" Jen says. She flips her planner open to next Saturday, and in neat block letters writes *Swamp Campaign, 1:00 p.m.*

Welp, guess it's official. I'd better get crackin'

CHAPTER 10

I COME HOME TO THE SOUND OF ENTHUSIASTIC AIR KISSES from the Almost Office. I follow the smacking sound and find Mom practically cuddling the monitor. "Love you, baby. I am so, so proud of you." She glitches, mid-smooch, capturing a most unbeautiful image on her side of the screen. One eye's squinted shut, the other's half open and gazing off to the side. Her mouth's pursed ridiculously, with just the tip of her tongue poking out.

"*Well, that's lovely,*" she murmurs, clicking the mouse, rapid-fire. Which, of course, does nothing to help.

"You got it working!" Yes! Phone calls are nice, but I've been dying to actually see Devin. Now that we can video-chat, maybe we could even do a game online sometime.

"About as well as our Internet will allow." She glances back at the screen. "Oh, thank God, I'm unfrozen." With a sigh of relief, she hops up from the computer and rolls me the chair. "Wanna talk to your brother? I gotta start dinner, and that's enough looking at myself for one day."

"Yeah!" I drop into the seat and twirl over to Devin. "Hi!"

He smiles and pushes his overgrown fluff of bangs out of his face, but it immediately falls back into his eyes.

"You need a haircut," I say, right as he says, "I read your campaign."

Better late than never, I guess. "Seriously? We just finished it, doofus."

"Aw, man," he says, shaking his head. "Sorry about that. I thought you downloaded a premade campaign like I told you to. I sent you links, remember?"

Well, I thought those were more of a suggestion than a told-you-to. "It's OK." I shrug. "I appreciate you reading it, *finally*, but everything went great!"

"Really?" His right eyebrow raises like a question mark.

Oh no. Doubtful eyebrows always make my stomach sink.

"Really," I say, slumping down in the chair. "You didn't think it would?"

"I'm glad it went well," he not-answers with a smile. A fake-looking smile. Like he doesn't believe me.

Why doesn't he believe me?

Why *wouldn't* he believe me?

There's only one reason he'd be looking like that, with his doubtful eyebrow and his phony smile and his disbelieving *Reallys* and his
patronizing *Glad-it-went-wells.*

"DID IT SUCK?" I whisper-shout into the monitor, leaning in so
close, his face blurs.

"Whoa." He recoils so fast you'd think I jumped through the screen.
"Sit down. Calm down. I didn't say it *sucked.*"

"You didn't say it didn't either," I say, not sitting and not calming.
I wish I *could* jump through that screen.

"Look, I liked it a lot. It's awesome you're writing your own stuff; it
reminds me a lot of the junk I wrote starting out actually."

"Junk?!"

"Not junk, you know what I mean. It's like a first draft. Isn't that
why you asked for help? To see how we could make it playable?"

First draft? Make it playable?

Crap.

My cheeks catch fire and a hard lump forms in my throat, but I
finally sit back down. I'm still not calm, though. I mentally run through
the campaign in my mind, from Lucy's first session to today's looting,
desperately searching for what went wrong.

"Riley? You there? Or did the Internet freeze?"

Nope. Not the Internet. Just me. "Yeah, I'm here." I swallow hard,
shoving the lump of shame down deep into my stomach. "How bad
was it?"

"It wasn't *bad*. It was a perfectly fine first attempt," Devin says. "Don't be mad."

"I'm not mad." Although "perfectly fine first attempt" is not the response I'd hoped for. "Everybody seemed to like it, though."

"Of course they did. They're your friends. They love hanging out with you. But they're all really new to D&D, right?"

I nod.

"So, here's the thing. Remember when you first started? You had no idea how to play. You were all over the place." He chuckles, like an old grandpa reminiscing. *Somebody get this boy a rocking chair.* "It took some time, and a whole lot of explaining for you to learn the rules. I'm sure it's the same way with your friends—they're still learning the game. Next time you should go a little more by the book. That way, they'll learn how to play for real."

Something about the phrase "play for real" strikes me as ridiculous, but what do I know? I'm the all-over-the-place DM with the junk campaign.

Why is my lip trembling? Devin's here with me, offering his help. I should be *happy*. Haven't I been bugging him for advice forever? I must've sent a million emails and, now that he's finally responding, what do I do? I cry-baby it up.

No way. No way am I wasting this time with him. Who knows when I'll get his attention again?

Biting my stupid lip, I grab a notepad and pencil from the desk drawer. "So. Help me out. What'd I do wrong?"

"Like I said, it's not terrible. The gnoll part was good." There's a smile in his voice, but I don't look up from the paper to see it. "But the dragon? No way. That red dragon would have roasted your little party in an instant."

"I leveled it down," I remind him softly.

"Yeah, but you can't really do that. It's not canon."

I'd kind of like to shoot myself out of a cannon right about now. My eyes flutter back tears, and the blue lines on the page blur. Why'd I think I could do this without help? I take a deep breath and a ferocious bite of my pencil's eraser. "OK," I say, spitting out a rubbery pink morsel. "What else?"

Within thirty minutes, I have three pages of scribbled notes, two broken pencils, zero erasers, a headache, a stomachache, and the confidence of a slug. It's bad enough to find out the thing that you made, the thing that you put your entire heart and soul into, sucks, but to find out *after* you've shared it with the people in the world that you most want to impress? Well, that's a special level of Hades. I'm just glad he doesn't know this campaign was originally for him. I can't believe I thought I'd surprise him with this junk. Now, *that* would have been embarrassing.

"So," I jump in, the second he pauses for breath because if I don't change the subject soon, I'll dissolve into a puddle of fail. "How're your classes going? What are you doing in Dr. Duncan's class?"

His eyes light up, and I prepare myself for the nerdalanche. "Oh! Yeah! I forgot to tell you! This is awesome. She wants to get to know us since we'll be working together over the next few years, so our first big assignment is to create a game-design document for our dream videogame. Like, what we would make if could make anything. We have to write up, in detail, the story, characters, level design, gameplay, interface . . ."

He kind of loses me at "interface," but I don't care. I'm just really glad we're done talking about my campaign.

▲ ▼ ▲ ▼ ▲

It's Thursday night, and I've got nothing.

This is *hard*. Way harder than last time. Of course, last time I had no idea what I was doing. I was just messing around, having fun. But playing for real is serious business, and now I'm wondering if maybe I'm not up for the challenge.

Every time I think I have a great idea, Google tells me why it isn't and I have to throw it away and start from scratch. The Almost Office trash can overflows with terrible plans, while the Binder of Adventure remains flat and empty.

I glare at my notepad of scrawled advice and flip through the *Monster Manual* for the thousandth time. That leaves me exactly two days to pull together an epic swamp campaign.

It'd really help if I could get off this hamster wheel of what-ifs and nopes that I've been running on all week, like the world's most anxiously indecisive rodent. Why'd I tell everybody I'd write the stupid thing? I should've kept my mouth shut and downloaded a free one like Devin told me to.

Not that I'd even run that right.

Oh, and of course Devin's been swallowed up by California again. The second he signed off on Sunday, he disappeared back into his world of school, work, and his precious videogame document. Out of sight, out of mind, and I'm on my own once again. Just me and my notepad full of corrections and suggestions that I have no idea what to do with.

Forget hard. This is heckin' impossible.

▲ ▼ ▲ ▼ ▲

Saturday comes, and I'm still not feeling any more inspired. After confirming that my email is, once again, email-less, I pounce on Mom. "Can I borrow your phone?"

"Sure, why?" She looks up from her coffee, and her eyes widen. "And why do you look like that? You've got dark circles down to your chin—did you even sleep?"

"Not really." I launch myself from the computer chair onto the couch next to her. "I was trying to finish the swamp campaign for today, but that's kinda hard to do, considering I haven't even started yet."

"A touch of the writer's block?" Mom smiles sympathetically and pats my leg.

"Something like that."

"It's probably hard to follow up on the unbridled awesomeness of that last one." Mom takes one look at my face and withdraws her leg pat, crossing her arms. "What? Don't roll your eyes at me."

"I'm not," I say, definitely rolling my eyes. "But that last campaign was not awesome. I made so many mistakes."

"Whatever." Mom rolls her eyes back at me. Hard. "I don't believe that. Even if you did, who cares? This is for fun, right?"

"Yeah."

"Well, right now, it doesn't look like fun. It looks like work. Not just any work, graveyard-shift-without-overtime-pay work."

"Feels like it too."

"It shouldn't. It called *playing*, right? Step back from the computer, wash your face, go down there, and wing it. Let your imagination fly, little birdie. I mean, dragonling. Phoenix? Griffin? Whatever your flying creature of choice is."

My laugh is quickly swallowed by a sigh. "I want it to be *right*."

"That's what you keep saying." She scoots closer and puts her arm around me, the faint scent of coffee over toothpaste tickling my nose. "But I'm pretty sure you're doing everything right and your friends think so too."

"But they don't know any better." I stiffen beneath her hug. "Can I use your phone? I need to run something by Devin, and he didn't answer my email. I have to text him."

"It's seven in the morning there, but you can try." She hands it over, stretches, and stands. "I'm gonna hop in the shower before work."

"All right."

"All right." She mimics my bummed-out tone and puts on an exaggerated frown.

"*What?*"

"Nothing, don't get snappy." She pulls me in for a rib-crushing hug, then swings me back out into a classic shoulder-grab, deep-look combo. "But do snap out of it. For real, get out of your own head. Your friends like you. They knock on the door all day and ring the phone all night. They help you do your *laundry*, for Pete's sake. I promise they'll like any campaign you make up just fine. Don't worry so much about being right. You already are. You're right for your friends."

"Thanks." I return the smile and the hug so that the obligatory pep talk will end. I know she means well, but she's never actually DMed a game. She doesn't know the rules, she doesn't know how it works, and she doesn't get it. One time, after Devin pulled an all-nighter with his group, she actually asked Devin if he won. He still laughs about it.

Once the shower's running, I shoot off a text. *Call me the second you wake up. It is an emergency.*

Devin can never resist an emergency.

Thirty seconds later, the phone rings.

"Hey."

"Riley?" Devin's voice is full of sleep-soaked panic. I woke him up *and* freaked him out. Maybe texting an emergency from Mom's phone was a step too far. Whoops, but also not whoops. "Where's Mom? Is everything OK?"

"No. I mean, yes. I mean *kinda*."

"What is it?" he asks gently.

"I need your help."

"OK?"

"I can't do this by myself," I burst out. "I'm supposed to run a game in an hour. *An hour!* But you know what? I don't have a campaign, I don't have a boss, I don't even have a starting point. Every time I try to think of something, my mind goes blank. So, now I'm going to have to go down there, cancel the game, and let everybody down."

"Whoa, whoa, whoa." Devin lets out an enormous yawn. "I haven't even had a coffee yet. Ri-Fi, girl, you've got to calm down. This is not life or death."

"I know that." I'm not stupid. "I just need a little help is all. It's not my fault you ignored me all week."

"I wasn't ignoring you, Ri-Fi." He sighs. "You have no idea how hard it is to keep up with everything here."

"You never have a hard time keeping up with things."

"I do now. Things are different in college." He sighs again, a long one that morphs into a groan at the end. "I'm *drowning*. You think you're having a hard time with your swamp campaign? This game-design document project is kicking my butt. Every time I come up with something, I remember that Dr. Duncan's going to read it, and I freeze."

"Oh." Well, now I feel bad. "Sorry."

"Don't be sorry. It's not your problem," he says. "And I shouldn't ignore you. I mean, I'm not ignoring you. At least, I'm not trying to. Don't go thinking I'm like Dad or anything."

"Never."

"Good." His voice brightens. "Just to prove it, why don't you let me run your game today?"

"Really?"

"Yeah. Why not? I don't have work until three, and I'm not falling back asleep anytime soon. Your little 'emergency' text about gave me a heart attack. So, yeah, put me on a video call and we'll do Monsters in the Marsh. That's swampy."

"Yes!" I screech. "I'll call Lucy and tell her to bring her laptop. We can use her phone for a hot spot. Ooh, and I can play!" This time, I'll pay real close attention to how Devin does everything, and I'll be sure to do it right next week.

"Sure," he says, another yawn lurking at the back of his throat. "Sounds good. Ping me when you're ready."

This is going to be *awesome*.

CHAPTER 11

THE BANDITS HAVE HOLED UP IN THE FORBIDDEN SWAMP, leaving only to pillage the townsfolk, stealing their goods, their food, and sometimes . . . even their lives.

Devin's soft voice is packed with drama and the promise of adventure, raising goose bumps on my arms. My friends are gathered around the folding table, gazing intently at the glowing laptop. It took a little convincing to get everyone on board with the switch—especially since they have no idea what a fail *my* nonexistent swamp campaign was—but now I'm sure they'll see what a difference having a real DM makes.

Having Devin here with us in the laundry room, even if he's just a glowing rectangle at the edge of a folding table, is the best Saturday I can imagine.

Fed up with the looting, the mayor has called upon your party to dispatch this troublesome band of miscreants—

"I like that word. 'Miscreant,'" Hannah interrupts, grinning at the Devin-head on the laptop. "Miscreant. Misssssscreant."

"You know, if the bandits were snake-people, you could call 'em hisscreants," Jen says.

"Oooh." Lucy tips forward in her chair, getting right up on the screen. *"Are* the bandits snake-people?"

"Um. No," Devin says, confusion covering his virtual face. "The bandits are bandits."

"Yeah, bandits are humanoid," I jump in, making sure Devin knows *I* know.

"But they *could* be snake-people, right?" Jen asks.

Out of the corner of my eye, I glance at the screen. Devin shakes his head. "No," I say. "Definitely humanoid."

"Hm." Hannah arches an eyebrow. "But what if they *are* snake-people? I think they just might be."

"Me too," Lucy whispers loudly across the table, then hollers, "Hisscreants for the win!" before turning to me. "You should put that in your next campaign, Riley."

My eyes flick back to Devin. His forehead wrinkles as he silently mouths something that looks an awful lot like *What the heck?*

"Uh, maybe," I say, a flush creeping up my neck. "Let's get back to this game, OK? We haven't even started yet."

"Yeah, yeah, yeah." Hannah giggles. "Time to get those miscreants, that might just be snakes."

Devin is not laughing. All the side-chatter didn't really bother me when we played last week, but Devin's really big on staying in character. This has to be grinding his gears.

"They're not snakes," I put in quickly.

"But they might be," she counters.

"Exactly!" Jen shouts, arm-smacking Hannah in agreement. "I mean, how do *we* know? We haven't actually observed the aforementioned miscreants. They could be anything, really."

Devin clears his throat and lets out an annoyed little cough, probably wondering why he got out of bed for this. He must think we are so immature. I slink down in my seat, my cheeks on fire. Why can't they drop it and play *right*?

"They're not snakes, OK?" I snap.

Jen's eyes widen, and her smile fades. "OK. Fine. Was just trying to be open to different possibilities, but I guess we're not doing that here, so . . . carry on, I guess."

Lucy and Hannah shoot me weird looks, which I ignore. "Let's just play, OK?" I say, turning back to the laptop.

It's not long before our party encounters our first bandit. "He's a tall, gaunt *human*," Devin says, heavy emphasis on the word "human."

He's dressed in worn leather, and at his waist is a long, sharp dagger. As he sees you approach, he pulls his weapon and shouts for backup. Two other bandits charge up behind him, brandishing similar weapons. They advance upon you, and the battle is about to begin.

"Let's get 'em, girls!" Jen says, reaching for her d20.

"Wait!" Devin says. "You all have to roll initiative first."

Jen does a slow blink at the laptop. "I *know*," she says. "That's what I was going to do."

"OK, well, I just wanted to make sure you knew," Devin says.

"I do," she says flatly. "Now, may I roll *initiative*, Dungeon Master?"

"Sure, go ahead." He shrugs. "All of you."

With Devin's blessing, we all roll. Hannah gets first attack and goes after the initial bandit with her usual enthusiasm.

"You're going down, human bandit-boy!" she shouts. "Feel the sting of my arrows!" She rears back and chucks her d6 at the table, *hard*. It ricochets off the surface, hits the door of one of the driers with a *tink*, then rolls . . . somewhere? We hop up from the table and start hunting for it.

"Where'd it go?" Lucy asks.

"Uhhh. . . I have no idea." Hannah crouches down and peers beneath the dusty drier. "Oh, yeah, I do. Look."

"Whoa, that sucker's way back there, in the Cavern of Doom," Lucy says, kneeling next to her. "There's no telling what Buffy rolled. I'm guessing a twenty, probably. Totally a crit."

"Yeah, right." I giggle.

"Try to get it out without tipping it," Devin says, his voice edged with impatience. "And next time, don't roll so wild, OK? Riley, didn't I get you a dice corral for your birthday? You should use that."

"Yeah, you're right." Why didn't I think of that? Hannah's rolls *are* pretty wild. "I'll get the die. I'll pull it out real careful so we can see what it was." Devin is *not* big on rerolls. He says it takes away from the authenticity of the game and it's basically cheating.

"No way are you sticking your hand under that nasty drier." Jen's nose wrinkles in disgust. "You have no idea what's living or growing down there. I'll whack it out with a hanger."

"No, don't," I say. "I'll get it."

Jen shoots me another *no way* look and grabs a hanger from my laundry basket. I grab her arm, but she shakes me off. "This is for your own good. It won't kill you if Hannah rerolls, but the germs under that thing might."

She tosses the hanger to Lucy, who catches it in midair. Swiftly, like she's swinging a sword, she swipes it beneath the machine. Hannah's die skitters out in a cloud of dust and cobwebs, its grimy face proudly displaying a twenty.

"See, told you," Lucy crows. "Totally a twenty!"

"That doesn't count," Devin and I say in unison.

"Why not?" Hannah gingerly picks up the die between two fingers, then rubs it clean on her shirt. "I think it should count *more*, considering how hard the poor die had to work to get it."

"I know, right?" Jen says. "That little lady had to go on a serious quest to earn that twenty."

Lucy nods. "Good point."

In a way, it is.

"Sorry, girls," Devin-head says. "That's not how it works. Come back to the table and reroll, since you weren't able to see what it really was. Not so wild this time."

Hannah, Lucy, and Jen look to me, each with raised eyebrows and hands-on-hips like Wonder Woman's pose. My eyes flick back to the screen. Devin's head is cocked to the side, just one eyebrow raised. "Yeah. . . you can't really do that. Go ahead and reroll. I'll bring the dice corral next time."

"If you say so." Hannah lets out a hefty sigh and heads back to the table. Lucy and Jen follow, shaking their heads slightly. Why is this even a thing? I mean, I probably would have let her keep the 20, and it *was* kind of funny, but that's not the point. The DM said reroll, so just reroll already.

Hannah cups the die between her two hands, then slowly and gently lets it fall to the table. "Oh, great. A one."

Even with Hannah's less-than-stellar reroll, we manage to beat the bandits and win . . . a piece of hardened cheese.

"Seriously?" Lucy asks. She shoots me a *can-you-believe-this* look, but I just shrug. It is what it is.

"Definitely not worth my HP," Jen says.

"But you got experience," I remind her. Devin cuts us off.

As the party argues over the piece of cheese, a crocodile emerges from the swamp's edge. Its teeth are sharp and curving, and it's poised to attack.

"Cool," Hannah says. "I'll shoot the crocodile."

"You can't shoot the crocodile," Devin says, just like I knew he would.

"Why not?" Hannah asks. "Isn't that what arrows are for?"

"You're out of range."

"Fine." She lets out a long, gusty sigh and moves her figure forward. "Now I'm in range."

"Not quite. You can't move that far in one turn." He points to a different spot on the board. "Riley, can you put her figure there, where it should go?"

"Sure." I reach across the table and grab Hannah's figure, moving it back three squares.

"Ooooh, power play," Lucy says, shaking her head at me. "That was wrong."

"Did you just move my guy for me?" Hannah glares at me.

"I was only trying to help."

"What if I didn't want to go there? I don't have to just because Devin said so, you know."

"Fine." I sigh. "Where did you want to go?"

"Well, I *did* want to go shoot the crocodile, but now I think I'm just gonna chill and let y'all take care of it." She picks up her piece and moves it back to its original spot. "I'll wait here."

Then, minus Buffy, the party proceeds to halfheartedly defeat the crocodile. We don't get any loot for that, but I mean, what do they want? It's a crocodile, for Pete's sake.

"Before we go any further," Jen says, "I'd like to cast Dancing Lights."

"What's the point?" Devin asks, eyebrows furrowed. "Why bother?"

"Why not bother?" Jen retorts. "What's the point of having a Dancing Lights cantrip if you don't use it?"

"Yeah," Lucy agrees. "It'd be pretty to look at, those glowing orbs hovering over the swamp. Good for morale."

"And we could use a morale boost," Hannah mutters. "And maybe a fun boost while we're at it."

"Also"—Jen leans in toward the laptop—"I'm considering using Dancing Lights once we entered the grotto. I'd like to try it out and study the effects first. Not that I have to explain myself to the DM. I get to pick what I do, right?"

"Yeah, of course," Devin says with a slight shrug. "But people don't normally cast it all over it the place."

Jen raises her eyes to the skies, then rolls them back to Devin. "I'm not casting it all over the place. I'm doing a test cast, which could potentially lead to a useful cast. But even if I did want to 'cast it all over the place'"—she air-quotes him—"I looked it up and cantrips are free magic. If I know a cantrip, I can cast it as many times as I want, whenever I want. Right?"

Devin looks like he's swallowed the world's buggiest bug. "Right. I guess. It's just that people don't usually do that."

"I am *not* usual people," Jen informs him. We all know she's not wrong. I also know an awkward silence when I hear one. And *this* is an awkward silence.

My brother and friends turn to me. Do they honestly expect me to weigh in on the great Dancing Lights debate? Like, what do I even say to all that? I have no idea what to say. Shrugging seems like the best option, so I go with that.

Wrong answer. Everyone looks annoyed, including Devin.

My shrug-fest continues when we catch sight of a bullywug, lurking in the cypress grove. I'm all set to go after it and investigate, but Devin's not so sure that's a good idea.

"Would Arwenna really do that?" Devin asks, rubbing his chin thoughtfully.

"Maybe?" I say, with yet another shrug. "You don't think she would?"

Hannah lets out a low whistle, Jen sighs, and Lucy rolls her eyes. All of which I ignore. Devin knows Arwenna; they don't.

"I don't know," he says, although I'm sure he does. "I don't think she'd go chasing after a bullywug like that. She's more cautious."

"Yeah . . . you're right," I say. "Um, I'll do a . . . what do you think?"

"You might want to do a Perception Check. Look for clues as to what they were doing, where they were going, that kind of stuff."

"You're right. I'll do that," I say, grabbing my d20.

"OK," Hannah says. "You can do that. But as soon as you're done, *I'm* running after the stupid bullywug."

"Don't worry," Jen says. "I've got your back. Maybe my *Dancing Lights* will distract it, as you attack. It's a cantrip, you know, so I can cast it as many times as I want."

Hannah and Lucy giggle.

It's not funny. "Come on, Jen."

"Come on, Devwenna," she counters.

"What does that mean?"

"What do you think it means?"

Devin clears his throat. "Uh, Riley. You wanna roll?"

"Yes. Yes, I do."

▲ ▼ ▲ ▼ ▲

The second Devin says goodbye and logs off, Lucy snaps her laptop shut and shoves it into its case. "Stingiest. Loot. Ever."

"Worst. *Game.* Ever," Jen mutters. She pushes in her chair with an ear-piercing scrape.

"What'd you say?" I get up and shove my chair in with a pretty loud scrape of my own.

"I said," she says, slowly emphasizing her words, "*that* was the *worst* game *ever*."

"No, it wasn't," I say slowly back.

"It was."

"No, it *wasn't*," I repeat, a little louder this time, as if that'll convince her.

"Did you play the same campaign as us?" Jen asks. "Because that was a nightmare."

"A nightmare?" I look to Hannah for backup. "No way, right?"

"One hundred percent *my* nightmare," Hannah says, one hundred percent not backing me up. "I mean, if I wanted someone telling me what to do all day, I'd go to school. I can't believe I wasted a Saturday on this."

Wasted a Saturday? We're lucky Devin took the time to help us out today. I glare at her, not feeling particularly lucky myself, but determined to defend my brother. It really was a big deal that he dropped everything for me today . . . even if it didn't turn out the way I'd hoped.

"Are you serious?" A hot flush creeps up my neck and covers my face. The fluorescent lights in here are not real forgiving, so I know everyone sees me going full tomato. Mortified, the flush deepens to a prickling burn.

"They don't mean it like that," Lucy says, shooting Hannah a look. "It's just, well, today's session wasn't very fun because—"

"Wasn't very fun?" I squeak out. *"Wasn't very fun?"*

I look around me, studying their faces, and I can see that it's true. They look miserable and annoyed, nothing like the happy, giggly crew I had last week. My eyes fill with tears, and I blink them back hard. Words fail me, and all can do is shake my head. After I stressed and freaked out all week? After I stayed up all night racking my brain trying to figure everything out? After Devin gave up his whole Saturday? After we did everything we could to teach them to play for real? After all that, all that time and effort, all they have to say is *wasn't very fun*? "Maybe if you guys played right, it would have been," I finally manage to spit out.

"Riley, we played just fine," Lucy says. Jen and Hannah nod in agreement. All of them are against me.

"You only think that because you don't know any better," I say.

"But your brother does?" Jen snorts.

"Um, yeah. He kinda knows everything about it."

"Not how to make it fun," Hannah says.

My hands tremble, and my throat goes dry. God, I hate arguing, but they just don't *get it*. I shove my hands in my pocket and gulp hard before spitting out, "Well, I always had fun playing with Devin, and if you all played right, without all the excessive cantrips and rolling wild and silly stuff, you would've had fun too."

"Yeah, who'd want any silly stuff *in a game*?" Hannah rolls her eyes and shakes her head. "Just saying, Riley, this was not awesome."

"Fine, since you're so smart, you tell me how to do it. Break it down for me, please."

"I never said I was smart." Hannah crosses her arms tight across her chest and glowers at the floor. "But I do know what fun is."

"Do you? Because this conversation is not."

"Hey," Jen says sharply.

"Hey, yourself," I say, every bit as sharp. "So, you totally hated it?"

"I mean, hate's a strong word. It's just that—"

"Fine." I cut her off and turn to Lucy. "What'd you think?"

"Me? I *tried* to tell you a minute ago. Remember? But since you're asking, I think you should stop being so defensive and listen for a minute."

"I'm not defensive. I'm over it."

"That's valid," Lucy says. "You can be over it."

"I am."

"I heard," Lucy says softly. She drops her eyes to the floor and gives a tiny shrug. "Maybe we should call it a day?"

"Fine." My eyes sting as I turn away. The door seems miles away.

"Riley, look," Hannah says softly.

No doubt trying to pull me back in so she can tell me how boring me and my brother are. Well, that's not going to happen. "Bye," I mumble, then I make a run for it.

CHAPTER 12

THE NEXT MORNING IS MISERABLE NOW THAT I'M BACK TO lonely Sundays. *Lonelier* Sundays, actually, because now instead of sitting alone on my couch missing Devin, I'm sitting alone on my couch missing Lucy, Hannah, and Jen too.

How did everything get so messed up? I tried to make it all so perfect, tried to do everything right, but instead I did everything wrong. Even with Devin's help. Or maybe because of Devin's help? No wonder I've never had any friends but my brother. I'm not good at this, and I never will be.

Suddenly, a soft knock on the door jolts me awake, and I almost fall off the couch. The throw blanket twists around my legs like a rope, and it takes a moment to untangle myself. In that moment, the soft knock grows into a full-out bang.

"Riley. I know you're in there!" Lucy hollers. "Don't make me bust down the door." What is she doing here? I thought she never wanted to talk to me again.

I run for the door and twist the knob. Lucy pushes her way in and slams the door shut behind her. I have no idea what to say to her, so I just stand staring. She stares back, arms crossed protectively over her chest. Her mouth is set in a firm line, but her brown eyes are giving me a gentle look.

"Can I talk and you just listen?" she asks.

I nod.

"Without getting mad or interrupting or running off?"

I nod again, although I'm certain that's going to be the hard part. She honestly can't expect me to sit here and listen to all the things she doesn't like about me. She leads me to the couch and sits, cross-legged, facing me. "First of all, I'm sorry if we hurt your feelings."

"What?" That is definitely not what I expected her to say.

"Seriously. Even though you *were* being kind of a butthead, we could've brought it up in a nicer way."

"Thanks?" I don't know what to do with that statement.

"You're supposed to be listening, remember?" Lucy says, then continues with a huff. "My point is that when we complained about yesterday's game, it was actually kind of a compliment to you as a DM. You'd know that if you'd listened and let us finish."

"How is 'your game's not fun' a compliment?"

"You're talking again." She waves a disapproving finger at me. "Also, it wasn't really your game, was it? That was all your brother."

"Yeah, which is even better."

Lucy purses her lips, like she's buttoning up a slew of words. She studies me for a moment, then says gently, "Look, I get that he's your brother and you love him. I'm sure he's a great guy, and it was nice of him to offer to play with us—"

"It *was*."

"Agreed. However, we liked it better when *you* were the DM."

"Yeah, but—"

"I mean it. You're fun, you're creative. That enchanted forest campaign was the best. It was new and different and cool and all you. It was perfect for us."

"But Devin said—"

Lucy raises a hand to stop me. "I'm sure Devin knows everything there is to know about that old rulebook. I'm sure he and his friends have a great time playing together, although I have no idea how. But *we* like how *you* DMed. We don't want you to be Devin 2.0."

"For real? You're not just being nice?"

"No, and I mean it. That's what I was trying to say yesterday, but you wouldn't let me finish."

"Sorry."

"It's OK." She smiles. "Family stuff's tricky."

Suddenly, my eyes well up with tears. "I thought you were never going to talk to me again."

"What? No way." She shakes her head so hard her curls bounce against her face. "I just wanted to let you cool down. Everybody was all fiery, and I didn't want anybody to say anything super mean."

"Thanks," I say. "But if they did, I would've totally deserved it. What kind of a friend am I that I didn't fight for the Dancing Lights and Hannah's twenty?"

"After that poor die worked so hard." Lucy laughs. "Speaking of Hannah, she's actually lurking right outside, waiting for the all-clear. Wanna head over to my place and call Jen?"

"Sure." I take her hand and let her pull me to my feet. When we open the door, we find Hannah as promised, sitting cross-legged on the ground playing an old Nintendo 3DS.

"Just hitting up a little Mario Kart. It soothes the soul," she explains, snapping it shut and jumping to her feet. "Everybody good? Got all the feels out?"

"Yeah." I grin. "All good."

"About time," she says. "Buffy dislikes conflict."

"Since when?" Laughing, we head off to Lucy's to call Jen.

After tossing her mountain of very decorative and very uncomfortable pillows to the floor, we pile onto Lucy's bed. She whips out her phone, dials, then puts us on speaker. Unfortunately, Jen's not the one that answers.

"Jen can't talk right now," Jen's mom's sharp voice crackles over the phone. "She'll be working on her STEM Club project all day. She'll see you at school."

Click.

Lucy stares at the phone in her hand, eyebrows raised.

Hannah let out a low whistle. "That doesn't sound good."

"Didn't she tell her mom she was done with it?' I ask. "So she'd let her come over?"

Lucy nods slowly. "I hope she's not in too much trouble."

Her mom can't be *that* mad, especially since she's finishing it today. My mom'd be over it in a minute, especially since it's not even for a class. "I'm sure it's fine."

▲ ▼ ▲ ▼ ▲

"You sure you're cool with me writing the swamp campaign?" Lucy asks, leaning across the lunch table and swiping a fry. So glad we made up yesterday. I don't think I could stand going back to eating alone.

"Totally," I say, grabbing one of her chips. "It was your idea to begin with, and I about lost my mind trying to figure out how to do it justice. I'll get the next one. Plus, I kind of want to roll a new character."

"Yeah? And say goodbye to Devwenna?" Hannah smirks.

"Too soon, Hannah. Too soon." I say with a weak giggle.

"For real." Jen drops into her seat with a heavy sigh, and our giggles fade. "I wish I'd never said that." She shakes her head and mutters, "Or a lot of things for that matter."

"No way!" I say. "I had it coming. You got my email, right? And the note I put in your locker? I'm really, really sorry, and next week'll be better. I promise."

"No, it won't."

"Jen." My stomach sinks. "Can we at least talk about it? We tried to call you last night but your mom—"

"*My mom.*" Jen glowers down at her lunch bag. "Now, that's someone that sure has a lot of things to say."

"Mine too." Hannah nods knowingly. "Like, all day and all night. 'Hannah, do your homework. Hannah, did you do your homework? Hannah, for real, do your homework. Blahbiddy-blah-blah, babysit the twins.'"

Lucy pats Hannah on the arm, then leans across the table toward Jen. "What happened?"

"I'm sorry," Jen says, her eyes filling with tears. "But Lovelace is officially *out*. The overbearing elven matriarch has dragged her back to the safety of the village, where she'll be held hostage for at least the next hundred years."

"Why?" I say, unsuccessfully hiding the panic in my voice. "Does this have something to do with the STEM Bowl project?"

"Kind of, yeah, but it's more than just that. Mom thinks D&D is a bad influence. She's not just mad that I lied to her about the project, she thinks the game is taking over my mind and making me lose focus on the 'important things in life,'" Jen says with air-quotes and an eye-roll. "Supposedly I spend too much time worrying about my character and not enough time worrying about my grades. Too much time drawing and not enough time reading. I'm late every time she comes to pick me up, which is way disrespectful. And, oh yeah, all we do is fight and she doesn't want me part of some mean-girl drama group."

"Oh, come on." Hannah snorts. "It was one little teeny-tiny disagreement."

"We talked it out," Lucy says softly. "That's not mean-girl drama."

"I know," Jen says. "I shouldn't even have said anything. I was upset when I got in the car, and I thought she'd give me some advice or something. Instead she got all offended and overprotective. Then when I got home, she wanted to see my project. Of course, there wasn't one. Then she was all like 'What else haven't you done?' and started digging through my backpack. She found a couple of elf doodles in my math notebook, a dragon in my history binder, and that picture of Buffy I was working on in my English folder. After that, it was all over."

Hannah's eyes widen. "Buffy put her over the edge?"

"Strangely enough, yes." Jen gives her a sad smile. "She was, like, stomping around the room with all these crumpled papers, waving them around, going, 'What even is this? Is this what I send you to school for? So you can draw big green monsters?'"

"How dare she? Buffy is *not* a monster."

"I know that, and you know that, but Mom does not know that." Jen shakes her head. "And I was not about to be the one to tell her. Anyway, I'm sorry but you're gonna have to go on without me."

"No, I'm sorry," I say, pushing my lunch tray away. I can't eat another bite. "This is all my fault. I caused that fight Saturday."

"It's not your fault," Jen says. "Like I said, it's a lot of things. All of which added up to Dungeons & Dragons is bad for me. She wants me to stay focused, to be successful like her, and she thinks this is going to get in the way. Cause bad habits."

"Are you even capable of bad habits?" I ask. "I've seen your D&D binder. Your character sheet, stat sheets, spell reference guide, and campaign notes are perfectly organized and in sheet protectors. You even have a table of contents."

"You use Cornell notes to track our progress," Lucy adds.

"You do all our in-game math," Hannah says. "For *fun*."

"Right? *Thank you*," Jen says, tossing up her hands in frustration. "That bothers me almost as much as being banned from playing does. I would have absolutely finished that project on time. There's no way I'd let Andrea Strickland beat me in the STEM Bowl. That girl's been out for revenge ever since I took her down in the spelling bee last year."

"Revenge?" Hannah's eyebrows raise, and she forces a smile. "Took her down? Man, if I'd known nerds were so bloodthirsty, I'd have started hanging out with them sooner."

"Well, it's too bad you waited so long." Jen blinks back a fresh round of tears. "Because it looks like you've got one less nerd to hang with. On the weekends, anyway."

"I don't want to play without you," I say, blinking back tears of my own.

Hannah and Lucy nod in agreement.

"I don't want you to play without me either. I want to be there." Jen rummages around in her lunch bag, avoiding our eyes. "It is what it is, though. At least we can still have lunch together."

"Yeah," I say, but no way is that good enough.

▲ ▼ ▲ ▼ ▲

"You going to tell me what's up?" Mom asks after work later that night, unclipping her name tag and tossing it on the counter. Her dark-circled eyes are narrowed as she attempts to peer into my soul.

"You going to say hello?" I joke, unable to muster a smile to go with it. I toss a bowl of ravioli in the microwave and jab the three-minute button.

"Hello." She yanks open the dishwasher and fishes me out a clean fork. "Now it's your turn. What's up? You were an emotional mess Saturday, all happy-happy joy-joy Sunday, and now you look like somebody died."

"Nobody died," I say, my lip trembling. "But we lost a member of the party."

"Oh, honey," Mom pulls me to the table and settles me in my seat. The microwave beeps and she brings my food over, waving away the rising steam. She smooths a paper napkin across my lap, then settles into the chair across from me. "Tell Mama all about it."

So I tell her.

"It's not your fault," Mom says as I blow my nose on my napkin. "You know that, right? You can have a disagreement without being toxic.

141

You took a break, cooled off, and talked it out. Lucy's right, that's not mean-girl drama."

"That's not what Jen's mom thinks."

"Which definitely presents a problem." Mom rubs her chin thoughtfully. "There's more to it than that, isn't there? Wasn't her mom mostly worried about her slacking on her schoolwork?"

"Which is ridiculous." I can't help but roll my eyes. "Jen has all A's, and that project isn't even for a grade. Her mom needs to chill—"

"—What are *your* grades like?" Mom cuts me off.

"My grades?" What does that have to do with anything?

"Yeah, your grades."

Well, that is a stumper. I haven't been paying much attention to the graded papers coming my way, and I have never once logged into my online grading portal. "I'm going to be real honest: I have no idea."

And because my mom is not Jen's mom, she laughs instead of freaking out. "OK, so maybe Valerie has a point."

"Valerie? You know her?"

Mom nods. "We went to high school together. She's always been"—Mom pauses, her eyes flicking back and forth as she searches for the right word—"*intense.* Nice, but intense. Also, incredibly driven. You know she got a full ride to UCA, just like Devin? Except she became a lawyer. She's actually a really big deal in town. You never saw her ad?"

"I don't know, and I don't care to," I say with a scowl, my heart sinking to the floor. Jen's mom literally gathers evidence and makes cases for a living. There's no way we'll ever convince her to let Jen play again.

"She's a good person, and she's done well for herself," Mom says, more to herself than me. "You can't blame her for wanting her daughter to be successful. I know I do." She looks at me before her words trail off and she lapses into silence, tapping her lip and staring off into space.

"Um, OK. I believe you," I say, after way too many moments have passed.

Mom snaps out of it and smiles. "Sorry, was plotting."

"Oh yeah?" My heart pulls itself up off the ground, cautiously settling back in my chest.

"Yeah. Val has a point, you know. I don't like not knowing what's up with your schoolwork either." She sighs. "When Devin was here, he kept track of all that stuff."

"No joke," I say. "He used to go through my homework, erase the wrong answers, and make me redo them. I couldn't fail if I tried."

"OK, that's a bit much. I didn't realize he was doing all that." She frowns. "That's way over the top. Kind of like your D&D game, huh?"

"Yeah. Kinda."

"I get it. I'm sure he was just trying to help and got carried away."

"I know," I say.

She nods, more to herself than me. "He always made me feel better, though. Like, if I had to work late, I knew you'd be all set. Since he left, I've done a terrible job of picking up the slack." She runs her fingers through her limp brown hair and gives me a wry smile. "I'm not going to lie, I have no idea what your grades are either."

"I'm sure they're fine."

"We're going to have to do a bit better than that."

What's *that* supposed to mean? "So, what were you plotting? To ban me from D&D too?" I groan. "Thanks a lot. Really glad I came to you."

"Simmer down, young one." She leans back in her chair, tenting her fingers. "I may have come up with a solution that will benefit us all."

"Yes?" I simmer down, just a bit, and lean in.

"Remember Devin's Intelligence Buffs?"

"Definitely." How could I forget? They were probably the geekiest thing this great, green Earth ever witnessed. Same concept as Jen's mother-required Study Boost, except the boy did it *willingly* and border-line obnoxiously. Since there was no way he could possibly spread out all his academic wares in his own room, he took over the whole kitchen, filling the table with his laptop, textbooks, binders, highlighters, and nerd cards—I mean note cards. Noise-canceling earbuds pumped a steady stream of lo-fi study music into his ears as he chugged quarts of ginseng tea, frowning and hmming at page after page. Oh, and if you dared to distract him by grabbing a glass of milk or zapping some pizza rolls, he'd glare at you until you scurried off to the living room.

He did this every Sunday afternoon without fail. It was half-funny, half-annoying, but also super effective, I guess. Who am I to judge? His grades were the stuff of Einstein's dreams.

"With your permission, I'd like to have a little chat with Valerie," Mom says, putting on her professional-woman voice. "I'll let her know that I, too, share her concerns, regarding my own darling daughter. By making an Intelligence Buff session a requirement for a D&D session, we'll ensure that our children are giving adequate time and attention to their studies and maximizing their full potential." She drops the fancy-lady talk and grins. "I can probably toss in some junk about how Dungeons & Dragons is rad for creative-thinking and problem-solving skills. There's gotta be some research on the Internet somewhere supporting that, right? Pretty sure that's how Devin got the high school to give him his club. Oh! I can even use Devin as an example! Get that UCA pride going."

"You think she'll go for it?"

"It's worth a shot. What about you? I'm serious about the study sessions. You're going to have to hit up that kitchen table, Devin-style, before either of you touch a die."

"I'll do it, and Jen already does anyway, so I'm sure she'll be fine with it."

Mom gives my hand a vigorous shake. "It's a deal then. I get off at four tomorrow, so check with Jen and make sure it's cool with her. If so," she says, rubbing her hands villainously, "I'll ambush Val at her office and make her an offer she can't refuse.

CHAPTER 13

"SO?" I JUMP OFF THE COUCH THE SECOND MOM CRACKS THE door. "How'd it go?"

"You have something decent to wear?" she counters, pushing past me into the living room. "You clean?"

I check my shirt for stains and sniff my armpits. "Lilac Breeze. But who cares? What happened? Did you talk her into it?"

"Riley, I don't know that anyone can talk Valerie into anything." She shakes her head, smiling slightly. "She totally deflected my ambush. I think I got a grand total of five words out before she shut it down."

"Oh. Rude."

"Oh, no, not with rudeness. With extreme politeness. She was all like, 'Oh, Robin. How *lovely* to see you, Jen's told me so much about your daughter. You must be here to discuss their *little game*. You must think I'm so unreasonable and overbearing.'"

"Yikes."

"Yikes is right. Like I'm going to tell *her* she's being unreasonable while I'm standing there, in her pristine office, to which I was escorted by her personal secretary, sweating my butt off in this lovely ensemble." She rolls her eyes, and gestures down at her green cashier's vest and wrinkled khakis. "So glad I kept my name tag on, so she'd know who I was. And she's standing there, perfectly put together, in a tailored white pantsuit. Oh, and get this, it was four fifteen, and there wasn't one coffee or ketchup stain on the whole thing."

While this is all very fascinating, it's time to move on from the fashion report and get down to business. "You look fine. I, um, like that dangly piece of hair that's falling in your eye. It's cute. So, then what? Did she call the secretary to throw you out before any mean-girl drama erupted?"

Mom pushes the dangly hair behind her ear. "No, she invited us to dinner."

"Really?!"

"Mm-hm. Tonight. In, like, an hour. Not sure if she's being nice or if she wants to cross-examine us and see if we're worthy of her daughter."

"Either way, we're going, right?"

"Of course. But, seriously, go find something nice to wear."

So I run back to my room and quickly change into a pair of khakis and a navy button-down, then pull my thin brown hair back from my face with a barrette. It's the most drama-free, wholesome look I can come up with, so hopefully Jen's mom finds me respectable.

When we get there, though, I'm wondering if my wholesome look is going to even cut it. Jen's house is *beyond* respectable. It's huge, beautifully decorated, and so clean you'd never know anybody even lived there. It's hard to keep my eyes from bugging out of my head as Valerie leads us back to the living room. I've never been in a house that has a dining room before. And by dining room, I don't mean a too-big table with mismatched chairs that swallows up half the kitchen. I also don't mean the couch.

I mean, like, an actual dining room, that has a long wooden table with fancy swirls carved into its legs. Where the chairs all match each other *and* the table. Where the plates are all made of white ceramic, with tiny yellow daisies circling the edges. Where the silverware is

already out of the dishwasher, gleaming against a pale-yellow placemat edged with white lacy-looking stuff. I put the matching napkin in my lap because that's what everyone else does, but, really, I'd rather anything I spill land on my pants. The napkin's way nicer.

If I make it out of here without breaking or staining something, I will call it a very good day.

Mom nudges me and motions for me to bug my eyes back into my head. Jen smiles at me from across the table. Her mom walks in, carrying a pan of lasagna between two matching yellow oven mitts. She sets it next to the bread basket, which radiates beautiful garlicky smells, then takes off the oven mitts and stacks them neatly by the pan.

Her shiny black hair is cropped into a fashionable pixie, and her makeup is flawless, but she's not wearing the white pantsuit anymore. I guess even she doesn't want to brave a lasagna. Instead, she's changed into a pair of expensive-looking jeans and a fitted UCA polo.

Perfect. Mom'll definitely be able to work the UCA/Devin angle.

"This looks amazing," Mom says. "How on earth did you find the time to whip this up?"

Jen's mom smiles as she begins to serve. "I made it on Saturday, actually. You see, I have a system. I pre-make my dinners over the weekend, freeze them, and then Jen pulls them out and pops them into the oven. That way, we always have a healthy, home-cooked meal."

"Oh." Mom takes her plate. "We should do something like that, Riley."

I shrug. It'd be nice, I guess, but also a bunch of work. "If you want."

"Do you cook, Riley?" Valerie asks.

Does pushing microwave buttons count? *I* think it does, but judging by this meal, Valerie doesn't. I still want to say yes, though, because maybe it'll impress her, but Mom's sitting right there, raising an eyebrow and smirking at me, so I say, "Not much, but I'd love to learn."

She nods, and hands me my plate, followed by the bread basket. "It's an important life skill. I've been meaning to teach Jen, but we never seem to find the time."

"You must be very busy," I say.

"We are. Between work, school, and Jen's extracurricular activities, there's not much time left over." She nods again, and I realize I've walked right into her trap. As in, there's not much time left over for D&D. *Curses.*

Jen sighs, picking the layered noodles apart with her fork. That's when I notice there's zucchini lurking inside.

Ew. Why?

"Don't play with your food," Valerie says, looking pointedly at her daughter's plate. Jen sighs again and shoves a smashed-up forkful into her mouth.

Without the slightest bit of playing, I slice off a neat corner with my fork and pop it directly into my mouth, zucchini and all. Bonus points to me for not dripping any sauce or leaving any cheese string dangling from my mouth.

"It's definitely a balancing act," Mom says. She smiles at Jen, who's still chewing heroically, then to Valerie. "Then trying to find time for creative exploration and social interaction, which we all know is so important for girls their age . . ." She trails off and takes a dainty bite of bread, chewing thoughtfully.

Nice one, Mom.

Valerie looks around the table, her brown eyes softening as they land on Jen. She's finally managed to swallow and has moved on to staring helplessly at her plate.

"All right, ladies. Enough beating around the bush. Let's get this hammered out. Jen hasn't given me a moment's peace about the whole Dungeons & Dragons thing, but I do have concerns. Valid concerns. One, I don't want Jen's grades slipping. And, two . . ." She looks up at the chandelier, searching for the right words.

"You want to make sure we don't have some Dungeons & Divas thing going," I say, helping her out. I pull the soft yellow napkin from my lap and tap the sides of my lips like polite people do in movies before continuing. "That part I can guarantee. Yes, we got in a little argument this weekend, and it was pretty much my fault. I'm really, really sorry Jen was upset—"

"It was not that big a deal," Jen hisses.

"But we talked it out, and I think the whole experience was a really good lesson in, um"—*What did Mom call it?*—"social interactions."

Valerie's eyes bore into mine. Instead of looking away like I want to, I widen them real big so she can see I mean it. My heart flutters, and I break out in a cold sweat. I would *hate* to be on this lady's witness stand. *Lilac Breeze, don't fail me now.*

Finally, she gives her verdict. "I believe you."

A sigh of relief comes whooshing out of my mouth, and I allow myself to blink. Under the table, I wipe my palms on my khakis. "My mom has a plan for the school stuff," I mumble, glad to hand it off.

"Really? I'd love to hear it."

"Great," Mom sails in. "I'd love to share it. So, here's my idea . . ."

Once they're deep in negotiations, Jen gives me a soft kick under the table. Her shoulders are so tight, they're practically at her ears, and her plate is a mess of squished noodles, meat crumbles, and saucy bits dotted with zucchini fragments. *I am so sorry*, she mouths.

It's fine, I mouth back.

So embarrassing.

I give her a big smile, hoping there are no parsley flecks in my teeth. *For real, it's fine.*

If anybody understands overbearing, embarrassing family members that care a little too much—it's me. Valerie and Devin could totally form a club.

▲　▼　▲　▼　▲

"Best. Possible. Outcome." Jen practically glows as she walks me to the car. "Not only is Lovelace back in action, but we get to study together!"

OK, I'll admit it. I was a little meh about all those extra homework hours coming my way. But hearing her say "together" like that, totally excited, makes an Intelligence Buff sound every bit as awesome as battling red dragons. "Right? It's perfect!" I glance back at the top of the driveway, where the moms are saying their goodbyes, and lower my voice. "I can't believe your mom went for it."

"Oh, I can," Jen whispers back. "You know what? While I was setting the table, I made sure Mom saw me drop a few tender tears into the napkins. She'll never admit it, but it totally cracked her armor."

"Weeping warfare. I like it."

"And it didn't hurt that Mr. Cameron called after school to tell her my STEM Bowl project was the best he'd ever seen from a sixth grader."

"Of course it was."

"By the time you got here, ol' Mom was ripe for the picking. Plus, there was no way she could refuse your mom's plan. Now, *that* was a stroke of genius."

I smile up the driveway at my mom, who's waving goodbye with one hand and shoving that dangly hair behind her ear with the other. "She *is* pretty awesome."

▲ ▼ ▲ ▼ ▲

I am celebrating, victory-dancing and jumping on the couch.

While Mom is cleaning.

"Stop that," she snaps. "Get down. What are all these crumbs from?" She bends down, narrowing her eyes at the bouncing specks. She brushes them into her palm, then stares down at them, mystified and annoyed.

"A lot of things, I guess." I jump off the couch and peer into her hands. "Like, the dark-brown ones are probably toast, but the light-tan ones are probably Pop-Tart. Oh, and the orange ones have got to be Doritos."

"OK, but why is all that crap on the couch?" She sprinkles them onto the carpet and wipes her hand on her jeans. "I'll vacuum that in a minute, once I get all the other junk picked up."

"Mom," I say, "it's, like, eight thirty at night."

"When else am I going to do it?"

I am so confused. Didn't we just have an awesomely successful night? Team Henderson saved the day, ensuring D&D for all, successfully completing a dinner party with no spills, stains, or choking. I think that qualifies.

Mom, however, does not look like she's feeling awesome *or* successful. Her hair is in a wild bun on top of her head, her hands are on her hips, and she's glaring at each at every corner of our apartment in helpless fury.

"Um. Now's good," I say, nodding like a bobblehead. "Now's great, actually." To show her I mean it, I pick up my hoodie off the floor and sling it over my shoulder. She still looks mad, though, so I drop to the ground and scoop up the rogue crumbs.

"I don't even know where to start." She shakes her head and stalks off to the kitchen.

I hop up and follow her, shoving the crumbs into my pocket.

"Look at this! It's gross." Mom shoves a plastic bowl under my nose, *my* bowl from this morning. Bloated Rice Krispies, accompanied by a dead housefly, float in a shallow pool of warm milk. A faintly sour smell tickles my nostrils.

"Gross," I agree.

"No way would this ever happen at Valerie's house." She dumps the bowl into the sink and flips on the garbage disposal.

Over the roar, I shout, "No fly would dare enter her lair!"

Mom flips the switch. "They've got no problem entering mine. Look at this place! That pan in the sink's been there since we had chicken *two days ago*."

I turn on the faucet, heating up the water. "You're right. I'll get it." *Just please stop freaking out.*

"You know Valerie asked me what clubs you were in?"

Mom starts pacing and I start scrubbing.

"I'm not in any clubs," I say.

"Good, that's what I told her," Mom says, pauses mid-pace and then starts up with even more fervor. "Actually, I told her, I didn't *think* you were in any clubs because I didn't actually know. And I *still* don't know what your grades are. Or even the password to log in to find out. I'm not even sure what your schedule is."

"It's fine, Mom," I say, squirting more Dawn on the world's stubbornest pan. "You're really busy. I get it."

"Like Valerie's not?" Mom snorts.

"Yeah, but she's *different*." An aggressive swipe of the sponge dislodges a layer of crust. "You know, like Devin. All about systems and processes and organization and junk."

Sighing, Mom drops into a chair and runs her hands over her face. "I miss Devin."

155

"Me too. It's always nice to have an organizer around the house." I rinse the pan and place it in the dishwasher, then shoot her a grin over my shoulder. She doesn't return it. "I'm sorry about the bowl and the crumbs and stuff."

"It's not just the bowl. It's *everything*." Mom drops her face into her hands, but not before I see the tears in her eyes. "I never realized how much he did around here, and without him, I'm drowning. I can't keep up. I'm not like Valerie."

I run over and wrap my arms around her, leaving wet handprints on her shirtsleeves. "I don't want you to be. I like how you are. In fact, Jen and I literally stood in her driveway today talking about how awesome you are."

With a small sniffle, Mom straightens. Then she wipes her eyes hard with her knuckles and gives me a sad smile. "Thanks for that, but you deserve better. A mom more like Jen's."

"No way. I only want a mom like you." I squeeze tighter, pressing my forehead into the groove of her temple. I'm trying to send her psychic messages telling her how great she is, and I really hope she receives them.

I feel her smile, and she squeezes me back. "A drama mama, you mean?" she says, rolling her eyes and shaking her head. "Sorry, Riley. You didn't need to hear all that. I should have kept that little freak-out to myself."

"Nope. I'm glad you told me, so I could tell you that you were wrong."

"You're sweet." She gives me a smile, an almost-real one. "Now, go to bed. It's getting late."

"Wow." I drop my jaw and widen my eyes. "That's *exactly* what a good mom would say. You have really got this down."

She laughs, a for-real laugh. "Go to bed, you nerd."

"On it. Love you."

"Love you too."

I head to my room and get ready to go to sleep, but it's kind of hard to sleep when your mother's up half the night blasting Fleetwood Mac as she scrubs every square inch of the apartment. Pretty sure our upstairs neighbors don't appreciate it either. About halfway through Mom's midnight vacuuming session, they start banging on their floor, which is our ceiling, yelling *Shut up!* through the vents.

Sorry, guys. I feel your pain.

When I wake up the next morning, the place looks amazing. After I finish breakfast, I make sure to scrape my cereal bowl and place it neatly in the dishwasher. Without anybody telling me to. Just like Devin or Valerie would.

▲ ▼ ▲ ▼ ▲

It takes a solid three hours to get through the whole Intelligence Buff thing, and by the time we finish, my brain literally hurts. Seriously, there's a stabby little twinge in my upper-right cerebrum that definitely wasn't there before. Also, I now know that learning, problem-solving, and reasoning *are* products of the cerebrum, so it could happen.

Mom insists on taking a picture of my note cards and study guides before we head to the laundry room. "Your brother is going to get such a kick out of this. I'm texting it to him right now."

Lucy nudges me in the ribs, "Yep, definitely sounds like his jam."

"Hey, it must be your jam, too, right?" I laugh. "Nobody forced *you* to come."

"True, true. You got me. I just couldn't resist the smell of fresh highlighters and sticky notes," she says. "Hannah stuck to her guns, though, huh?"

"Yep," I say. "I called her one more time this morning to be sure. She said she'd rather rub pollen on her head and stick it in a beehive, then she hung up. She'll meet us for the game though."

Laughing, Lucy and Jen pack up their backpacks while I gather the laundry stuff. "You sure you got it?" Mom asks.

"I'll be down there anyway," I say. "Might as well."

She gives me a rib-crushing squeeze, then hops onto the couch, grabbing her library book and a bag of Oreos off the coffee table. "A day off that's actually a day off?! What is this sorcery? Just for that, girl, I'm ordering us a pizza. Be back at five? We can watch a movie or something since your homework's all done."

I nod, and she gives me a thumbs-up before diving into her book.

"Your mom's cool," Lucy whispers, once we're outside. "Mine would never chill with me at home on her night off."

"Thanks. Sorry. Thanks," I whisper awkwardly back. Jen gives us a curious look, and we head off to Hannah's apartment.

A knock at the window stops us as we pass Lucy's. A second later, her dad bounds out the door, grocery bag in hand. "Rations," he says, handing the bag to Lucy. "To fortify the party. That's what you call them, right? Rations?"

"You got it." Lucy takes the bag and a hug. "Thanks."

"Let me get that for you." He takes my heavy laundry bag and slings it easily over his shoulder. "I'll run it down for you while you grab Hannah." Whistling, he strolls off toward the laundry room.

"Thanks!" I call after him, then whisper to Lucy, "Your dad's cool. Mine would never bring me rations or carry my laundry."

"Thanks. Sorry. Thanks," she whispers back.

"What are you two whispering about?" Jen asks, *not* in a whisper. "I am literally standing right here."

OK, yeah, that's rude. I definitely see her point, but I also don't really want to get into the whole reason why we're whispering about each other's parents. "Sorry. We're just admiring each other's parents."

"We admire yours as well," Lucy adds. "I like her commercial. It's fierce."

Jen laughs. "I don't know. Maybe I should tell her to step it up a bit, though, donate some snacks or something, I don't want her left out of any whisper sessions."

"Your mom is cool," I loud-whisper in Jen's ear. "Even if she puts zucchini in her lasagna."

"You're weird," Jen says.

"Who's weird?" Hannah pops out of her apartment before we even knock.

"You," Lucy says.

"Cool, cool." Hannah nods agreeably. "Y'all finally ready?"

"Yep," I say. "You should've come. It was fun."

"I'd bet Buffy's bow and all her arrows that it wasn't. Besides, I'm sure you got done way faster without me." Her mouth tightens, and she gives a little shrug. "Let's go play already. I've been waiting for ages!"

▲ ▼ ▲ ▼ ▲

"All right, Riley." Hannah smiles at me from across the table. "I want to hear about this new character. Get up there and do your thing, but don't be boring, OK?"

"I'll do my best." I grin back, thrilled that we're all back together again, ready for a new adventure.

I don't have a binder with sheet protectors or an epically drawn character portrait, but I do have a scribbled-up spiral notebook and what I think is a pretty cool new character. All eyes are on me as I stand in front of the group.

"OK, so." The laundry room is really bumping on this fine Saturday afternoon, and every last drier is whirring behind me.

"I can't hear you!" Jen shouts, cupping a hand to her ear.

I clear my throat and start again, louder. "OK. So. My character's name is Sutherland, and she's a gnome. She's very small, only about three feet tall. Her light-brown hair is short, sticking out in every direction, and her eyes are a deep forest green. She is seventy-five years old, which is young in gnome years. They can live to be five hundred, you know."

"I did not know!" Hannah slaps her hands to her cheeks, shocked.

"Well, now you do, and knowing's half the battle," I say, sticking out my tongue. "Anyway, Sutherland's an orphan and a rogue, who has made her living pickpocketing. Her weapons of choice are her trusty daggers and her wits. Recently, back in her home village, she attempted a break-in at the mayor's house. I say 'attempted' because she was caught and thrown into jail. Using her lock-picking skills, she escaped and is now traveling the world as a treasure hunter."

"Nice!" Lucy gives me a literal round of applause, clapping in a circle. "We could use a rogue. Can you detect traps?"

"Yep," I say. "If I roll high enough."

"Good, you're gonna need that," she mutters. She shuffles the papers behind the DM screen and shoots us a threatening look.

"Definitely not boring." Hannah gives me two thumbs up, followed by finger guns.

"Oooh, I'd like to draw a gnome," Jen says, rubbing her chin thoughtfully.

"Just not in any of your school notebooks," I remind her.

"Definitely not!" she agrees. "Now, roll her up!"

I roll my stats, and together we fill in the character sheet, bringing Sutherland to life.

"All right, kids," Lucy says. "You know what time it is. Get ready to sing!" She pulls out the obligatory character birthday cupcakes. This time, they're chocolate with green frosting and plastic football rings on top. She passes them out, popping a white candle into each. "Sorry, these were all they had. I guess it's football season or something?"

"Lucy? I got your text, but where the heck are you?" Uncle Jay calls from the laundry-room door. He must be tagged in today.

"Back here!" She stands up and waves.

He strolls to meet us in the back, shaking his head and chuckling to himself. "You're so weird," he says, then leans forward to light the candles.

"Be nice," Lucy says, sticking out her tongue. "Or I won't give you one."

Uncle Jay puts a finger to his lips and steps back, the model of good behavior.

We sing "Happy Birthday" to Sutherland, my heart swelling with pride and excitement. When it's time to blow out the candles, I don't make a wish because this time I don't need to.

CHAPTER 14

"COME HERE, KID," MOM BECKONS ME FROM THE COUCH THE
second I walk in the door. I close it quickly behind me to keep out the
cold November air and toss my backpack in the corner.

"What's up?"

"We need to talk about Thanksgiving."

Yes, we do! I was planning on grabbing my bucket to give the laundry room its Friday cleaning, but that can wait. I take a flying leap onto
the couch, giving Mom a little bounce when I land. I love me some
holidays. Of course, I still get a little teary-eyed whenever I remember
Devin won't be here, but it'll be OK. Mom and I can still do and cook
all the things. We can have an awesome breakfast, watch the parade,

cook all afternoon, eat dinner, moan on the couch about how full we are, make hot chocolate, eat *more* pie, and then watch *Elf* to ring in the Christmas season. "We need to go shopping," I tell her. "Thanksgiving's in six days, and you haven't even bought the turkey yet. I mean, where's all the food? Don't you work at a store?"

"Yes. Yes, I do." Mom sighs. "That's kinda what I need to talk to you about."

I pause my mental grocery list and look Mom over. She loves holidays as much as I do, but her eyes are not shining with joy at the upcoming celebration. They're downcast and shifty. "What is it?" I ask. "Go ahead, you can tell me."

"I have to work," she mumbles.

"WHAT?!" The saddest scene in the world flashes through my mind: me, on the couch, picking at a microwave turkey dinner, staring miserably at the flickering TV screen.

All. Alone.

"Baby, I'm sorry." She grabs my hand and squeezes it tight. "I put in for the day off six months ago."

"Then they should let you stay home." My lip is trembling, and I'm on the verge of a selfish, immature meltdown. I take a deep breath, but it doesn't help a whole lot. I can't do a holiday by myself. *I can't.*

"*Should* doesn't mean *will.*" Mom's mouth sets in a hard line, and she glares at the ceiling. She takes a deep breath of her own, then looks back to me. "They're starting the Black Friday Sale at six o'clock this year—"

"On a Thursday?"

164

"Yes, on a Thursday," Mom spits out.

"That doesn't make any sense." My voice rises and cracks. "You can't leave me all alone on Thanksgiving! It's a family day. It's bad enough Devin's gone—"

"Don't I know it?" she mutters.

"Why can't you call out?" I'm whining and I know it. *But seriously, Mom, it's* Thanksgiving.

"Because, Riley." A hard edge creeps into her voice. "I can't afford to get fired right now. I'm not a partner at a law firm. I don't have a ton of money in savings. Instead, apparently it's my life's purpose to get to the store at noon, on Thanksgiving Day, to rearrange the store and hang up dumb signs that say crap like 'Seasons Savings!' and 'Ho-Ho-Hot Deals!' Oh, and the *door prizes*! I have the special honor of hiding the stupid freaking door prizes! You know, important things like Santa bobbleheads and Rudolph keychains. Things no one should live without. Ooh, and then, *then* I get to decorate all the fake Christmas trees, to really get everybody in the holiday spending mood." She pauses her rant long enough to draw breath, then cusses her boss to the skies.

With, like, *really* bad words.

Startled by her venomous, not-holiday-friendly outburst, I freeze. My eyes are wide and any tears I thought about spilling have sucked themselves right back up into my eyes and marched deep down to the depths of my soul. The meltdown I had brewing is nothing compared to what Mom's got going on here. She's still squeezing my hand, a little harder than she probably means to, but I don't pull away.

"I'm sorry," I say, picturing her trapped at work, doing all sorts of hokey, fake holiday stuff, and then having to open up the store and smile in a bunch of overexcited deal-hunters' faces. Now is not the time for a Riley pity party.

"I want you to know I tried." She sighs and loosens her death grip on my hand. Her voice wobbles, though, and it hasn't quite lost its hard edge. "I just really, really need this job right now. No matter how crappy it is."

"I get it." I hug her tight and nuzzle my head against her shoulder, then pull back and force a smile. "I do. Thanks for, you know, working and buying me food and stuff."

"Riley—"

"I mean it. I wasn't being sarcastic," I say quickly. Meltdown Mom is kinda freaking me out, and all I want to do is to make her feel better. "Anyway, you don't have to go in until noon, right? That's plenty of time to watch the parade, right?"

Mom nods.

"Maybe we could make a special breakfast? You could make your quiche, and I can make this thing I saw on Pinterest. You take a cinnamon roll and stick pieces of bacon up in the back like a tail, then you make pretzel feet, and a candy-corn beak, I forget how you do the eyes. . ." I'm babbling, and I know it. I just want her to feel better.

She nods again, this time with a glimmer of a smile.

"It'll be fine, Mom."

She throws her arms around me and gives me another squeeze. "You're awesome. Sorry to freak out on you like that. You should see your face. I feel terrible. Did I scare you? I'm the worst." She stands up, pacing a little. "When your brother was here, he used to listen to all my work rants. I guess I've been a little pent-up, and I exploded."

"It's OK, really." And the cuss-fest *was* kinda funny . . .

"Speaking of that boy." She glances toward the calendar with a shake of her head. The dates are all empty boxes without Devin to add notes and appointments. "I really wish he could've come home for Thanksgiving break."

"Me too."

"Dang it, Devin." She shakes her fist in the air. "If you weren't having such a great time, I'd drive on out to California and drag you back by the ear."

I giggle. "Right? I call shotgun."

"You can ride shotgun on the way to the store. Let's go plan our extra-special, one-of-a-kind, no-freak-outs-allowed, cinnamon-roll-turkey-with-a-bacon-butt Thanksgiving breakfast."

"You got it."

▲ ▼ ▲ ▼ ▲

The trip to the store with Mom was fun, but later that night, I can't help but indulge in a teensy-tinsy sniffle-fest as I scrub the folding table. The newly replaced and hideously bright fluorescent light is glaring down on me, and rogue lint bunnies keep bumping my ankles, but at least most of the bugs left with the warm weather. I'm not feeling up to a show-down with a spider today.

Poor me.

All alone on Thanksgiving.

No Mom.

No Devin.

No turkey.

All my friends will be off with their families, and I'll be alone in my apartment.

Completely and utterly alone.

For real, poor me.

"I think it's clean." Lucy reaches over me and grabs my filthy, used-up Clorox wipe. "However, this thing is not." She balls it up and chucks it into the trash can.

"Hi! I didn't see you there!" I give her what I hope is a wide, friendly smile.

"Whoa." She backs up, holding her hands out in front of her. "Scary smile. Don't ever do that again. What's up?"

"Nothing's up!" I singsong. "Just doing a little cleaning." I giggle so she knows I'm fine.

Lucy scrunches up her nose and stares at me hard. "What are you giggling about? That's even creepier than the smile. You're being weird. Something's wrong."

I can't think of anything to say, so I revert to blinking.

"Come on, sit down." Lucy guides me into a chair and pulls another up next to me. "Tell Mama all about it."

"It's dumb."

"That's fine."

"Like, First World problem dumb."

"That's OK. It's bothering you. That's enough for me."

▲ ▼ ▲ ▼ ▲

"I know it's not a big deal." I sniffle. Lucy fishes a Kleenex out of her purse and hands it to me. I'm not, like, crying-crying or anything, so I pat my eyes and then start to rip it into little shreds. "It's just everything's so different and lonely this year."

"Yeah, I get it," Lucy says. "I'm not really all that pumped either."

That doesn't sound good. A couple days ago, Lucy *was* pumped. Her mom actually showed up for her last two visits, and it was her year for Thanksgiving. They'd made all kinds of plans. "What happened?"

"My mom's going to her boyfriend's parents'."

By the look on her face, I can tell Lucy is not invited.

I roll my eyes and shake my head. I have no words. Not any nice ones anyway.

"I know," Lucy says, fully comprehending my eye-roll/head shake. "She even fooled Dad this time too. He signed up to work a shift at the hospital so he could get holiday pay, and Jay's opening up for the Black Friday sale. Dad's trying to get a buddy to switch with him, but I don't know, last I heard they were looking for a babysitter. *A babysitter!*"

"Why so serious?" We hear Hannah before we see her. She flops into a chair and sprawls out. Eyebrows raised, she examines us closely. "Am I missing something? Or maybe y'all are. Like the part where we have a whole week off from school coming up?"

"OK, that's *one* good thing about Thanksgiving." Lucy attempts a smile in my direction.

"Thanksgiving-Shmanksgiving." Hannah dismisses the holiday with a wave of her hand. "Totally overrated."

"How can you say that?" I ask, shocked to my soul. "Thanksgiving is a huge deal—"

"It's a huge expense, is what it is. That's what my mama says, anyways. We don't really do Thanksgiving, and that is fine by me."

"Really?" Maybe some of her fine-ness will rub off on me.

"Really. My daddy's like, 'You want me to blow all my money on random extra food you're just going to eat up and decorations you're going to throw away, or you want me to put that in the bank for Christmas presents?'" Hannah grins and nods to herself. "I say Christmas presents, every time."

"You're not doing anything for Thanksgiving?" Lucy asks.

"Other than being thankful for vacation days? Nope! Why? What are y'all doing?"

Lucy shrugs. "Nothing."

The tiniest inkling of an idea slithers up my brain stem and sets up camp in my mind, lighting a little fire of inspiration.

"Nothing *yet*," I say.

"What do you mean?" Lucy asks.

"Well. . ." I say slowly, letting my little spark of an idea grow into a full-blown flame. "All three of us have some extra time off, and all three of us have zero family plans for Thanksgiving, plus all three of us could use some holiday cheer—even you, Hannah."

"Do I now?" Hannah says. "It's not like I'm the grinch of Thanksgiving or anything."

"I don't know, you could be." I laugh. "Right now, you're all *Thanksgiving-Shmanksgiving*. How long before you're sneaking into houses, robbing folks of their cranberry sauce and green-bean casserole?"

Hannah's eyes widen. "You're right, I can see it now. Except I'd never steal green-bean casserole." She crosses her eyes and sticks out her tongue. "Nasty. Anyway, how do you propose to save me from that lowly fate?"

"Yeah," Lucy says. "Whatcha got in mind?"

"OK, so. I'm thinking that maybe we could do a Friendsgiving-slash-D&D-party instead. Like, I could decorate the apartment, write a special campaign . . ."

"We could all bring something to eat," Lucy adds.

"And Buffy will learn the true meaning of Thanksgiving!" Hannah shouts, clutching her heart.

"Precisely." I nod. "So, you in?"

"One hundred percent," says Lucy, while Hannah shoots me enthusiastic finger guns.

"So, now we just need to call Jen," I say. "Fingers crossed, her Thanksgiving plans are as boring as ours."

"For real." Lucy whips out her phone, and we call Jen on speaker.

"Do you have plans for Thanksgiving?" I blurt out in response to her "Hello."

"Um, hi, Riley," she says, reminding me I should have greeted her first. "And, yes, of course I do."

"Oh." I try not to sound disappointed, because that'd be rude and weird.

"Oh yeah? What are you doing?" Hannah leans in and asks.

"Um, hi, Hannah. Going to my granny's for the Early Bird Special, as usual."

"What's that?" Lucy asks.

"Oh, hi, Lucy." Jen laughs. "You're all here, huh? Anyway, Early Bird Special's what my mom calls it. For some mysterious, it's-a-tradition reason, my granny insists on getting up at the crack of dawn to put the turkey in, so we end up eating a huge Thanksgiving lunch. Then she gets tired and goes back to bed."

"Oh? Then what?" I ask hopefully.

"We go home. Mom turns on football, then dives into her laptop. She refuses to go to the store on Black Friday, but that doesn't stop her from cross-referencing every last online sale." She lets out a long, dramatic yawn. "So boring. Not that I mind the presents, of course."

Lucy, Hannah, and I exchange glances. Boring online-shop-fest is promising, and points to Valerie for boycotting Black Friday. "So, you'd be home by . . ."

"Four, probably? Why?"

"Here's the thing. Hannah, Lucy, and I aren't doing *anything*. It's actually kind of pitiful, so we were thinking we could throw a Friendsgiving party, with a special campaign and a potluck dinner—"

"YES!" Jen blasts out my right ear. "Yes, this is happening. Your apartment is on the way home from Granny's, and my mother *will* free me from her sportsball/shopping prison or face the consequences."

"What are the consequences?"

"Hm. Good question. Probably me, sitting in the corner sobbing and whimpering until she caves. She acts all big and bad, but we all know she can't take it when I cry."

"Solid plan."

"I'm going to go call my granny and tell her to make extra pie. I'll bring that and some drinks. You all sit down and figure out the rest of the menu."

"Yes, ma'am."

This is going to be the best Thanksgiving, I mean Friendsgiving, ever.

▲　▼　▲　▼　▲

That Sunday night, the computer can't boot fast enough. Devin and I are meeting up for a video-chat, and I can't wait to tell him about my Friendsgiving plans. Unfortunately, as soon as the call connects it is clear that my brother has other ideas.

"Is Mom OK?" Devin Head on the screen looks pale, with dark circles under his eyes to rival Mom's. His forehead's waved with worry wrinkles, and his mouth sags into a frown.

"Are *you* OK?" I ask. He looks skinny—skinnier than usual, even.

"I'm worried about her," he says, ignoring the question. "She seems so stressed."

I bite my lip. Mom *is* stressed, and the phone call I overheard late last night between her and Dad-guy proves it. But what's Devin going to do? He's thousands of miles away. I shrug, trying to blow it off. "Oh, you know Mom."

"I do know Mom. That's why I'm worried."

"She's a little bummed about the holidays, but—"

"I knew it!" he shouts, loud enough to make me jump, and slaps his desk. Wincing, he lowers his voice. "She feels awful about Thanksgiving, and she thinks she let you down, doesn't she?"

I wave *that* bit of silliness away with my hand. "Oh, we worked that out. We're fine."

"I'm not so sure." Devin shakes his head. "She's probably just pretending to be fine, so you don't worry."

"For real," I say. "We've got plans for the morning. I've got plans for dinner. It's all good. Plus, it ended up being a good thing, skipping the turkey and all that stuff."

"How could that be a good thing?"

"Save money, you know? Especially helpful when Dad-guy skips out on not only his familial but economic responsibilities as well."

"He didn't send his child support?" Devin's cheeks go from vampire-white to tomato-red. Oh no, I figured Mom had told him; otherwise I wouldn't have brought it up.

"Didn't sound that way," I say, then roll my eyes and blow out my lips to make a rude noise. Talking about Dad-guy always makes me immature.

"How do you even know that? Did she tell you?"

"No." Devin's not *totally* wrong about her pretending to be fine. "She doesn't talk to me about him at all. I overheard her half of the conversation late last night when I got up to go to the bathroom. She told him off, but . . . it doesn't matter." I force a smile. "Point is, we saved money. So, really, skipping Thanksgiving dinner's a good thing."

"Yeah, like hurricanes and heart attacks are good things." Devin stares at me like I've grown an extra head.

I stare back, my fingers itching. For a minute, I contemplate turning off the monitor and sending him to black. That way, I wouldn't have to look at him looking at me like somehow he doesn't believe that I could be telling the truth.

"She'll be fine," I repeat softly. That's what Mom would want me to tell him. I'm pretty sure, anyway.

He doesn't say anything else, just chews his bottom lip and blinks up at the ceiling.

Which, not surprisingly, gets boring and awkward almost immediately.

"So . . ." I rack my brain for something to say. Something, anything, that'll tear him away from his ceiling gazing. Oh! I know! "How'd your project go?"

"What project?"

"You know, the game-design thingy for the illustrious Dr. Duncan? Did you knock her geeky little socks off?"

Welp, I'm successful on one count. Devin stops staring at the ceiling, but now he's staring at the floor.

"I have to redo it," he mumbles.

"What?" My ears must be clogged. Devin's never had to redo anything. Ever. Like, he spits on a piece of paper, turns it in, and the teacher tacks it up on the bulletin board for all eternity.

"I said"—he enunciates every word, extra-sharp and pointed—"she told me to *redo it*. As in, delete it, start from scratch, and do something completely different. She hated it, and if I don't come up with something better by the end of the semester, there's no way I'll make a good grade in her class."

"I don't believe that. You are, like, the ultimate teacher's pet. I almost got you an engraved dog collar for your birthday: *If you find this nerd, please return to the Science Lab.*"

He doesn't laugh. Instead, he just shakes his head and studies his keyboard.

I narrow my eyes and lean in. "Is this like the time you got a ninety percent on your chemistry test and told Mom you failed?"

"For real, Riley. She hated it," he spits out. His reddened cheeks flush deep purple. "She said it lacked originality. That it sounded like a *Lord of the Rings* rip-off."

"What a jerk!"

"The thing is, she's not a jerk." Devin sighs. "She's right. It *is* a rip-off, and a bad one. There was nothing new or fresh about it."

Well, crap. The only reason I'd brought it up was to give Devin a chance to brag. I was *trying* to distract him with success and nerdery, not make him feel worse.

"That's OK." I slowly pull the chair back to the computer, my heart sinking. He looks like he's about to cry, and I don't know if I can take that. "It's not that big a deal, Dev. It's just one project."

"Yeah, but . . ." Suddenly he is almost whispering, and there is a tone in his voice that I've never heard before. "Some people's were good. *Really good.* Stuff I'd never even think of doing. Mine was literally the worst."

"I'm sure that's not true."

"It feels true. I *failed.*"

"Devin, it is literally one grade. I don't know. You said she's nice. I mean, she's letting you redo it. That sounds nice to me. Maybe she's trying to help?"

"I don't want to be the guy that needs help." He slaps the desk, and his keyboard and mouse rattle. "I've never been that guy."

I stare down at my own keyboard, racking my brain for the right words. It's true. He's never been that guy. I can't remember one time in my life hearing Devin ask for help with anything. He's always been the *helper*, while I always loved being the *helpee*, but that doesn't mean he didn't need help then, and it doesn't mean he doesn't deserve help now. I just wish I knew how.

Devin sighs and mathematically straightens his keyboard. "Sorry to dump all this on you. Evie's usually my sounding board, but . . ."

This time I think I see tears glistening in his brown eyes. "But what?!"

"We broke up."

Aw, crap. "No. Why? What happened?"

He shrugs, blinking rapidly. "Nothing, really. It's hard being so far apart, and we're both so busy with school, and we're on completely different schedules, not to mention time zones. She thought it'd be better if we took a break for a while to focus on ourselves." He forces a smile. "I get it. I really do. She's got a lot on her plate with the whole pre-med thing, and I don't want to hold her back. It's just hard, you know?"

"Oh, Devin. . ."

He shakes his head again, then pushes his hair back out of his face. "Enough about that. I called to ask about Mom, not whine about me. Stop making that face, OK? I'm fine. I'm just really, *really* ready for winter break."

"Me too." I make a desperate effort to stop making "that face" and smile at him. "Winter-Con, baby!"

"That's right." He smiles back, but it's not a real one.

We talk for a little bit longer, but it feels hollow and like neither one of us really knows what to say. When we say goodbye, I can't help but think that he is just like Mom, pretending to be fine. And just like Mom, he's really not. I'm the only one that seems to be genuinely OK, and it makes me feel really, really weird.

CHAPTER 15

BALANCING PRECARIOUSLY ON THE ARM OF THE COUCH, I TAPE Octavia's turkey form to the boring white wall. The poster-board cut-out, garbed in aluminum-foil chainmail and brown construction paper breeches, wields a cardboard axe in her feathered fingers. I cock my head to the side, examining my newly repurposed Thanksgiving decoration. But something's missing.

I hop down off the couch and pluck a red Sharpie from the mess of art supplies covering the coffee table like a rainbow ooze. With one quick stroke, I add the signature scar across the bird's goofy face. *Perfect.*

Next up is Lovelace. She's wearing a flowy white dress of tissue paper and carries a twig of a wand in her small yellow beak. The best part is the little tiara I fashioned out of foil and wrapped around her turkey head.

Buffy Van Orckingham's turkey took the longest. It took forever to color that whole stupid turkey green, so Hannah better appreciate it. Not to brag, but the bow I made out of a rubber band and flexible stick is pretty amazing.

I position my own turkey a little below the others, creeping out from behind the couch, then decorate the rest of the room. A cornucopia turned battle horn. A bowl of mashed potatoes colored to look like the eye of a beholder. A dish of cranberry sauce chopped up into rubies, nestled in pumpkin-pie treasure chests.

Standing back, I survey my work. Something's still missing.

I grab the googly eyes from the table and glue a set to each member of the turkey party.

Now it's perfect.

"Riley." Mom rubs the sleep from her eyes and does a 360, giggling at the newly decorated living room.

"Yeah?" I ask, stifling a yawn. I was up half the night making this stuff.

"I . . . I have no words. Which one's you?"

"The littlest one with the dagger in its talons, of course."

"Ah, yes. The rogue." She moves forward to examine my handiwork more closely. "I see now why we had to make that emergency run to the dollar store last night. I mean, what Thanksgiving—"

"*Friendsgiving*," I correct her.

"Right. Of course. I mean, what *Friendsgiving* is complete without personalized turkey cutouts arrayed in their finest battle garb?"

"Exactly." It is a stroke of genius, to be honest.

"Is it weird I feel jealous?" Mom asks. "I mean, where's my turkey?"

"Hold on! I got you." I run to the kitchen to grab my more delicious creations.

Mom's eyes widen when she sees cinnamon-roll gobblers, in all their Pinteresty glory. "I thought I smelled bacon. These turned out so cute! I can't believe you got up and made them yourself." She pulls out a meaty tail feather and chomps down. "Amazing! I remember when you couldn't even use the microwave."

"I could always use the microwave," I say, rolling my eyes. I clear a spot on the coffee table and gently set down the tray.

"Could've fooled me." She smirks. "I'm gonna go reheat my quiche."

"Already in." I say, checking her face for signs of not-fineness. She's smiling, and her voice has been light, but Devin's got a point, there's something sad about her eyes.

"Can I least make the cocoa?" she asks.

I grin up at her, throwing my arms around her waist and squeezing. "Sure, just don't forget the marshmallows."

Mom hugs me back and hustles off to the kitchen. I grab the remote and jump onto the couch, pulling a soft fleece blanket around my shoulders. Mom and I are going to watch this parade, we are going to eat our breakfast, and we are going to have a great time. By the time we're done, there'll be no doubt in Mom's mind that our celebration is beyond fine, Devin will see that he had nothing to worry about, and my friends and I will have the best Thanksgiving ever. There are plenty of ways to celebrate, and plenty of ways to make things special.

Mom comes back in with the cocoa, her quiche, and plates, setting them down on the coffee table. Then she joins me, snuggles up in my blanket, and together we eat and watch the parade.

"This is nice," she says as the giant turkey float comes rolling down the street by Central Park.

"It is," I say, resting my head on her shoulder. We stay like that until Santa comes and goes, the credits roll, and a cheesy old movie comes on the screen.

When Mom reluctantly leaves the coziness of our couch, she's smiling. "Thanks for a great Thanksgiving, Riley."

"Thank *you*," I say. "Your quiche was epic."

"*This* was epic." She squeezes my hand, and I think maybe we really are fine. It's a little hard to say goodbye when she goes to work, but knowing my friends will be there any minute makes it easier.

So much easier. Just as the quiet of the apartment starts to get me down, the party arrives, filling the place with life, chatter, and food.

"This is awesome." Lucy leans back on the sofa and takes a huge bite of pizza. She points up at Octavia-turkey and mumbles with her mouth half full, "Can I haz that?"

"Of course."

"The ultimate party favor." Jen grins and grabs another soda from the cooler next to the coffee table, which is pressed up against the wall of the living room, holding all the food. Before she left, Mom helped me drag the kitchen table into the middle of the room for gaming. My DM screen was adorned with red, yellow, and orange feathers surrounding my HAPPY FRIENDSGIVING! sign.

"Are y'all ready, or you gonna keep stuffing your faces?" Hannah asks, shoving a forkful of pie in her mouth.

"I don't see why we can't do both," Lucy says. Pizza in one hand and dice in the other, she hops up from the couch and takes her place at the table. I settle in behind my screen and check my notes as the others grab their seats.

"Everybody ready?" I ask.

Three excited nods and we're off.

You wake at the campsite, just as the sun is rising. The forest is still and silent, without even the faintest trill of a bird. As the light grows, you notice that Sutherland's bedroll is empty.

"Where'd that tricksy little gnome get to?" Hannah puts her hands on her hips and narrows her eyes at me. "She'd better not be off pick-pocketing. I've been working hard to raise that kid right."

I shrug innocently. I'm in Dungeon Master mode now, which means I'm out of character. Lucy and I've been taking turns leading the campaign, so whenever it's our turn to DM, we send our characters off on random little side quests that put them out of the action. This time, though, I decided to make it part of the action.

"We should search the area," Jen says.

"Yeah, and call for her," Lucy adds.

Hannah nods and cups her hands around her mouth and hollers, "Sutherland! Girl, where you at?" She sounds exactly like her mother, and a very un-DM-like snort-laugh erupts from my nose. I swallow my giggles and continue.

There is no response. You conduct a thorough search of the area and find Sutherland's pack has been left behind, her daggers laid neatly next to it in the grass.

"Sutherland would never leave her daggers," Lucy says.

"Let's search the perimeter for tracks," Jen suggests.

You examine the grounds. Large three-pointed tracks lead away from the campsite toward an uneven dirt road. Behind the tracks is a long, unbroken groove in the dust.

"That's weird." Lucy chews her lip thoughtfully. "I wonder what that is."

"Could be some kind of weird creature dragging something," Hannah says.

"Or *someone*." Jen takes a sip of soda.

"Sutherland." They say in unison.

"Welp." Hannah finishes her last bite of pie, licks the whipped cream from her fork, and pushes her plate away. "We'd better go after her."

▲ ▼ ▲ ▼ ▲

The farmer says he hasn't seen anything out of the ordinary.

"Yeah? Well, the farmer's a liar." Lucy scowls. "The track led us right up to his property. How does he explain that?"

"Let Buffy handle this." Hannah grins. "I grab the farmer by his suspenders and jack him up into the air. 'I'm gonna ask you one more time, corn-shucker,'" Hannah growls. "Where's the gnome?"

Your hot orcish breath shrivels the hairs in his nostrils. He gags, retches, then begins to cry. "I don't know what you're talking about," *he wails.*

"Ugh. Fine. I drop him."

He lands on his butt with a thud.

"Then you won't mind if we search the grounds," Jen says coldly.

Still sobbing and clutching his nose, the farmer nods. "Do what you will. Just don't let the green one breathe on me again."

185

"Stay out of our way, or she just might," Lucy threatens. "Now, let's go search the cornfield."

As you make your way through the cornfield, the terrified cawing of crows stops you in your tracks. The flock whooshes over your head like a speeding black cloud. Within moments, they are gone, leaving nothing behind but a few glossy black feathers that have fallen to the stalks.

"I grab them and put them in my pack," Hannah says. "I can use them for my arrows."

As you're collecting the feathers, a large shadow looms over you.

"Ah! What is it?"

You turn and discover what frightened the birds so badly—a scarecrow. Coal-black eyes glitter menacingly from behind his face of scratchy burlap. An evil laugh drips from his dark gash of a mouth, and he reaches for you with straw hands tipped with sharp, curving claws.

"Oh, uh-uh," Lucy says. "This guy's going down. I grab my axe and advance. Let's beat him up a little bit and see if he knows anything about Sutherland."

"All right," I say. "Roll for initiative!"

▲ ▼ ▲ ▼ ▲

"You think he was telling the truth about the barn?" Lucy asks.

"I do," Jen says. "That was a good plan, by the way. To get him down and sit on him, then rip out his stuffing till he talked."

"Ruthless." Hannah shakes her head.

"Hey, I put him back together. And he attacked *us*, remember? Now, let's try to open this barn door."

The door doesn't budge. It's as though it has been blocked from the inside.

"Nothing's ever easy," Hannah mutters.

As you lower the rope through the hole you've cut in the roof, you hear a small shout. "It's about time! Get down here! This bird's diabolical!"

"Wait, what?" Jen wrinkles her nose. "Let's get down there and check it out."

As you reach the floor of the barn, you are immediately overtaken by an enormous turkey. She puffs out her brown-feathered chest and flares her red-and-gold plumes intimidatingly. Her beady eyes glow with an unearthly light, and her beak is blackened and decayed. In a high-pitched crackling voice, she shrieks, "Excellent! More food for my harvest feast! Turning the tables is such fun!" She laughs then, harder and harder, until her cackles turn to gobbles.

Behind her, Sutherland jumps up with a snicker of her own: "Oh, please. There's nothing delicious about that group."

"Hey, I take offense to that," Hannah says with a grin. "Nice to see you, by the way. Never thought I'd have to rescue you from a bird."

"I know, I know," she says. "It's embarrassing. But it's not just any bird, in case you haven't noticed. The talking? The size? The rotting beak? Obviously, it's bewitched and corrupted. Now, quick, throw me my daggers and we'll fight our way out of here."

"Um." Lucy side-eyes the group. "Did we bring her daggers?"

Jen shakes her head.

Sutherland stamps her tiny foot. "You guys are the worst."

"Oh, please," Hannah says. "You're the one who's always talking about how great you are in a fistfight. Time to put up or shut up."

"I'll never shut up." Grinning, I pick up Sutherland's dice and prepare for battle. "Let's do this!"

▲ ▼ ▲ ▼ ▲

Lovelace's spell removes all signs of corruption from the turkey, returning it to its normal state. Exhausted, the bird collapses onto the floor as you call for the farmer's wife. The farmer's wife approaches slowly, then drops to her knees and pets the sleeping turkey. "Poor Puffkins," she says. "Thank you for showing mercy and sparing her life. She really is the sweetest bird."

"When she's not possessed," Lucy says.

"It must have been that witch that came through town." The farmer's wife shakes an angry fist. "She threatened to curse us if we didn't give her half our stock. Of course we refused. I never thought she'd take it this far. I didn't believe she could."

"We're lucky I learned Dispel Magic last week." Jen pats herself on the back smugly. "I knew that'd come in handy."

"Where's the farmer?" Hannah asks.

He sends his thanks.

"Is he avoiding me?"

Yes. Yes, he is.

"Fair enough." She laughs. "Now, aren't you going to give us a reward or something?"

Once the loot is divided and the food's all eaten, the party disbands, and everyone heads home. Lucy's the last to say goodbye. She stops at the door, turns, and throws her arms around me.

"Thank you," she whispers fiercely in my ear. "This could have been the worst day, but you made it the best day. You're a really good friend, and I'm glad I moved here." Before I can answer, she's out the door.

Shortly after everyone leaves, Mom walks in. She moves slowly, shoulders slumped. "How was it?" I ask.

"Don't ask," she says, flopping onto the couch with a sigh.

"Are you hungry?" I ask, tucking a blanket around her. "I just made popcorn, and there's some leftover pizza. I can heat it up for you and we can watch a movie."

"Too tired to eat," Mom says. "But a movie sounds good."

I grab my popcorn, turn on *Elf,* and cuddle up next to Mom on the couch. Buddy had just set off for New York when a loud knock rattles our front door. It's more of a thump than a knock actually.

Mom jolts awake, her soft snore punctuated by a startled snort. "One of your friends forget something?" Mom asks, untangling herself from our cozy blanket fort.

I shake my head. "I don't think so."

Mom squints through the peephole, then screams, which causes me to launch my giant bowl of popcorn from my lap and scream in solidarity.

A shower of kernels rains down on the couch, floor, and coffee table. My bare feet grind some of the butter-soaked bits into the carpet as I rush to her defense. I grab the empty popcorn bowl and brandish it like a club, prepared to face this threat in my snowman pajamas.

Still screaming, Mom flings off the chain lock and yanks the door open so hard it about flies off the hinges.

I take a step back. Because A: this green plastic bowl is not much of a weapon. And B: nobody needs to see me in my Frosty jams. Oh, and C: Mom's *opening* the door to let the stranger in?! Then I see someone step over the threshold.

It's *Devin*!

I let out an earsplitting shriek of my own. The neighbors above us bang down at our ceiling, while those down below bang up at our floor. Those cold, unfeeling monsters.

"Nice to see you too." Devin grins at us behind a stack of aluminum pans. "You want to help me get these, or you just going to stand around screaming all night?"

"Of course, of course," Mom practically sings. She grabs the entire stack of pans and gestures wildly at the door with her head. "Oooh, these are warm. Smell good too. Come in, come in!"

He can't quite make it in, though, because the second Mom moves her butt out of the way, my arms are around him, squeezing him to little itty-bitty bits. He laughs softly and ruffles my hair. "Miss me, Ri-Fi?"

"You know it!" I drag him in, hugging his arm and tripping his feet.

He doesn't mind. He laughs and stumbles along beside me, careful not to step on my toes or bonk me with his swaying duffel bag.

"What about you? You miss me?" I ask, breathless.

"More than you know." He slings his bag to the floor, then smiles at us both. "Surprised?"

"So surprised," I say, grinning so hard my face hurts. He literally drove across the country, just to bring us Thanksgiving? I still have his arm in a sweaty death grip, but he doesn't pull away. "I thought you couldn't get away."

"Oh, I got away all right." His smile dims for a split second, then returns full-force. "You ready for a real Thanksgiving?"

"Oh my gobble, Devin!" Mom hollers from the kitchen. "You are too much! Where did you get this? There's a full Thanksgiving dinner in here! Like, a perfect one—not like one I'd make. It looks a Butterball commercial or something!"

"It's from Silver Slipper," he hollers back, leading me into the kitchen.

Mom's speed-setting the table. Her eyes are shining and she's definitely not too tired to eat now. "No way! I would have thought those would be all sold out by now."

"I ordered it a week or so ago. At first, I thought I'd call you and tell you to pick it up as a surprise. But"—he shrugs, then smiles—"this seemed like a way better idea."

"It is! It is!" Mom coos, then snatches his free arm in a death grip of her own. "Best Thanksgiving I could've asked for."

"I'm really glad." His voice is thick with emotion, which is absolutely not his normal state. I sneak another peek up at his face. The dark circles are still there, and there is a flush of red blooming across his cheeks. He smiles down at the both of us, but his eyes still look sad. "You ready to eat?"

"Yes!" Mom squees, clapping her hands.

I nod and smile, even though I have literally been eating since nine o'clock this morning and my stomach is perilously close to exploding. I'm already regretting the three tiny pieces of popcorn I ate—not to mention that fourth slice of Jen's granny's pie.

If Devin can drive thousands of miles just to bring me some food, the least I can do is eat it. I can do this.

Stomach, don't fail me now.

CHAPTER 16

THE NEXT MORNING, I WAKE TO THE SMELL OF BUTTER AND sweetness. I sniff the air and my stomach growls. Devincakes. After last night, I thought I'd never be hungry again, but . . . well, here we are. I throw on some clothes and make a beeline for the kitchen.

"When do you get your report card?" Mom asks, reaching for the syrup.

At the stove, Devin winces. He flips the pancake a little too soon, and the batter splats out and ruins the perfect circle. "Ugh, this one's messed up," he mutters.

"I'll eat it," I volunteer, grabbing a plate. "It's going to get messed up in my mouth anyway."

"Nah, I'll make you a good one." He scoops the perfectly edible pancake up with his spatula and launches it into the trash can. "You don't get report cards in college, Mom. They post grades online at the end of the term."

"Oh, OK." Mom floats her pancakes in a hefty layer of syrup, then cuts them into tiny triangles. "I'll wait. You could print it for me. That'd be like getting a report card. I'll put it on the fridge." She points to an empty spot next to her UCA magnet.

Devin's back stiffens as he white-knuckles the skillet. His back is to Mom, so she doesn't see his face turn twelve shades of purple. Something tells me the game-design project redo is *not* going well. I didn't want to ask, but I was hoping he'd have come up with something by now, something that would help him get a good grade in the class and not be so stressed-out. From the look on his face, though, I don't need to ask.

"Here you go." He hands me a plate with two impeccably crafted pancakes.

"Perfect!!!" I gush, with extra exclamation points and wide eyes. Maybe my enthusiasm will cheer him.

Unfortunately, my enthusiasm does not seem to cheer him.

"At least I can do *something* right," he mutters to the oven.

I end up biting into my lip instead of pancakes as I watch him. It's kind of weird that Devin drove all the way from California just to be crabby, and then he's just going to turn around and drive the whole way back. I'm happy to see him and all, but maybe his time would have been better spent taking a nice, long nap. Or better yet, redoing his stupid project. The semester's almost over, and he's obviously worried sick about his grades and impressing Dr. Duncan, so why is he in our kitchen making pancakes? He doesn't have time for this.

I start to ask him if he's OK, but then I glance over at Mom. Somehow, she's completely missed all the grumbles and cringes, and her mood and appetite are blissfully intact. She looks so happy getting down on all that syrupy goodness, so I keep my mouth shut for now. There's no point in stressing her out. She's got enough on her plate. Literally and figuratively.

▲ ▼ ▲ ▼ ▲

Mom heads off to work, and Devin heads to the couch—only after meticulously cleaning the pan and loading the dishwasher, of course. So, I sit on the opposite end, waiting. Though I'm not really sure what I'm waiting for. Which is fine, I guess, since it seems that Devin has no clue what he's doing either.

He turns on the TV, flips through the channels, and turns it off again. He pulls out his laptop, types who-knows-what, sighs furiously, then slaps it shut. He snatches up his phone, scrolls his feed too fast to even register what he's looking at, sighs again—even more furiously this time, with a big throat-burning whoosh—then tosses his phone on the coffee table.

"So," I try to start the conversation with intelligence and wit. "Hi."

He looks up, eyes wide, like he just realized I'm here. "Hey, sorry. I'm being boring, huh?"

"No, of course not." I smile, scooting closer to him on the couch. I pull my legs up, crisscross-applesauce-style, and face him. "You're probably tired from your drive, and I'm sure you're dreading driving back."

"You got that right." The words burst out, hot and peppery, then he nods, a quick snapping motion that has to hurt.

"It was nice of you to come home, though," I say, trying to get a handle on his shifting mood, quell some of the agitation I don't understand. It's definitely not something I'm used to, and it scares me a little. "Mom's happy you came. So am I."

"Yeah?"

"Yeah." I smile at him, even though my temples are tight. I send warm, fuzzy vibes his way, emanating all the love and light. Right when I'm about to crumble, he cracks and smiles back.

"Good. Good." He nods again, more to himself than to me. Just when the nodding's gone on so long it's getting weird, he snaps out of it, with a literal snap of his fingers. "Hey! You want to play some D&D? You should call your friends up. Now that I'm back in town, we can get a real game going."

"Oh, um . . ."

Methinks this is a bad idea.

Like, a really, *really* bad one.

"Come on, it'll be great!" He grins at me, his first actual hon-est-to-goodness grin since he walked in the door last night.

And how can I say to no to that?

"Sure!" I say, even though I'm not sure. "It'll be great!" I say, know-ing it probably won't be.

Even if I can get everybody to agree, who's to say it won't be a com-plete disaster like last time? This boy's so clueless, he doesn't even know it *was* a disaster, and my Spidey senses are telling me that now is not the best time to tell him.

"Awesome! I'm going to go get my stuff!" In one swift motion, he propels himself off the couch and heads to his room.

I slowly drag myself from the couch and head to the phone.

▲ ▼ ▲ ▼ ▲

"It'll be fine," Lucy says. "He's probably homesick out there in the big, bad city and wants to relive his glory days as Master of the Dungeon."

"But—"

"It'll be fine. Don't stress, Riley. For real. He's your brother and you love him. You've told me a lot of nice things about him, so I know he's not a total butt."

"He's really not."

"I know. I get it. We'll be nice and play along. He'll be scooting on back to California in a day or so anyway, and we can get back to our own game. Ooh, hey! Did I tell you I had an idea for an epic pirate adventure?"

"No, you did not," I say. "You holding out on me?"

"Just retaining my air of mystery."

"Ah, yes. I should never underestimate the mysteriousness of Octavia's air."

"Or the fierceness of her friendship," she says. "Now, go hang with your brother. I'll call Jen and Hannah."

"Really?!" My voice leaps three octaves, along with my heart. I can't even begin to describe how much I dreaded calling the others. Not after what happened last time.

But Lucy's not the kind of friend you have to describe those things to. She already knows.

"Yeah, I got this," she says. "Meet us in the laundry room at one o'clock."

▲ ▼ ▲ ▼ ▲

"Why does it have to be the laundry room?" Devin wrinkles his nose and shakes his head. "It's filthy down there."

What I want to say is *Excuse me, sir, but we are doing this for your benefit. If you got a problem with my laundry-room locale, then maybe we should squash it now.* Instead, I smile sweetly and say, "Not anymore. I cleaned it."

"*You* cleaned it?" He looks skeptical.

That offends me. "Yes. *I* cleaned it."

He huffs and hoists his duffel bag up onto the couch and pulls out the latest D&D campaign book. The hardback is glossy, shiny, and official with a gorgeous griffin on the cover. A far cry from my raggedy binder and mountain of sticky notes. His map is cool too. It's actually a bunch of precut tile pieces that pop together in whatever shape you want—you can even draw on them with a dry-erase marker to show where stuff is. Those would really come in handy . . .

"Riley, you listening?"

"No." Full honesty. "I was admiring your map tiles."

He grins. "I understand. I was asking one more time: Are you sure we have to do this down there? I mean, we could set up in the kitchen."

"Nope, sorry, it's nonnegotiable. In case you haven't heard, us girls put the dungeon in Dungeons & Dragons."

"Ahhh, I see. And I can take the girls out of the dungeon, but I can't take the dungeon out of the girls?"

"Now you get it." I smile, then take a deep breath, still trying to figure out the best way to say what I need to say. "Um, Devin? One more thing."

"What else? You have even more weird rituals?"

"No. Well, probably, but that's not what I wanted to say."

Devin puts his book to the side and looks at me, eyebrow raised. I study the floor. There's still a popcorn kernel from last night, just out of reach under the couch. The lone survivor from Devin's midnight cleaning raid. The second we finished dinner last night, he was all over it, loudly commenting on my spill and the bugs we were sure to attract as he swept up the pieces and rubbed grease smears out of the couch. I'd have done it, but he insisted on doing it himself so he could make sure he got it all.

"Riley? What's the one more thing?"

"Oh, I just wanted to say . . ." I swallow and try again. "Try to be nice to everybody this time, OK?"

His eyebrows furrow as he pulls away, shaking his head. "What are you talking about? I'm always nice." He flings his arms out to the side in a *what-the-heck* gesture, and stares at me with narrowed *how-dare-you?* eyes.

My cheeks flush, and I backtrack. "I know. I know. It's just something we always say before a game. 'Be nice out there, kids! And remember it's only a game!'" I do a hokey PE-coach voice, then clap my hands. "Now, hustle!"

"Oh," Devin says, then chuckles. As the tension in his face drains, the burning sensation in my cheeks follows. "It *was* another weird ritual."

"Yeah, I guess."

"Now that you've got that out of your system, let's go have some fun!" His smile is soft and kind, and I know he means it. He really does want us to have fun.

Maybe this time we will.

▲ ▼ ▲ ▼ ▲

I skip down the stairs, swinging my dice bag in one hand and gripping my figurine in the other.

"What's that?" Devin's not skipping because he is too busy trying to get his big wooden DM screen, campaign book, binder, and map tiles down the stairs without busting his butt. I offered to help carry something, but of course he said no. I swear he thinks I'm a klutz or something.

"It's my guy."

"Your guy?" He snorts.

"Yeah." I unfurl my fingers and show him. Lucy gave each of us a miniature of our characters after her last campaign, as super-extra-special bonus loot, and mine's perfect. It's a small copper gnome, with pointed ears peeking out from the folds of her hooded cloak. In her teensy little hands, she holds two curving, red-hilted daggers.

Devin scrunches his eyebrows, shifting the weight of all the things from one hip to the other. "That doesn't look like Arwenna at all."

"It's not. It's Sutherland. My gnome, remember?"

"Oh, yeah, I forgot you changed." He looks all bummed-out again, like I ruined something, and I feel bad. He did spend a lot of time on Arwenna. He made her stat sheet, helped write her backstory, and took her through so many dungeons. There's a lot of Devin in her. I don't want him to feel like I don't appreciate him, but . . . I really like playing a character that's all me, like Sutherland is.

In the laundry room, Devin sits at the head of the table; his book, dice, and notes are hidden behind his wooden screen. He's scooted so far forward in his seat he's practically sitting on air. He rests his hands briefly on the table, then pulls them back awkwardly, looking like a derp T-rex. I *told* him I scrubbed everything down with a Clorox wipe, so there's no reason for him to be mincing around like the room's made of plague.

Or is it?

I look around the table. At the opposite end, Lucy's arranging the chips and sodas, not the slightest bit concerned when her fingers touch the table. Across from me, Hannah and Jen throw practice rolls, completely oblivious to any hidden germs.

OK, yeah, pretty sure it's fine.

I shrug and turn to Devin, who's now opted to stand. He clears his throat, and Lucy drops into her seat. Hannah and Jen corral their dice.

In his best, most mysterious DM voice, Devin begins.

The four of you are gathered around the table, breaking your fast on porridge and honey, when—

"I like your shirt, Devin." Hannah interrupts. She smiles at him, then across the table at me, like *See? I'm being nice!*

I smile back, wondering what Lucy said to her.

We all lean in to take a closer look at said shirt, as Devin glances down to see what he's even wearing. It's a faded black classic Super Mario Kart tee, with boxes that show each of the main characters. Pretty cool.

"Uh. Thanks," he says, giving her a small smile. "Anyway, like I said, you're in the tavern—"

"You know what's weird?" Hannah continues. "I've played Mario Kart probably a million times, but I've never actually *been* Mario."

"Is it even Mario Kart, then?" Jen asks. "Or would you say you're, like, playing Luigi Kart or Bowser Kart?"

I rub my chin, mulling this over. "I'd be playing Toad Kart, for sure. Toad's my go-to."

"Same! Up high." Hannah leans across the table, palm up, and I slap it. "Toad sisters unite."

Devin clears his throat again, looking around the table then back down at his shirt helplessly.

Crap, we're doing it again.

Or *he's* doing it again.

Part of me thinks I should tell everyone to pipe down and concentrate, but the other, bigger, part of me wants to know who Hannah's and Lucy's favorite Mario Karters are. I open and close my mouth a couple times, little froggy gulps that don't make a sound or pick a side.

Then, thankfully, Lucy saves me.

She echoes Devin's throat clearing and clasps her hands in front of her on the table, like a good little student, and the others follow suit. "Pardon us, Wise Dungeon Master. Please continue."

▲　▼　▲　▼　▲

"I'd like to launch Sutherland at the troll's big, fat ugly head," Hannah announces after some pondering.

"Launch me how?" I ask. "I might be tiny, but there's no way I'm gonna fit in your bow."

"No, hop up, I'll show you." She dashes over to me and pulls me away from the table. "Now, stand in front of me, facing the monster, aka Devin."

"All right," I say, following directions. The girl is literally a head and a half taller than me, so I'm really feeling like a gnome now.

"Take out your daggers."

I wait for the next part.

"I said, *take out your daggers*," Hannah repeats.

"Oh, right." I unsheathe my invisible daggers and smile at her. How's that for staying in character?

"Good. Now, one-two-three, here you go!" She picks me up by my armpits, and I dangle there for a moment, hovering above the floor. Then with a grunt, she propels me forward and releases. I don't get much air, and I don't make it very far, but it definitely illustrates our move. My ankle gives out as I land, and I slide to the floor, giggling hysterically.

"Yeah, we can do that," I gasp out. "But higher, faster, and more intimidating. And, like, I do some flips in the air, OK?"

Devin reaches down and pulls me to my feet. "Be careful," he says, not amused. "You're gonna get hurt."

"Danger is my middle name," I inform him, then bare my teeth menacingly.

"What's Sutherland's last name then?" Jen asks.

I think this over. "Us."

The room goes silent for a moment, then Lucy busts out. "I see what you did there! That'd make you Sutherland Danger Us. Sutherland Dangerous!"

"That's right." I nod smugly, and we laugh some more.

Well, Devin doesn't laugh. He just shakes his head and looks annoyed.

His annoyance only grows as we make our way through his dungeon.

"I'd like to consult my beholder," Jen says. We're at a standstill at the edge of the griffin's lair, unsure of what to do next.

"Your what?" Devin says.

"My *be-hold-er*," Jen repeats, slowly pronouncing each syllable. She gives him a tiny, pursed smile, then breaks it down for him further. "You know, the large floating orb with one big eye, lots of little eye-stalks, and awesome magical abilities? I could draw you a picture if you need me to."

"I know what a beholder is," Devin says. There's a slight edge to his voice, like he can't believe he just got D&D-splained. "I don't get how you have one."

"I found it. In a little clay jar in the cellar of a haunted castle. We think it's a baby."

"You can't have a beholder for a pet. They're too powerful."

His tone sets my teeth on edge. *I mean, I love you, Devin, but you can't be coming up into my laundry room, telling people what they can and*

205

can't have. Especially if I'm the one that gave it to them. "It's from one of my campaigns. We never let it out of the jar—there's protective magic on it."

"I'm sorry." Devin shakes his head. "I don't think a level-two wizard can consult a beholder. That doesn't even make sense. You should do Detect Magic."

My cheeks burn, and I can't help but roll my eyes. Welp, at least I've figured it out, once and for all. Devin's the one ruining the game. I'm 100 percent sure of it now.

Jen leans back in her chair, arms crossed. Her eyes narrow, and she's about three seconds from losing it on him. She shouldn't have to, though. He's *my* brother, and while it's not my fault he's being bossy, it *is* my fault we're all down here being bossed.

"Hey, Devin." My voice wobbles and cracks. I take a deep breath and try again. "The DMs not supposed to—"

Lucy clears her throat, and she and Jen carry on some sort of tele-pathic conversation with their eyes.

"It's fine," Jen says, waving it off. "I can be open to feedback. OK, I'll detect magic or whatever."

It's nice of her, but it's not right. She should stand up to him, and I should back her up. His feelings aren't worth more than hers. Before I can argue, Devin carries on. I lose my nerve and the moment passes.

For a while the game continues without much trouble, but then, as we finally enter the griffin's lair, I have the misfortune to sniffle. So, Devin pauses the game, roots around in his pockets for a small pack of

Kleenex, then tells me to blow my nose. In front of all my friends like I'm three years old or something.

My cheeks flush as I take the tissue, but a wave of annoyance sweeps away my embarrassment. I look him dead in the eye and blow the biggest, honkingest, Sutherlandiest wad I can into the tissue. I contemplate handing it back to him, shoving it right into his palm, but that's more gross than satisfying, so I walk it slowly and deliberately to the trash can.

"I think Sutherland's allergic to griffins," I say, flopping back into my seat.

Then, as we're dividing up the loot, which is kind of stingy, if you ask me, I reach for another soda.

"It's a little late for all that caffeine," Devin says, intercepting my hand. "And it's too close to dinner for more snacks."

I snatch my hand away. I don't need him to monitor my soda and snack consumption. I am quite capable of deciding what and when to eat and drink. Obviously, since he's been gone for months and somehow I'm still alive.

Then the most awkward silence falls over the laundry room.

"So," Lucy comes to the rescue, clearing her throat and asking, "Who wants the leather waterskin?"

I sit back as they sort out the rest of the items.

I guess Devin's right about one thing. I *have* changed, and more than just my D&D character. And this, *this* is not *fun* for me. Devin thought the laundry room was gross, acted like my friends were annoying, treated me like I didn't know how to play D&D, and embarrassed me. No wonder everybody had a miserable time at his swamp campaign. Devin was way out of line then, too, but I just didn't want to see it. Not only was Devin a jerk then, but I was too. But even after all that, they still agreed to play with him again. They worked so hard to keep the peace today, so I wouldn't feel bad. Jen didn't even try to fight him on the beholder thing. *They* could tell he was stressing me out, so why couldn't he? Was he so busy trying to have everything his way that he didn't even notice?

I wish he was as worried about my feelings as he was about how many Cokes I drank.

CHAPTER 17

BACK IN THE APARTMENT, DEVIN DOES NOT BECOME ANY MORE fun. If possible, he becomes less fun.

His eyebrows furrow to a dark, cartoonish V as he embarks on the world's hangriest scavenger hunt. With a grunt, he yanks open the pantry door and pulls out two cans. He glowers at the offensive tomato soup and ravioli, then tosses them back on the shelf. Sighing, he heads to the fridge. I mean, back to the fridge. He's already looked in there three times. But who knows? Maybe this time will be different.

"There's not even any milk," he grumbles.

"Do you want some milk?"

"No, but that's not the point. You're going to need it in the morning for your cereal."

"I could eat a Pop-Tart."

He shakes his head. "That's a terrible breakfast. What are you going to have for dinner? Where's Mom, anyway? It's dark. She's been gone all day. Is she always this late? She didn't used to be."

"You want me to answer the Mom question or the dinner question?" I snap.

He flings the fridge door shut and eyes the darkened window. "The Mom one."

"First of all, it's not *that* late. It's only, like, seven o'clock. It gets dark fast in the winter, remember? It's not like she's out partying till midnight or anything." Unlike Lucy's mom, mine's always legit working, so I try to have a good attitude about it. Plus, that lady is stressed, and I am not about to give her a hard time. "She's trying to go for assistant manager, so she's been picking up extra hours. She doesn't really have a choice."

"Because of Dad skipping out on child support?"

I roll my eyes. "Yeah, you know how it throws stuff off. Even when he does send it, it's less now anyway. He made sure to get it adjusted ASAP. You're not technically a child anymore, and he wanted to make sure he wasn't accidentally supporting you or anything."

"Oh." His cheeks flush crimson, and his jaw sets in a hard, trembly line. He jams his hands in his pockets and stares at the linoleum, shaking his head and chewing his lip.

"It's fine, though," I say, nodding as hard as I can, like it'll counter-act his bummer headshaking. "She works really hard. They'd be silly not to make her assistant manager." I shrug. "Anyway, he's supposed to send November and December this week, so that'll be cool."

Devin clears his throat. It's his *Yeah, right* throat-clearing.

"Let's go back to the dinner question, OK?" I say. "I'll heat up the tomato soup. You make grilled cheese. If you *must* have a vegetable, there's some leftover green-bean casserole. For dessert, there's ice cream in the freezer and snowflake sprinkles in the cabinet above the sink. We're fine."

"I guess." Devin doesn't look convinced, so I promise him that there is nothing wrong with a grilled cheese for dinner. It is fine. It is more than fine.

On Saturday I wake up, not to the smell of pancakes but to the sound of Mom's shrill voice hollering into the phone. I run to the living room, bumping into a plaid-pajama-clad Devin on my way.

"I'll be there as soon I can." She paces a frantic path back and forth across the living room, her face pale and her forehead furrowed. When she sees Devin, the wrinkles smooth and her voice softens. "Oh, that's right. My son's here. I'll be right up." She slips the phone in her back pocket and lets out a shuddery sigh.

Devin springs into action. "What's wrong?" He guides her gently to the couch.

"There goes my promotion," she mutters, rubbing her temples. Then she shoots back to her feet, wiping her blurry eyes. "Sorry, Dev. I need your car. Mine's busted; it straight-up won't start."

"Do you need a jump?"

"No. Riley's friend's dad came out and tried that. He thinks it's something with the engine. Which I'm sure will cost hundreds of dollars to fix." Her voice rises harshly, her fast-paced sentences wobbling and breaking at the end. "Hundreds of dollars I absolutely don't have. Not even on a credit card. I used it up last month when that jerk "forgot" to send his support. Wonder what excuse there'll be this month. I don't even know how I'm going to do Christmas presents." She lets out a few cusses, then stops short. "Sorry, I didn't mean to bring him up."

"It's fine," I say, stepping toward her. "And I don't care about present stuff. I—"

"—I'll take care of the car," Devin cuts me off, putting an arm around Mom's shoulder. She looks up at him, and the lines in her forehead smooth. "I have some money in savings, and it doesn't look like I'm going to need it anytime soon."

"I can't let you do that."

"You can't stop me." He smiles down at her. "Besides, there's no time to argue. You told them you'd be right up. Go wash your face, take some deep yoga breaths, and Riley and I'll take you to work, OK? I need to grab some groceries anyway."

Mom nods, then scurries off to the bathroom.

"That was really nice," I say softly.

Devin just shrugs. "Dad's the worst," he says through gritted teeth.

At dinner, though, Devin's all smiles. A dinner, I might add, he made me wait until eight thirty for, so that Mom could eat with us. "First things first," he says, spatula poised over the chicken broccoli casserole dramatically as his family starves. "Your car should be ready by Monday."

"You're too much," Mom gushes. "I'm going to pay you back, you know."

"Don't worry about it." He waves her comment away with the spatula, which is apparently no longer used for serving food. "That's not what I wanted to tell you."

"Yeah?" Mom is interested, but I can barely hear him over the rumbling in my stomach. I lean across the table and swipe a forkful of food. Devin doesn't even notice—he's too busy building suspense.

"Yeah." He pauses once more before plunging the spatula into the casserole with a flourish saying, "I'm not going back to California. I'm staying here. For good." He gives Mom a big, cheesy grin, but she doesn't return it.

Instead, she just stares at him with flushed cheeks, chewing on her bottom lip, her eyes flicking back and forth across his face. "Is this because I freaked out earlier?" she asks quietly. "Because I'm fine, Devin. I mean, yeah, the car thing stressed me out a bit, but—"

"It's not about the car. Or a perfectly justified freak-out." Devin smiles. It's a tight, weird smile, though, and not one that I recognize.

I shake my head. "I don't get it."

"Nothing really to get," he says. "I've been thinking, and you know what? UCA . . . it's not for me." His smile wavers, for a split second, then returns at a thousand megawatts. "I've been going back and forth about it for a while but, now that I'm home, I know this is where I belong. So, my mind is made up and I'm staying."

"But why?" Mom asks.

"It's going to be great," he barrels forward, ignoring the question. "I called up Admissions at Coast Community College earlier this month, and they can have me enrolled next semester. All I had to do was fill out the application. Full scholarship. Honors program. Oh, and listen to this. After they reviewed my records, they said I'd be perfect as a math tutor at the Learning Commons. They practically begged me to take the job."

"I'm sure they did," Mom says slowly. "Everywhere you applied practically begged you to come, but you chose UCA for a reason. You had them picked out since you were thirteen. Coast is great, but they don't have a game program, remember? They don't even have Computer Sciences."

I look at Mom and then Devin, my hunger forgotten for the moment. I spent eight months of my life trying to convince Devin to go to CCC. I even bought him a bumper sticker. He just laughed and blew me off, then practically wallpapered the back of his truck with UCA stickers. He even had the nerve to buy me one.

"Yeah, well, I'm not a hundred percent sure that's even my thing anymore." He shrugs, dishing a scoop of casserole onto Mom's plate. "You know how many people out there want to be a big-time game developer? Just 'cause I used to like playing games doesn't mean I would be good at making them, you know?"

"But you're good at it—"

"Actually, I'm not," he says loudly, jabbing the spatula into the pan, like a knife to the heart of his hopes and dreams. "No offense, Mom, but you haven't played a computer game since Oregon Trail. You don't know what games are like anymore."

I flinch. Devin has never raised his voice like that before—especially not to Mom. I watch her as Devin sighs, and he sounds tired now when he says, "I'm sorry. That's not the point anyway, OK? The point is, I want to move back home, I want to go to CCC, and I want to be here for you and Riley. I thought you'd be happy."

She stiffens as if the words stung her and she looks down at the table, chewing on her bottom lip. Finally, she looks up at Devin. "I am," she says. "I just want to make sure that you are. That this is what you really want."

"It is, Mom." Devin takes her hand and squeezes it gently.

Then he looks at me, eyebrows raised. I must be making the wrong face, so I force a small smile and say, "Me too, I'm glad you're back." It's true. I am, but I'd be more glad if he was acting like his old self. With the way he's been acting lately, I'm not even sure if I like him.

Maybe he just needs time to settle in.

"Good!" He settles Mom back into her seat and rambles on, completely ignoring the strange tension in the room. "Oh, and listen to this, Riley, when I talked to the people at the college, they said I can bring you along in the afternoons. You can hang in the library while I'm tutoring. You know, finish your homework, mess around on the computer, read, whatever. Then we'll come home and make dinner. You won't be by yourself anymore."

Hold up. It's one thing if Devin wants to completely uproot his life, but it's a totally different story if he thinks he's going to squash mine in the process. "I wasn't by myself," I remind him. "I have my friends and our games."

"Yeah, but their parents shouldn't be watching you. I should."

"I don't need anybody to *watch* me." The idea of spending my afternoons trapped in a college library, separated from my friends, waiting on Devin, is a nightmare.

I look at Mom, but she's too caught up in her own thoughts to help me out.

"It'll be great," he says, holding out a plate to me.

"Mom?" I don't take the plate, and Devin leans forward and places it gently on my place mat. The silverware is out of the dishwasher, ready and waiting, in perfect formation.

"I don't know, kiddo," she says slowly, looking at me. "This will definitely be a big help."

"And just like old times," Devin chimes in.

"Yeah, exactly." She smiles warmly at him and gestures around the table. "And I mean, look at this! This is just like dinner at Valerie's. You always make everything so nice, Dev."

There is still a tense feeling to her voice, but it has a brighter and more pleased ring to it than I would have liked. It's almost impossible to keep from rolling my eyes, remembering how not-nice he made my last D&D game. "Mom," I say, trying to be the voice of reason, "this is not necessary."

"Let's just try it, OK?" she says firmly.

It's not OK, but I can tell now is not the time to push it. Mom's not even looking at me. Her eyes are on Devin, a small, hopeful smile on her lips. Does she really think this is a good idea? Because I don't. I don't think it's even worth a try.

▲ ▼ ▲ ▼ ▲

Hannah, Lucy, and I are waiting at the bus ramp when a shrill, yet official, voice cuts through the crowd. "Riley! Riley Henderson!"

I look up from a deep conversation on the intricacies of the Demogorgon's evil powers to find the assistant principal shrieking my name.

Why on earth would she be looking for me?

"Um, I'm Riley?" I half raise my hand.

"You sure about that?" Hannah murmurs with a smirk.

"Hush." Lucy smacks her, then drops her hand as Mrs. Williams approaches.

"You're supposed to be at car pickup." She points an accusing walkie-talkie at me.

I don't want to correct her, but I also don't want to miss my bus. "I don't go to car-riders anymore. That was only at the beginning of the year," I say softly.

Her deep-red lips press together in a hard line. "Then why is your brother down there holding up traffic waiting on you?"

"Oh . . . I'm sorry. I didn't know."

"You'd better scoot."

"OK. Sorry," I say before turning to Lucy and Hannah and giving them a quick wave and a "See you later." Then I scoot.

It's nice of Devin to pick me up. It's super thoughtful and all that. And it's definitely a lot warmer than the bus, and it certainly smells better.

I shouldn't be annoyed, but I am.

After we get home, Devin makes me a peanut butter and jelly sandwich, cut into four triangles, crusts off. I feel ridiculous, but eat it anyway, keeping quiet about the fact that he made it wrong. Since he's been gone, I've found I like my PB&J's heavy on the jelly, light on the peanut butter, and all in one piece with the crust *on*. He wouldn't know that, of course, so I just thank him.

"Go ahead and grab your homework," he says after rinsing my plate and sticking it in the dishwasher.

"I was going to run to Lucy's."

"Homework first."

▲　▼　▲　▼　▲

Unfortunately, I never make it to Lucy's.

Instead I spend the afternoon trapped in the Almost Office, listening to an hour-long lecture on the Pythagorean theorem, then write, and rewrite, my English paper to Devin's specifications and standards.

"What about *your* classes?" I burst out, after reworking my thesis statement for the third time while Devin lounges on the couch scrolling through his phone. I am more than a little over this.

"My classes?"

"Yeah, your classes." I spin around in the computer chair and roll toward him. "You know, the ones you were so pumped to take? The ones that you *are* taking? You can't just not go to school, right? You're going to fail, and the Devin I know would rather walk on boiling lava than wreck his precious GPA. Don't you care? You're going to get all F's." I lean forward, waving an accusing finger in his face.

For some reason the thought of Devin with all F's is very satisfying right now.

"I'm not getting F's." He pushes my finger away. "I'm getting W's."

"What's a W?" Definitely not a win. For either of us.

"It's what you get when you withdraw from a course."

"They should give you a Q."

"A Q?"

"Yeah, for quitter."

His jaw drops, shocked that I dared speak to him that way. "You don't get it." Per usual, he is muttering.

"Then explain it to me."

"I already did. Last night, at dinner," he snaps. "That's all there is to say, so drop it. Now, you need to come up with another supporting detail. Your third one's basically the same as your first one."

"I'm going to my room." I speed-roll the chair back to the desk, grab a stack of notebook paper and a pen, then storm off before he can stop me. "I'd rather write it than type it, anyway!"

"Fine!" he shouts after me. "Bring it back when you're done!"

I slam the door behind me, whispering a nice, long medley of Mom's favorite cusses.

▲ ▼ ▲ ▼ ▲

By ten p.m., my hand is cramped and achy and I've got the beginnings of a headache, but at least my paper's finished. I slide it into my backpack, unchecked and uncorrected. I'd informed Devin at dinner that he would *not* be reading the final draft, and I'm standing by my statement. Besides, he already went to bed. Without saying good night to me, I might add.

I'm exhausted, but sleep refuses to come. I lie in bed, fighting the anxious twinges in my stomach and wondering what went wrong. Things have been so awkward with Devin since he got back, and I hate it. We haven't had one fun day yet. Just bossing and crabbiness and weird moods that I don't get.

I miss him more now than I did when he was in California.

I creep through the darkness to his room and knock softly on the door. He doesn't answer, which is pretty normal. When he's in his room, he's usually brain-deep in the computer with noise-canceling gaming headphones glued to his ears. I push open the door and peek through the crack.

In the glow of the laptop, Devin is tipped back in his chair with his drawing tablet propped up on his knees. With his stylus, he adds details to the character sketch displayed on the computer screen.

It's a man, or man-like figure, anyway, dressed in ripped jeans, red Vans, and a black Final Fantasy T-shirt. The body is completely humanoid, down to the knobby knees that poke through the ripped denim; however, the head is anything but human. Instead, a mouthful of fanged teeth surround a slobbering crimson tongue, and a large brown eye fills the rest of the lumpy beige face, kinda like a beholder from D&D. But instead of eyestalks, scaly green snakes spring Medusa-like from his scalp. Each snake is poised to strike in a different direction, with four little dripping fangs bared. On top of each snake's head is a small, glowing golden eye.

Now, *that's* the Devin I know. No wonder he was so offended by our pet beholder in a jar. Apparently, he has quite the affinity for the things. I guess I should treat them with more respect, especially one as cool-looking as this. I'm about to bust in and tell him how great it is when he exhales loudly, half sighing, half growling. He tosses his tablet and stylus on his desk, then slams his laptop closed. The room plunges into darkness. "Stupid," he mutters.

I hover in the doorway. Maybe I should give him a minute?

I guess I stand there too long, breathing too loud, because he hollers at me in a super-snappy voice. "It's late, Riley, go to bed. And close the door behind you, please."

"Fine. Jeez. Good night." I ease the door shut slowly. Slow enough that he'll have plenty of time to apologize for snapping and let me in.

Without turning on the light, he throws himself into bed with a mattress-squeaking thump. "For real, go to bed. I'll see you in the morning, OK?"

"*OK*." I shove the door closed with a vicious click. "Your guy looks really cool, by the way," I mutter as I trudge back to bed. "Not that you care what I think."

CHAPTER 18

"I'M CHECKING THE MAIL!" I HOLLER, THEN BOOK IT OUT THE door before Devin can stop me. I don't care about the mail, there's never once been anything in it for me, but after a week of Devin's homework boot camp, I will do anything in my power to escape. Even if it's only for a minute.

On my way to the mailboxes, I pass the laundry room and can't help but take a peek. The flickering fluorescence combined with the smell of Fresh Meadow Bounce and mildew is soothing. I take a nice deep breath.

"Taking in the crisp, cool air of freedom?" Lucy taps me on the shoulder from behind. I knew checking the mail was a good idea.

"Why, yes. Yes, I am. I'm currently on a top-secret letter-retrieval mission."

"Cool." Lucy smiles, but her eyes are bleary.

"What's wrong? What are you doing down here?"

"In the crying corner, you mean?"

"Yeah."

"It's so stupid." She blinks rapidly, then drops her eyes to her fidgeting hands. "I should've known not to get my hopes up."

"Your mom?" I ask, my heart sinking. Lucy's mom was supposed to get her for a week over the holiday break. Lucy said over and over that she didn't believe it and she didn't care anyway, but I know under all that, she was hoping her mom would come through.

"Yeah. She's going out of town with the boyfriend. So. You know. *Whatever.*" She sniffles, then lets out a frustrated sigh. "It's not like I even one hundred percent wanted to go. It's way more fun here with you, and Dad and Jay are actually the ones that'll do stuff with me, it's just . . ."

"It's just that you want her to be different." I get it. "You want her to want to spend time with you."

"Exactly."

"It's not you, you know that, right? She—"

"Riley!" Devin's shout cuts me off. "Riley, where are you?"

"Are you *kidding me*?" A hot wave of annoyance breaks through me. With Devin in town, it's impossible to be the friend I want to be. "It's literally been five minutes."

"It's OK," Lucy says. "You better go."

"Riley?!" Devin calls, closer and more aggravated this time. "We need to go the store!"

I groan, "He can wait a hot minute. The store's not going anywhere."

"I'm fine," she says, then gives me a quick hug. "We've had this conversation a thousand times. I'll just replay it in my mind. Besides, Jay ran out to buy me sympathy tacos, so for real, I'll be fine. We're playing tomorrow, anyway. Unless . . ." She clutches my arm, dropping her voice to a whisper. "Your brother's not going to wreck it, is he?"

"No! Mom at least had my back on that one," I whisper back. "She told him we were fine to play in the laundry room by ourselves."

"Whew." She smiles, wiping imaginary sweat from her forehead.

"Riley!"

"I'm coming!" I shout, storming out of the laundry room. "Hold your heckin' horses!"

▲ ▼ ▲ ▼ ▲

I trail behind Devin as we walk down aisle five, pushing the cart like a good little helper/prisoner. I'm too busy glowering at the scuffed floor to notice when he pulls up short, and I ram directly into his calves. Serves him right.

"Ouch, Riley." He shoots me a fire glare over his shoulder.

"Sorry."

Then, I actually am sorry, once I see why he froze so suddenly. Evie, Devin's ex, has materialized in our path, carrying a bag of Combos and a bottle of sparkling water. Her hazel eyes widen, and she nibbles her bottom lip, doing some serious damage to her bright-red lipstick.

Devin stares at her, doing weird things with his own mouth. He opens it, closes it, then opens it again and lets it hang there. I shove my hands in my pockets to keep from shutting it for him.

Something tells me they haven't spoken much since the breakup.

Something tells me they may *never* speak again.

Decades from now, we will be here still, a permanent fixture in the cereal aisle. A blinking, gaping, awkward statue of two, orbited by a stranded, frustrated, and soul-crushingly bored baby sister.

"Ah-heh-heh-HEM." I clear my throat like I'm about to make a real big announcement.

Neither of them looks my way. Evie pushes a pink-tipped strand of hair behind her ear, but that's the only movement I get.

"Aaaaaaaaaaaaaaa-HEM!" But it's not me this time. It's a little old lady with a mountainous cart. She looks like she might ram Devin herself if the star-crossed lovers don't get the heck out of her way.

They do. Slowly, like they're underwater, but they finally do. Thank heaven for little old ladies.

She bustles past them, and in the lingering scent of muscle cream and lavender, Evie speaks.

"Devin, hi! I didn't know you were in town! It's good to see you." She smiles like she means it, even though her lipstick is a hot mess and her face is a shade of red not often found in nature.

"You too." He smiles back, but when he takes the cart from me, his hands are shaking.

"Yes, yes," I jump in, walking off toward the end of the aisle. They've lapsed back into awkward silence again, and I'd love to leave this store sometime today. "Fancy meeting you here. This is quite a coincidence, isn't it? We're buying food. You're buying food. At a supermarket. And now . . . now it's time for us to check out. Time for you to check out. Coincidences abound."

They laugh and follow, murmuring stuff and I don't even care, I'm just glad we're moving. By the time we get to the checkout line, all their awkwardness has evaporated. They're not all smoochy or anything, but they're *definitely* extra-special friends. Evie's stuff is in our cart and the two of them are hotly debating who would kick whose butt in a game of Mario Kart.

Oh, *now* he wants to talk about Mario Kart. I see how it is. Whatever. At least we finally made it to the register. Maybe, just maybe, I'll get home in time to check on Lucy.

"All right, well," Evie says, slinging her canvas grocery bag over her shoulder. "I'd better run if I'm going to catch the bus."

"Wait," Devin says. "We can take you home."

We can?

"You don't have to that," she says. "I still have some errands to run."

Good.

"We'll tag along." Devin smiles. "It'll be fun."

It is not fun. I'd much rather be home, hanging with *my* friends, than driving Devin's ex/bestie all over creation on a never-ending quest for essential items. Essential, can't-live-without items, like comfy sweatpants, a BPA-free water bottle, sticky notes, highlighters, the latest textbook on human anatomy, and a lavender-scented candle.

Of course, it's dark by the time we're finished. Devin and Evie sit up front, chatting and giggling and having a grand old time, while I'm in the back, third-wheeling it up.

"Oooh, hey! Stop here!" Evie shouts, slapping Devin's arm. She points out the window at the Natural 20. "I want to grab the new Daredevil comic. You know Elektra is doing the Daredeviling now, right?"

"I hadn't heard the news." Devin smiles and does an abrupt U-turn into the parking lot. The comic shop's sign, a glowing blue die, twenty-side up, shimmers against the purplish-black sky. The store lights up the block, its long series of windows crowded with posters, comic-book racks, and cardboard cutouts of Captain Marvel and Black Panther. The marquee up front reminds me in bold black letters that Winter-Con is next week—not that I needed a reminder. OK, so maybe this outing isn't a total bust. I'd never say no to a trip to the Natural 20.

A silver bell, dangling over the door in a gargoyle's stone claws, rings as we enter. The owner, Cat Serling, looks up from the display of buttons she's arranging by the cash register. There's a Shuri one that would be perfect for Lucy's backpack.

"Welcome to the Natural 20," Cat calls out, her voice husky and smooth. "What can I roll you for?"

If anybody else said that, it'd sound nerdy as heck, but not Cat. She is the coolest person I've ever seen in real life. Or on TV, for that matter. She's tall, confident, with platinum-blond hair shaved close to her head and a dragon tattoo snaking up her arm and around her neck. Coppery steampunk gears hang from her ears, and she's dressed in a flowing red maxi-dress, cinched at the waist with a brown leather utility belt.

"Just grabbing some comics," Evie says. I smile and nod, completely tongue-tied.

"Great. Let me know if you have any questions."

Because Cat can answer them. She knows everything there is to know about comics, gaming, and movies, and can come up with the perfect recommendation for anybody. One time I saw her completely roast this obnoxious know-it-all guy who tried to argue with her about the date of the original Peter Parker comic. Like, dude was nothing but a pile of ash and shame by the time she was done with him, but then she turned around, sweet as pie, and helped Devin find the perfect vintage comic and matching T-shirt for Evie's Valentine Day's present.

And did I mention she owns the whole store *and* runs Winter-Con?

Yeah, I might be a little bit in awe of her.

I mosey around the store, reveling in the perfect mix of fantasy and geekery. I'm going to have to take my friends on a field trip here someday soon. On a day that Mom can drive us, of course. No way we're going with Devin. For now, I settle on bringing them back a few souvenirs.

"Nice picks." Cat looks approvingly at my choices: the Shuri button for Lucy, the d20-shaped sticky notes for Jen, and the ranger sticker set for Hannah.

"Thanks," I say softly.

"You a ranger, punkin'?"

I shake my head, whispering, "My friend." As she rings me up, I cringe at myself. I could've at least told her about our party or said I had one. *Or* I could've said I was a rogue. *Or* mentioned our last campaign. *Anything* would've been cooler than squeaking out "my friend" like a nervous little mouse.

She smiles, not unkindly, and hands me a bright-purple bag and my change. "I'm sure they'll love those."

"Thank you." I take my bag and scuttle off toward Evie and Devin, who are already waiting at the door.

"Look what I have!" Evie waves a pale-blue slip of paper, printed with snowflakes and frost dragons under Devin's nose. I squint at the undulating gothic font until I make out the words "Winter-Con." "You should get your ticket, too, while you're here."

Yes! Good plan!

Devin gives a little shrug. "Nah. I'm skipping it this year."

Or not.

"Skipping it?" Evie sounds as surprised as I feel. She glances over her shoulder at Cat, then lowers her voice. "You love Winter-Con. Don't you at least want to check out the computer stuff?"

He swallows hard, turning from her toward the door. "Nah, I'm good," he mutters.

"Come on." She gives him a playful punch on the shoulder. "I was talking to Cat a second ago and she's going to take those big meet-up rooms in the back and fill them with gaming laptops this year. All the indie games your little heart could desire—"

"Yeah, no." Devin cuts her off and pushes his way out the door. The gargoyle bell dings a sad goodbye. "I'm not feeling it, OK?"

"Oh. OK." Evie gives him the side-eye on her way out, but lets it drop.

I give her a little bit of the ol' side-eye myself. If she's so concerned about Devin's attendance at Winter-Con, why'd she break up with him in the first place? Pretty sure that was a contributing factor in all his weirdness. Besides, if anybody gets to be salty about him skipping it, it should be me. And, trust me, I am. "But you said we'd go together this year," I say, hustling up between them. "You promised."

"Riley," he huffs. "You heard me. I'm not feeling it. Drop it, OK?"

I let out a gusty sigh, which Devin ignores, and climb into the car.

It's a very quiet, tense ride home.

▲ ▼ ▲ ▼ ▲

Evie stays for dinner, which is a very smart move by Devin. I'm sure he doesn't want to hear about how he *promised* to take me to Winter-Con, but then decided to "skip it" without even bothering to tell me.

She provides an excellent buffer from my wrath. But that's OK, I know where he lives.

I glare at him over my tacos, picking off pieces of shell and crumbling them to dust. Devin takes his eyes off Evie long enough to glance my way. "You might want to turn in early tonight if you've got a game tomorrow. You look tired."

I just stare at him. It's 8:17. On a *Friday*. I am not four years old, and I do not need him telling me when it's time to go sleepies.

But you know what? I am tired—tired of being treated like an infant. I think I've had enough Devin for one night.

"If you say so." My hip bumps the table as I stand, slowing my smooth exit. Fallen shreds of cheese and lettuce bounce off my plate.

Devin eyes the mess with annoyance, but I leave it. If he wants to be the boss of everything, I'm gonna let him. All the way down to my half-bitten scrippety-scraps.

▲   ▼   ▲   ▼   ▲

It's eleven o'clock, but Devin and Evie are *still* chitchatting away, the rise and fall of their voices carrying down the hall and to my room. I'd spent the last few hours perfecting tomorrow's campaign, and *now* I'm ready for bed. Also, I'm thirsty. Since Devin hasn't bothered to offer me so much as a glass of water, I decide to go get one, making sure he knows I'm up. Halfway to the kitchen I start to really hope I don't interrupt anything important.

"I don't see how you could give it up," Evie says softly. "I'm happy to see you, but I never wanted you to quit. You know that, right?"

I freeze in the hallway, flattening myself against the wall by the door.

"I know," Devin says, and I can tell he means it. "You were right about taking time to focus on our own stuff, and we'd always be friends, no matter what. It's not about that, though."

Evie exhales in relief. "Good. But what is it then? Developing games is all you've talked about since you were my adorkable lab partner in seventh grade. You took the SAT *three* times to get your scores high enough for UCA. You are literally in one of the best, most competitive programs in the country. You've got the best teachers in the country. The best connections. *Everything.*"

"Yeah, well, I'm *not* one of the best students," he snaps.

"So?"

"So, I'm making C's! *C's!*" He moans tragically. You'd think he accidentally downloaded ransomware to his precious PC or something.

"Oooooh," Evie snorts. "Big deal. I made a C on my calculus mid-term—should I drop out of pre-med?"

"That's different, and you know it."

"How?"

"It just is. Anyway, if I didn't withdraw—I might've even made a D in Duncan's class. I was almost there, you know. I had a seventy-two percent. My last assignment was beyond pitiful, and I never finished my project."

"Why not?"

"I just . . ." He trails off, leaving them both in a tense silence. Does *he* even know? After what seems like ages, he sighs and continues softly. So softly I have to lean in to hear him. "I just couldn't. Everything I tried to come up with was try-hard or stupid. Definitely not up to UCA's standards. It was barely up to my trash can's standards."

"I'm sure that's not true."

"I'm sure it is, but who cares? There're a lot more important things than chasing stupid dreams that are never going to come true."

"Really? What's so important you're willing to toss everything for?"

"My sister. My mom."

I suck in a breath and hold it. This isn't what I want. Maybe it was, back when I was scared to be without him. Not anymore, though.

"They seem fine," Evie says softly.

We are *fine.*

"I'm not so sure about that," Devin says. "When I left, I told myself it'd be worth it. Like, I'd go out there, be a huge success, get an awesome job, make a ton of money, and nobody'd have to worry about anything ever again. But that's not gonna happen. I *suck*, Mom's *stressed*, and Riley is on her own all the time. I never should've left them. It was selfish and stupid."

"No, it wasn't—"

"*Please*. I'm just like my dad," he says, cutting her off, a hard edge to his voice. "Running off across the country, ditching everybody. And for *what?*"

My stomach clenches, and every bad thought I ever had about Devin evaporates. I peek around the corner. His head is in his hands and his shoulders are hunched and tight.

Evie puts an arm around him. "You are not like your dad."

He sniffles and straightens. "You're right. I'm not, because I'm going to take care of my family. Whatever it takes."

My heart swells and the sharp prickle of tears stings my eyes. That is the sweetest thing I have ever heard. It is also the most unnecessary. I don't want him to take care of me, and does Mom really need him to take care of *her*? I don't think so. What we need him to do is take care of himself.

He's the one I'm worried about.

CHAPTER 19

EVENTUALLY, THE TOSSING-TURNING NIGHT FADES AWAY, AND my room lightens with the pinkish-gray of early morning sun. I'm already awake, so I might as well get started. I get up, get dressed, put my pajamas in the laundry basket, brush my teeth, floss, and comb my tangled hair into a neat ponytail. I decide my room's up next—no easy feat. Luckily, I have a little extra time this morning. Terrified Devin would try to "help," I'd opted out of today's Intelligence Buff, leaving Jen and Lucy to study on without me. Hopefully, that'll give me enough time to conquer Mount Crap.

I love my room, but it looks like a bomb went off in here. A bomb that showered the room with dirty clothes, crusty bowls, and crumpled bits of paper. If I'm not careful, Devin's gonna be all over it. Sorting things, organizing things, *touching* things.

I'll be danged if I let him. The sooner he figures out I can do this stuff on my own, the better. *For real, I can clean my own room, Devin.* Just because I *don't* do something doesn't mean I *can't*. I'm capable of a lot more than he thinks I am.

▲ ▼ ▲ ▼ ▲

After wrangling my room into orderly submission, it's time to tackle Mom. I've got to make her see what's really going on; the huge mistake Devin's making and why he's making it. He might actually listen to her. I hit the kitchen, fire up the coffee maker, and wait for her to appear. She appears in seconds, rubbing sleep from her eyes. It's better than a summoning circle.

"Oooh, coffee." Mom grabs the freshly brewed pot and pours herself a cup. "You made this?"

"You see anyone else here?" I say, taking a pointed look around the room. "I can handle making coffee, you know."

"All right, all right." She blows into the cup, steam curling around her face. "I see that, but *how does it taste?*" Slowly and dramatically, she brings it to her lips and takes a sip. She smacks her lips, tilts her head thoughtfully to the right, then to the left, takes another sip, then smacks her lips some more. "Hmm. . ."

"Well?" I say. "Don't leave me in suspense."

After another lip-smacking sip session, she gives her verdict. "Better than mine, that's for sure. I'd say this was on par with Devin's."

Walked into my trap there, didn't you? "So, what you're saying is that I can make coffee every bit as good as Devin's?"

"Sure." Her eyes narrow. "It's great. Now you want to tell me why you're being weird?"

OK, so maybe my lead-in wasn't all that smooth, but no point dragging this out. Devin will be up any minute. "Don't you think I can do a lot of things every bit as good as Devin?"

"Oh." Mom slides into a chair and pats the one next to her. "Have a seat. And yes, of course, I think you can do a lot of things as good as Devin."

I drop into the chair. "What about you? Do *you* think you can do things as well as Devin can?"

Mom's face goes blank, except for a slight flush in her cheeks. "What are we talking about, Riley?"

"We were fine when Devin was in California, weren't we? We don't actually need him here supervising us every little second, right?"

"Of course, but—"

"I think Devin thinks we do. Actually, I *know* Devin thinks we do." Her eyes widen, and I should probably apologize for interrupting, but instead I take a deep breath and keep going. "Like, he's literally giving up everything he's ever worked for to come home and babysit us. All his hopes and dreams in the trash can just so he can help me with my homework and make sure we hit the four food groups daily. It's sweet, *I guess*. But don't you think it's weird?"

"He's always been protective."

"I know." I snort. "Trust me, I know. But this . . . this feels like some next-level smothering. And now he's somehow got the idea in his head that if he leaves again, he'll be deserting us, just like Dad."

Mom sucks in a breath. "He can't think that."

"He does," I say firmly. "I heard him tell Evie."

Mom rubs her hands over her face and then stares at the table. I force myself to keep quiet, giving her time to mull it over.

"He has always put a lot pressure on himself to do everything right," she says finally. "But I know him, and I really think there's more to it than you, me, or your dad."

I blink hard to keep my eyes from rolling. "What? That college is hard? That he's not the superstar?"

"Yeah, realizing, for the first time ever, he's not the superstar." Mom gets up and softly closes the kitchen door. "It's probably eating him up."

"That's silly."

"Maybe." Mom shrugs, then crosses her arms tightly over her chest. She leans back against the closed door, a faraway look on her face. "But that doesn't mean he feels it any less. He's seeing other people doing things, things he feels like he can't do. Their success makes him feel like he's failing, and . . . it hurts. I get it. He wants to succeed at something, even if it's just taking care of little old me." She shakes her head at our rickety kitchen table, and I know she's comparing herself to Valerie again.

"He's not failing." There's a quiver in my voice, and I swallow it away. "Neither of you are, just so you know. And feeling bad or sad or whatever doesn't mean you should quit. It means you should try harder. Or be nicer to yourself."

"Maybe." Mom sits back down at the table and gently takes my hand. "Or maybe it means it's time to take a break." She sighs, and then continues, "I don't know. I really don't, Riley, but for right now I'm going to trust Devin. If he says he wants to be home, then that's what he should do. Maybe he needs us just as much as he thinks we need him. Maybe he needs to be needed."

"But Mom—"

"Just so we're clear, I don't need Devin to babysit me," she says, her brown eyes swimming. "But I do need him to be OK."

How can I argue with that? I can't. Even if I still think they're both wrong. All I can do is nod and squeeze her hand. There is a small click as the door unlatches and I take a deep breath to clear some of the emotions puddled up inside me.

"Is that coffee I smell?" Devin says, popping his head into the kitchen, blissfully unaware. "And why was the door shut?"

"Yep! Let me grab you some." Answering his first question and ignoring the second, I make him a coffee in his favorite Zelda mug, complete with his favorite salted-caramel creamer.

"Nice," he says, after taking a sip. "Almost as good as mine."

Mom hops up out of her seat and ruffles his hair. "I'd say it was just as good as yours," she says with a slight sniffle. "I'm gonna get ready for work. You two be good."

"Don't worry about the laundry!" I call after her. "I've got that. Have a good day. I love you." *I'm sorry I stressed you out before work.*

While Devin fixes himself breakfast, I gather up Mom's and my laundry. "Dost milord have any garments in need of cleaning?" I inquire, dragging the heavy bag into the kitchen.

"Uhh . . . no." He shakes his head. "I'll get them myself."

"Right-o!" I salute, then turn on my heel and drag the bag toward the door.

"Let me get that for you!" He reaches for the bag, but I jerk it away before he can lay a finger on my Chore of Responsibility.

"Nope. Nope. I got this! Do it all the time," I holler over my shoulder, picking up the pace so he can't get his shoes on in time to catch me. "You sit back and relax. I'll see you after the game, and with fresh towels! Oh, and I grabbed your towels! Just gonna run them through, on the hot setting, of course. That's how you kill off all the germs and dust mites, you know. I read that on the Tide website and—"

And I'm out the door.

I quickly slam it shut behind me and chuck the laundry bag down the stairs. I grab my DM gear that I'd left waiting by the door and skip down after it, picking up a few stray socks as I go.

"And then," I muse, tossing Devin's stinky towels into the washer, "she wrapped it all up with the ultimate parting shot: '*I need him to be OK.*' Like *I* don't care if he's OK or not."

"OK, I see what she's saying. But . . ." Lucy pours a capful of detergent into the machine. "Say he does stay here? He goes to CCC, micromanages you and your mom into safe, sweet oblivion, proves to himself that he's not his dad, tutors folks at the college, all while sitting on the sidelines and watching his ex-girlfriend ace pre-med. Is all that going to make him OK? Or is he going to wake up one day, definitely not-OK, wondering why he gave it all up?"

"Right?" I shove four quarters in the slot and slam down the lid. "That's exactly my point. It's, like, the world's most unwanted sacrifice."

"Is it even a sacrifice then?" Lucy asks, twirling the knob to Hot. "Or an obligation?"

I press Start. "Feels like an obligation to me. He thinks it's a sacrifice, though."

"Which is easy to make 'cause he thinks he's failing."

"Exactly, but I still think he'll regret it."

"Me too." Lucy boosts herself up onto the washer, sitting cross-legged. "I looked it up and UCA really is the best. He must be amazing if he got in, let alone scored a full scholarship."

"He is." I climb up on the one next to her, a lump rising in my throat. "I do want him to be OK, you know. It's not just that I'm mad he's taking over my life. Yeah, I'm frustrated, but I also get why he's doing it now. Even though I hate it, I don't hate him. Mom's not the only one that's worried."

"I know." Lucy takes my hand. "What are we going to do?"

"I don't know. I mean, I know I've got to show him that Mom and I'll be fine if he goes back, but that's not enough. I've got to figure out a way to show him that *he'll* be fine if he goes back."

"Yeah. . ."

"Where you nerds at?" Hannah busts into the laundry room with Jen in tow. "We're ready to wreck face!"

I drop Lucy's hand and wipe my eyes. "Right here!" I shout, forcing a smile. "Prepare to get owned!"

△ ▽ △ ▽ △

So, either I was off my game or the party is getting wiser. My carefully crafted final boss, an evil mutated shocker lizard, went down pitifully fast. So embarrassingly quick was his demise, I worried the party would be disappointed, but no—they were having way too much fun gloating.

"How'd you like that plan?" Hannah asks smugly. "Gormek the Devourer didn't stand a chance."

"I'm kind of hurt," I say. "I can't believe y'all did Gormek like that. It was both sneaky and dishonorable."

Also, *genius.* Jen cast her Mage Hand cantrip, causing a spectral floating hand to appear, just outside the mutated shocker lizard's lair. She taunted him with this ghostly, magical hand, luring him away from the protection of his home and pack. Not only that—it tricked Gormek into discharging his lightning at an illusion, in the complete opposite direction of the party. Once they'd gotten him where they wanted him, the party sprung from behind and made short work of my poor, scaly shockinator. The way I'd planned it, they were going to have to fight Gormek *and* his pack. Hannah totally outsmarted me.

"Yes!" Jen says. "So smart to suggest Mage Hand. I've had that cantrip forever and never thought of a way to use it."

"I hereby pronounce you Buffy the Brilliant!" Lucy crows.

Hannah blushes. "I don't know about all that," she says softly. "I'm definitely not brilliant."

"Oh, you are," Lucy says. "I've hereby pronounced it, and there's no take-backs to my proclamations."

"You're so weird." Hannah's cheeks are bright pink, but she smiles.

"Let me let you in on a little secret." Lucy leans forward, elbows on the table, hand cupped around her mouth. In a loud stage whisper, she tells us, "We're *all* weird here."

Giggles fill the room as everybody makes their weirdest, most unbeautiful face. My eyes are crossed and my tongue is curled up toward my nose when a scary realization crashes over me and fixes my face. Today is the first day since Thanksgiving that I've felt like myself. Felt free enough to be myself. Since Devin got home, I've been following his moods and rules, wavering between frustration and fear. I'm frustrated by his smothering but scared of hurting him while he's down.

I can't live like that, and neither can he.

Because he's doing the same thing. He's so overwhelmed by his fear of failure, and of letting Mom and me down, that he's constantly on edge and frustrated with the world.

It's not enough to show him I can make it on my own. I have to show him that he can too.

"Riley?" Lucy asks. "You all right? You look so serious. Whatcha thinking about?"

"Nothing. Just that I love you guys."

▲ ▼ ▲ ▼ ▲

I'm surprised Devin's laptop hasn't burst into flames, because his eyes are *blazing*. If I look close enough, I can almost see sparks shooting from them to the PC balanced precariously on his stomach. Flat on his back on the couch, still in his pajama pants and ratty old robe, he hits the space bar, sighs, taps Escape, and sighs again, louder this time. After that, a flurry of manic typing followed by a vicious assault on the backspace button. Oh yeah, and another sigh.

"What're you working on?" I ask, leaning over his shoulder. "Anything cool?"

Pretty sure he didn't hear me come in, because he jumps about a foot in the air, lands, and slams the laptop shut. "No," he growls, which is an upgrade from the sighs. "It's nothing. Literally."

For the next few hours, the house is thick with mood. Everywhere I go there's an edge, a heavy buzz in the air that makes it impossible to relax.

"Dinner's ready," Devin says, knocking softly on my door.

I tried to tell him I could make it. It was just mac and cheese, but he snatched the box from me, snarling, "I can handle *this*, at least." I've been hiding in my room ever since, trying to think of a way to get him back to his old self.

He smiles at me across the table, like maybe he realizes that he way overreacted about some powdered cheese and elbow noodles.

"Yum," I say, smiling back, although I like the way I make it better. I add two more tablespoons of butter than the box says, a dash of pepper, and a generous sprinkling of paprika. Now *that's* yum.

"How was your game today?"

"Awesome!" What a perfect lead-in to my idea. "You know what you should do?"

He wrinkles his nose. Maybe annoyed, maybe amused. Who knows these days? "What should I do?"

"You should call up your old D&D club. Get a game going." I nod, agreeing with myself. "Today was amazing. Exactly what I needed— really made me feel like my old self again. You should try it too. Don't worry, I'll stay out of your way when you're playing with the big boys. You won't even know I'm here. Or..." I add with a wink, "I might even be persuaded to loan you the laundry room."

He shakes his head, *not* agreeing with me. "One: what do you mean 'feel like your old self'? You're twelve, Riley. That's ridiculous."

"I don't think that's ridic—"

"And two: everyone's busy. They all have lives of their own. Most of them aren't even in town. They're off at college, doing great things. In fact, I doubt I'll even see Evie again until after finals."

I wince, wishing I could recall that stupid idea back to my mouth.

I'd forgotten that everybody was gone and that the semester wasn't over yet. It's only Devin who's home, and I went and rubbed it in his face.

If I thought the atmosphere was dark before dinner, now it's absolutely opaque. It's wild how some people's feels can fill up a whole apartment. Do the neighbors feel it too? I mean, we do share a wall. A deep gloom settles over the place, broken only by sporadic, angry typing. Typing that I am not allowed to look upon or merely glance at without Devin snapping the screen shut with the obligatory gusty sigh.

"I just remembered," I say. "We left the laundry room a total mess. I'm gonna go clean up before Ms. Hannigan has a fit." The cleaning bucket's slung over my arm for believability; in actuality the laundry room's as clean as it's ever gonna get. I just really, really want out of this apartment.

"I don't think so," he says, not looking up. "It's dark."

"That's what we've got lights for."

"I don't want you down there by yourself, and I don't feel like going down there right now. I'm trying to do something."

"Oh? What're you trying to do?"

"Nothing."

What? That makes no sense.

"Mom lets me," I say, moving on from his nonsense. "I can call *her* and ask."

"Do not call Mom over something dumb like that. She's at work."

"Then let me go clean up." I pull myself up to my full height and gaze at him with all seriousness. "It is my responsibility."

"Fine. Be back in half an hour." He pulls his phone out of his back pocket and hands it to me. "Call me if you need me."

Pretty sure I won't, but I take it anyway. I can use it to watch YouTube while I'm hiding in the laundry room.

CHAPTER 20

A LOUD, WET SNIFFLE ECHOES THROUGHOUT THE LAUNDRY room, and my heart drops to my stomach. I run to the back and find, not Lucy like I expected, but Hannah slouched down at the folding table. Shiny tears make tracks through her freckles down her beet-red face.

The whole scene is so *wrong*. Seeing Hannah cry is like watching the sun shoot raindrops. It shouldn't be happening. My mouth falls open, and I drop the cleaning bucket.

Hannah jumps, startled, then rubs her eyes hard with her knuckles. "What are you doing here?"

"Are you OK?" I kick the bucket out of the way and run for a chair. I pull it up right next to Hannah and put an arm around her shoulder.

"I'm fine. I guess." Her voice is quieter than usual, thick and husky, and she keeps her eyes on the table. "Or not."

"Do you want to talk about it?"

"Not really." She shrugs off my arm and rolls her damp eyes. "But I guess I should tell you I won't be back after finals."

"Why?!" I shriek, my mind running wild. Is she sick? Is one of her brothers sick? Is she moving? *What?!*

"Remember when Jen's mom wanted to make her quit D&D? Because she's such a genius and it was interfering with her overachieving?"

"Yeah?"

"This is kind of the opposite. *My* parents are gonna make me quit because I'm stupid."

"Really?" I give her a skeptical look.

"Yes. *Really.*" She bugs her eyes out and gives me an annoyed look in return.

"So, your mom came up to you and was, like, 'Hannah, girl, you're stupid. Buffy's out!'" I do my best impression of Hannah's mom, really emphasizing her loud Southern twang, but Hannah doesn't laugh.

"No, but she might as well have. Dad too. They went in my backpack today while we were down here playing, supposedly to get a pencil for my brother, and found a note from my math teacher . . . and my last test."

"It was bad?"

"Horrendous, but definitely nothing new. The problem is that they've been on me about my grades all semester. They even took away the TV last month, but who cares? Like, 'Oh no, please don't take away my *Paw*

Patrol and *Blue's Clues*.'" She rolls her eyes. "But today they must have gotten a fiendish burst of inspiration when I was down here. They *know* how much I like playing with you guys, so they're taking it away. They've really got me this time." Her jaw sets in a hard line, and she shakes her head. "If I don't pass my next math test and all my finals, I'm out."

"How long?" How could we play without Buffy? There's no way I'd have any fun, knowing Hannah was upstairs, alone in her apartment and miserable.

"Until my next report card, but only if it's a good one. So, basically half-past forever."

"That's not true," I say. "You can pull your grades up."

"No, I can't. I'd better enjoy these next couple games while I still can."

"Hannah, come on. I know you can do this."

"Do you?" she asks. "Do you even know why I'm not in any of your classes? Or Lucy's? Or Jen's?"

"Um, because you have a different schedule?"

"Heckin' right I have a different schedule. My state test scores were crap last year, like they are every year, so they put me in all remedial classes. Then, the guidance counselor decided I was so dumb I needed an *extra* math class and yanked me out of art." Her eyes fill with tears, but she blinks them down hard. "I'm not smart, OK? I'm not like you guys. You know what? It's probably best my parents are pulling me. I'll just slow everybody down."

"That's not true."

"It *is* true. I'm just glad Jen divided up the gold for us today, instead of waiting on me. I'd still be sitting here, trying to figure it out on all my fingers and toes."

"Hannah—"

"Face it, Riley. It's over. I'm out of the party. My grades are never coming up. I was hanging on by a thread in elementary school, and now I'm lucky I don't have all F's."

I'm on the verge of bawling myself. I *know* Hannah is smart, but if she leaves the party and we're not there to prove it to her, she'll never believe it. We have to keep her in the group.

"Why don't you come to our next Intelligence Buff?" I ask. "We could hold it at Lucy's, so you don't have to worry about Devin annoying you. We could even have an emergency session tomorrow."

She crosses her arms and leans back in her chair. "No way."

"Why not? It's fun."

"It's bad enough *you* know I'm an idiot, but I don't need Lucy and Jen to see my ignorance firsthand."

"You're not an idiot, and they're your friends. They're nice."

"I know they're nice. I love them to bitty bits, and I'm going to miss them so much. But I'd like to keep this between us, OK? It's embarrassing."

"It's not embarrassing to ask for help."

"That's nice." Hannah rolls her eyes. "Real nice. Why don't you put that on a poster for the guidance counselor?"

"It's true."

"Maybe," she says. "But I'd still rather cover myself in trash and jump in a wild raccoon's den than show them how much help I *really* need."

"They wouldn't think anything bad."

"They might think *different*, though," she says. "Today, Jen dead-serious called my plan 'so smart.' Like, not sarcastic at all. And Lucy 'hereby pronounced me Buffy the Brilliant.'"

"Well, you *are* Buffy the Brilliant."

She shakes her head. "You know how many times I've been called smart before? Exactly zero. Nice? Sure. Funny? All the time. But intelligent? Uh, no. Finally, I've got people believing that I might have half a brain, and I'd really, really like to keep it that way." Her face falls. She's not crying anymore, but she looks totally defeated. "Even if it's not true."

My heart twists. All this time, I thought Hannah was the most confident person I knew. "It *is* true, and I'm going to prove it to you. But I understand if you're nervous, and I won't tell anybody. What if we do it, just us?"

"What do you mean?"

"I'll come over tomorrow and help you."

"I have to study?"

"Well, yeah. It's the only way it'll work. You can't *roll* your grades up."

"You sure about that?"

"Pretty sure," I say, pretending to think it over. "Even if you could, would you want to risk it? I mean, you might roll a one and regress to total infanthood."

"That doesn't sound so bad. It'd get me out of schoolwork."

"Come on. You want to play or not?"

"Of course I want to play."

"All right, then." I hold out my hand.

Hannah examines it suspiciously. "You really going to come? Devin's going to let you?"

"Of course he's going to let me." I shrug. "Well, actually, Mom will let me. She's off work tomorrow and Devin's going Christmas shopping. I'll call you every day after school, too, as soon as Devin frees me, and we'll go over stuff. Then next Sunday, we'll spend the whole day cramming for finals."

"You mean it?"

"Yes, I mean it. Now, stop leaving me hanging and shake my hand already."

She grabs my hand and shakes it so hard I feel it in my shoulder. "I think you're going to regret this," she says, grinning.

▲ ▼ ▲ ▼ ▲

Sunday night, when Devin says I look tired at dinner, he's not wrong. My study session with Hannah didn't go quite as smoothly as I expected. Not only was there a mammoth stack of old assignments to tackle, there was her crushing self-doubt that reared its ugly head every time she picked up a pencil. Talk about some tackling. *Seriously, what do you think erasers are for? I promise you can make a mistake and I won't think you're stupid.*

I'd never thought I'd say it, but Hannah and Devin have a lot in common.

Despite all that, we did it. *All of it.*

With no bloodshed, no hard feelings, and no tears.

Well, minimal tears.

"Yeah, you're right," I say with a yawn. "I'd probably better get to bed soon—especially if I'm going to be up in time for the bus."

"Don't worry about that," Devin says. "You know I can drive you."

"I know you *can.*" I glance over at Mom, making sure I've got her attention. "But it's a matter of, *should* you."

"Why shouldn't I?"

"Yeah, why shouldn't he?" Mom shoots me a sharp look, like I'm attempting to dismantle Devin's OKness or something. "It's a nice offer."

"Oh, I know!" I say, smiling around the table like I actually believe that. "It's just that I've been thinking a lot about my carbon footprint. You know, the greenhouse-gas emissions caused by my actions?"

I *have* been thinking a lot about it. Ever since 3:19 this afternoon, when Hannah and I discovered this very interesting fact in her science book and decided to use it to our advantage.

"OK," Mom says, her face softening. "Tell me more about your gas emissions."

"Mother, please."

"Excuuuuuse me," she says, giggling.

"What are you talking about?" Devin says, not giggling.

"This: It seems a waste for your truck to burn up all that gas and send all that carbon dioxide into the air for little old me. Especially when there's already a mode of transportation heading to and from my exact destination. Did you know"—I check my pen-scribbled palm under the table—"that a typical passenger vehicle gives off over 4.6 metric tons of carbon dioxide per year?"

"Whoa," Mom says.

"Whoa is right. I just want to do my part."

"I think that's great," Mom says, her little tree-hugging, butter-soaked heart thoroughly touched. "I totally support you."

I feel a little bad. I mean, I love the Earth as much as the next girl, but my main objective here is riding the bus in peace with my friends and showing Devin I can take care of myself. Saving the Earth is an awesome bonus, though.

"Yeah. Me, too, I guess," Devin says, although he looks more irritated than impressed.

"Oh, come on," I say teasingly. "You'll love it. You won't even have to deal with me until, like, three thirty."

"I like dealing with you," he says nicely, and I get a warm, fuzzy feeling at him. "And after the break, you can ride the bus in the morning, and I'll get you in the afternoons on my way to the tutoring center."

Oh, yeah.

I'd almost forgotten about that ridiculous plan.

I don't want it to, but that warm, fuzzy feeling nosedives fast into a cold, prickly one.

"So, yeah," I gather up my dirty dishes and head toward the sink. "Big day of saving the Earth tomorrow. I'd better get to bed."

"You can leave those," Devin calls after me. "I'll get them."

"I've *got* them! They're *my* dishes!" I holler back.

▲ ▼ ▲ ▼ ▲

"Read it and weep." Hannah slaps a red-inked paper down on the cafeteria table, then drops into the seat next to me. "Tears of joy, that is. Happy Friday!"

"You got a C!" I shriek, thrilled our week of hardcore studying paid off. "In math!"

"Which, they tell me, is a *passing* grade." Hannah grins.

It's amazing what a little perspective can do. On one hand, I've got Devin, ready to drop out of school and spend the rest of his days crying in a corner, babysitting his rapidly aging kid sister. All because he made some C's. On the other hand, I've got Hannah, about ready to jump out of her freckles with pride, all because she made a C.

Because she did something hard.

"You're amazing."

Am I gonna cry?

"Are you gonna cry?" She peers into my eyes, a small smile playing on her lips.

"I'm just really happy."

"Well, get out your hankie, kid," she says. "Because my English teacher loved the book report you helped me write on *Catwings*. I got an A!"

"That was all you," I say, perilously close to needing a hankie. "I just told you to read it so we could talk about it."

"Yeah, but it was such a good talk. Made it so easy to write."

That's how it used to be with Devin and me. Hashing out book reports was one of my top ten things to do back in the day.

"It was the *perfect* pick," Hannah says. "Short book. Flying kittens. I feel so seen."

Yeah, exactly. That's how I always felt when Devin picked out the perfect book for me. He hasn't suggested anything since he's been home, well, except to knock off the soda or blow my nose, and that does *not* count.

"What's that?" Jen pops up behind Hannah, peeking over her shoulder.

Hannah snatches up her math test and crumples it into a tight ball. "Nothing," she says, shoving it in her pocket.

She might as well have crumpled up both our hearts and shoved them in her pocket. That is *not* nothing. It's so much hard work, and I know Jen would understand that if Hannah gave her the chance.

I open my mouth to brag on her, but Hannah sends me a fierce warning look. My mouth snaps shut, keeping my promise—this is just between us. But I know, deep down, that she has nothing to be ashamed of and her pink cheeks are a waste of blood and energy.

I wish I could say the same thing to Devin and his C—if only he'd listen. Hannah is just as special as Jen, and Devin is every bit as special as anyone at UCA.

But insecurity is a beast.

Hannah might have crumpled up our hard work, but by the end of Saturday's D&D session, she was ready for more.

"Hey!" she tugs my sleeve on the way out, pulling me back into the laundry room.

"Yes, matey?" We've just completed Lucy's epic pirate adventure, and I'm finding it hard to lose my brogue.

"We still on for tomorrow, Captain Smartbeard?" she whispers.

"You got it, my brilliant buccaneer!" I whisper back.

"High noon, right? I gotta take over twin patrol at five, and I need all the time I can get. Especially on that math. I mean, *maths*." She rolls her eyes. "What better way to help out the dumb kid than by giving them double the work?"

"You are not dumb," I remind her, for the million and fourth time. "Seriously, you've got the remedial one down. I have not been spending my nights with a phone glued to my ear for nothing. And, dude, we are so close on that pre-algebra. . ."

"You think so?"

"I know so."

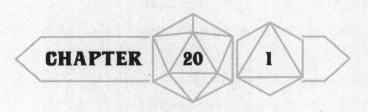

CHAPTER 20 1

I SPEND MOST OF SUNDAY MORNING HOLED UP IN MY ROOM. There's no way I was going to let Devin ruin my study session with Hannah, so I figured the best course of action would be to keep my mouth shut about it. I ran it by Mom, of course, but planned to wait until the absolute last minute to tell Devin, so he couldn't try to stop me or, worse, make us study here.

At exactly 11:45, I slide on my backpack and venture out into the living room.

"Surprise!" Devin shouts, sending me about three feet out of my skin. My backpack slides off my shoulders and hits the floor with a heavy thud. My jaw drops, and I can't open my eyes wide enough to take in the sight before me.

"Oh, wow," I manage to whisper.

"You should see your face," Devin says. "I knew you'd be surprised!"

He's not wrong. I force my mouth into what I hope is a smile and swallow hard. My stomach tightens as I look around, both wondering and dreading what he's up to. Blue and silver streamers twist and stretch from corner to corner, and sparkling silver stars dangle from the ceiling. Devin's collection of pewter dragons line the counter, accompanied by bowls of favorite snacks and a six-pack of Cherry Coke. On one end of the table is Devin's DM screen and his kobold incense burner. On the other end is my Arwenna figure, my Sutherland figure, and my dice, accompanied by a brand-new RPG journal and a set of spellbook cards, fully detailed and beautifully drawn.

The room is not the only thing that's decorated for . . . whatever this is. Devin is waiting for me, wearing his old wizard hat, a long black cape, and a T-shirt that says WHEN THE DM SMILES, IT'S ALREADY TOO LATE.

He smiles at me. And his shirt is right, it's already too late.

My plan completely and totally backfired. I should have let him know I had plans today. I could have prevented all this.

He grabs the journal off the table and shoves it into my hands. It's a soft green velvet, with golden stars embossed across the cover. The letters *RRH* glimmer in the bottom right-hand corner. Riley Rhiannon Henderson.

He had it *engraved*.

"You like it?" he asks, gleefully certain that I do.

And I do, but . . . "It's beautiful," I say softly. "I love it."

"Good," he says, then cocks his head and looks at me thoughtfully. "Things have been kinda weird between us lately, huh?"

"Yeah." *A lot weird, actually,* this latest manic shift being the least of it.

For a minute, I think he's about to apologize, but all he says is, "We just need to cut loose and have some fun!" He bows and offers me his hand. "So, please, my dear rogue, or my dear sorceress, if you're feeling so inclined, please join me at the table. Like you said, there's nothing like a good campaign to get us feeling like our old selves!"

OK, that's not exactly what I said. What I said was: I really like playing with my friends, so he should go play with his.

But this is the first time I've seen him smile for real in ages.

And he bought me an engraved journal.

And Cool Ranch Doritos.

And more than two sodas.

But most important, he's smiling.

When was the last time I saw him smile like that? My heart twists, and I know I can't hurt him. Mom was right—he needs us. He needs to feel loved and important, and whether he knows it or not, he needs to be convinced he's awesome. What if this game is a golden opportunity to show Devin just how cool and creative he really is? To show him he's got amazing stories and games to share? To show him it's time to go back to California and be the developer he was meant to be?

Hannah might never forgive me, but I've got to try.

"Where you at?" Hannah asks, popping her gum in my ear. "These expressions are not going to evaluate themselves."

"Um." I pull the phone into the living room, trying not to puke. Devin's in the kitchen, happily shuffling his papers and humming, probably patting himself on the back for making my day. And, really, on any other day, it would totally have been made. His timing just sucks.

"Um, what?" Hannah asks sharply, her voice suspicious. "Is Devin trying to tag along? Because I am not having that snootypants smartypants all up in my Mediocrity Buff."

"It's an *Intelligence* Buff, and you know it," I remind her. "But, um, that's not the problem."

"Then what is it? Can you spit it out already, because it makes me nervous as bees when you 'um' all over the place like that. Like, I want to jump in and finish your sentences so bad, but I have no heckin' idea what you're trying to say."

My throat is tight, but I spit it out: "I can't come over, but, um." I wince. *Stop umming, Riley.* "I'll call you tonight."

"Why not?" Hannah's voice climbs, a note of panic in her question mark. "He won't let you?"

"Not exactly. He just, um . . ." *Crap. Another "um."* "Made plans, and I can't back out. Not without hurting his feelings real bad, and I think I might be able to help him."

"What about my feelings?" Her voice is tiny. "What about helping me?"

"I care about your feelings, Hannah. So much," I plead. "I'll call you tonight. I promise. I'll talk to you until two in the morning if you want."

"I don't want."

"*I'm sorry*," I say.

"Not as sorry as I am."

"Come on, Hannah," I say. "We've been working every day. You have all the notes and everything we made. You said so yourself, all you need is a little boost on pre-algebra. I'll call tonight, we'll go through it."

"That won't work. I'm watching the twins till bedtime, remember? I can barely remember my own name when I'm dealing with their racket."

"We can try."

"There's no point," she says, her voice wobbling. "I have to be on them every second, you know that. But won't you even *try* to come over? Just for an hour or two?"

My throat is dry and sticks when I swallow. "I wish I could . . ."

"Not as much I do," she says. "Or as much I wish that I was like you guys. It must be nice to know everything all the time and not have to depend on other people to explain it to you over and over again. I can see how that'd get annoying. It's fine. I get it. Go hang with your brother."

Crap. I *really* hurt her feelings. "It's not that. I like studying with you."

"Riley, for real, it's fine," she says. "Just don't tell the others why I got kicked out, OK? I'll come up with a story."

"You're not gonna get kicked out of the party."

"Pretty sure I am."

"Riley," Devin calls from the kitchen. "You about ready?"

"You better go, Riley," Hannah says.

Then she hangs up. Not hard or angrily or anything, just softly and sadly.

I feel awful.

▲ ▼ ▲ ▼ ▲

I go with Arwenna for the game.

Devin goes with Devin, the real-live actual brother that I know and love.

It'd be so much fun if I wasn't sick inside over Hannah.

▲ ▼ ▲ ▼ ▲

Along with the loot, Devin hands out an apology. *Finally*.

"I'm sorry I've been so crabby," he says, neatly adding five gold to my stat sheet. "It's not you. You know that, right?"

"It's not?" I mean, I didn't really think it *was*, but I'd like to hear more. I'm fragile right now, and I'll take all the love and apologies I can get. Besides, he owes me.

"Of course not." He sighs, but not angrily. "I'm humiliated. I ran off across the country, left you and Mom hanging, and for what? So that I could find out what a failure I am? That I'm only a big deal in *high school*?"

"That's not true."

"It is, but I don't want to talk about that right now. I want to talk about you," he says, reaching over to squeeze my hand. "Just because I'm stressed doesn't mean I have to pass it on. I shouldn't be taking my stuff out on you."

"I get it, though."

"I don't *want* you to get it. I know you're growing up, but I don't want you to worry about those things. I want you to be happy. I want you to have fun, and right now, you're not. You're hiding in your room. You stopped bringing your friends over. And apparently, I'm such a cranky old butthead that you'd rather endure the smelly old school bus than ride with me."

"Dude, seriously, I love the Earth."

And riding with my friends.

"Yeah, me too." Devin smiles, shoving his bangs out of his eyes. "But mostly I love you. You and Mom are my Earth. I'm sorry I've been putting you on edge. I'll do better. *Promise.*"

My ribs tighten, squishing my heart to jelly. I love this guy so much. "Stop worrying about doing better, Devin. You're good enough, you really are. For me. For Mom. For UCA. For young gamers everywhere."

He chuckles, a little sadly, then forces a grin. "Thanks, Ri-Fi. That's really sweet."

"It's not sweet. It's true," I say, seizing the moment. "I mean, you wrote this whole campaign, and it was amazing. Everything you do is. UCA will figure that out before you know it. You just need a little more time."

"I don't—"

"It's like with Hannah," I babble on. "She was legit failing math, not just a little old C or something like you got. But anyway, we've been working and working, and now she's doing great. I'll bet she even aces her final tomorrow." *Please let her ace her final tomorrow. Then maybe she won't hate me forever.*

Devin exhales slowly. "No offense, Riley, but this is a little more serious than a sixth-grade math test."

"I know, but—"

"We had a nice day. Like old times, right?" He stands, gathering up his dice bag and notes. "I like being home. I like being here for you and Mom. It's important to me, OK? So, can you please just drop it?"

No, I really can't. Not while he's determined to ruin his life (and mine).

▲　▼　▲　▼　▲

For the first time ever, I'm thrilled when my alarm goes off on Monday morning. After a long, sleepless night of second-guessing myself, that obnoxious beep is an absolute relief.

Part of me is sure I made the right choice. Devin and I needed that talk, and I feel like I know him again. More than ever, I'm determined to find a way to show him how special he is and how lucky UCA is to have him. To prove that, YES!, I am growing up and he can trust that Mom and I are safe and sound on our own.

The other part of me is devastated because I let Hannah down. I tried to call her as soon as Devin and I finished playing, but she was already babysitting. The conversation was one-sided and went a little something like, "I'm sorry, ex-tutor Riley, but Brantley is currently attempting to shove green LEGOs up his nose. You know, to make boogers. I'm afraid I haven't time to discuss the maths. *Brantley, put that down right this minute!*"

Click.

It was hard, and it hurt my feelings, but I'm not letting this exam, or this friendship, go down without a fight.

I throw on some clothes and check the clock—5:30, Monday morning. There's two hours before the bus leaves—just enough time for a pre-algebra boost. I grab a piece of bright-yellow construction paper and write a note in black Sharpie.

I went to Hannah's to study. I will be back in time for the bus.

Love, Riley

I scribble Hannah's apartment and phone number down at the bottom, then leave the paper on the coffee table, right on top of Devin's laptop, where he's sure to see it. I bolt out the door and hightail it to Hannah's.

The blinds are drawn, and her apartment is dark. I tiptoe up to Hannah's window and knock softly on the glass. There's no answer, so I knock a little louder, feeling like the world's creepiest creeper.

A pale finger pushes down a slat in the blinds, and a blinking brown eye peers out. Within seconds, the blinds are up, along with the window. Hannah yawns, her hair sticking up every which way like a campfire.

"Who are you? Romeo or something?" She grins, smoothing her frilly pink pajama top.

Oh, good. A grin.

Suppressing a giggle at her super-girly jams, I grin back. "Something."

"You scared the mess out of me, Something. What're you doing here?"

"I am so, so sorry I couldn't come over yesterday . . ."

"So, you got up at the butt-crack of dawn, marched over to my house, and rapped on my windowpane?"

"Um, yeah." OK, maybe that was a weird thing to do.

"That's a really nice thing to do." Hannah says, gesturing into her room. "Please, enter."

Heaving a sigh of relief, I climb through the window. "You hate me?"

"Of course I don't hate you. But. . ." She peeks out the window behind me, then slides it shut. Dropping her voice to a whisper, she says, "Don't tell Jen's mom or anything, but I *was* kinda mad at you yesterday."

"You were disappointed. And scared. *And* I backed out on you. I get it."

"Buffy never admits fear." She puts her hands on her hips, Wonder Woman–style. Then she drops them, rolling her eyes. "But *Hannah* was terrified."

"You had every right to be upset. I broke a promise."

"Yeah, but I know you, Riley. If you say you needed to stay home, then I'm sure it was the right choice. And you're here now. Once again, you're just trying to make everybody happy."

"*Is* everybody happy?"

"Pretty happy," she says. "Just so you know, though, you didn't have to do this. Even if I failed my test, I wouldn't have blamed you."

"You are not going to fail," I say. "I needs my Buffy. Now, get out your math book."

"OK," she says, rummaging through her backpack. "No offense, but this might just be the worst pajama party ever."

"Yeah . . . it's kind of like an un-slumber party, huh?"

"Exactly. Surprise! Wake up and math!" She rolls her eyes and sticks out her tongue. "You could have at least brought doughnuts."

"I've got gum," I say, reaching into my pocket.

"That's so not the same, but I'll take it. My orcish morning breath is singeing my own nostrils." She snatches the gum and leaps onto the bed, notebook in hand. "All right, my trespassing tutor, let's do this!"

Two hours flies by, but I'm incredibly pleased with myself as I climb back out Hannah's window. To her complete and total shock, she breezed through the test review. All those study sessions must have finally paid off and, honestly, she could've done the whole thing on her own. She just had it in her head she couldn't, so she didn't even take out her backpack until I came knocking.

I tiptoe quietly back into the house, but Mom's already up and in the kitchen, finishing a bowl of cereal. She looks up at me, one eyebrow raised. "Man, I thought Devin was a nerd, but you must be a *super* nerd: sneaking out of the house to do math like that."

"I didn't sneak out," I say, grabbing a bowl. "I left a note."

"Before creeping out into the darkness." She gets up and pours me some Cheerios and milk, then hands me a spoon, but she's not smiling. "What time did you leave?"

"Five thirty. It was morning," I say defensively.

"Technically," Mom says. "But it was still dark. And you didn't actually ask me if you could go out."

"I thought it'd be OK," I say.

"Look, Riley," she says sharply. "I see you. I get it. You're becoming more independent and I'm proud of you, but that does not mean you can go prowling around the apartment complex in the pitch-black darkness. It doesn't mean that you can just come and go as you please. You're still a kid, and if you want to go somewhere, you need to run it by me."

I want to be annoyed, but she does have a point. Plus, I'm too tired to argue and it's way easier to just apologize. At least she said I had to run it by *her* and not Devin. "Sorry. I didn't think about it like that," I say meekly. "I won't do it again."

"Good." She smiles and the sharpness melts away. "How was the mathing? Hannah getting it?"

"She really is," I say. "I think a lot of it is a confidence issue."

"Could be." Mom nods. "Lucky you were there to help her."

"Kinda like with Devin," I can't help but add. "I still think he needs someone to help him get his confidence back."

"I'm not sure this is the same thing," Mom says, taking her bowl to the sink.

"Yeah, that's what Devin said."

Mom takes a deep breath, then exhales slowly. "So, maybe drop it for now," she says, a hint of annoyance creeping in. "Don't push him too hard, OK?"

I'm really, really sick of everyone telling me to drop it. It's obvious the boy needs a push, but she's too busy blowing me off to see it. I don't want to stress her out before work again, though. "I won't."

Mom checks the clock, grumbles softly, then grabs her keys and phone from the counter. "I gotta go to work. Bye, baby," she says, dropping a goodbye kiss on my forehead. At the door, she pauses and turns. "I do wish I could help him, you know. Like how you helped Hannah."

"I know, Mom." And I still think we can.

She heads out, leaving me with half an hour to kill before the bus comes. I take the opportunity to grab Devin's laptop to play some games. He's got all the good ones, and his laptop actually runs fast enough to play them. I settle into the couch and type in the password. Lucky for me, but kinda sad for Devin, it's still Evie3000.

It boots directly to a start screen for a game. The title, Cry of the Beholder, runs along the top of the screen in a bold, red font. Beneath it is the character I saw him working on. Same ripped jeans, same T-shirt, same creepy bulbous eye and fearsome mouth crowned by hissing snakes. Except this guy's 3-D, and he stands in a desert wasteland, beneath a starry purple sky cut by shadows. Swirls of dry sand blanket his sneakers, and his pale, scaly arms cradle the army-green fanny pack at his waist protectively. When I peer closer, I can see a tiny eyeball peeking out.

What the heck? This is pretty weird, Devin.

And by weird, I mean awesome.

I press Start.

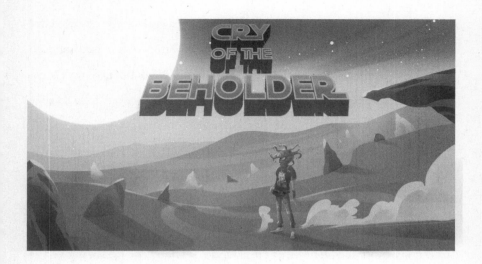

The game opens with a cut-scene. A family of these serpentine beholder-type creatures lounge among the stars, minus their humanoid bodies. The snakes are relaxed, lying limp like hair, and the oddly expressive eyes are calm as they float serenely through the universe. But not for long.

A rumble shakes the screen, and a flash of blinding light rips open the sky. Amid a chorus of shrieks, the humanoid beholders tumble into darkness.

Then a soft glow returns to the screen, and Devin's character is shown standing in the desert. A small slip of white floats toward the ground and is immediately scooped up. He pops it into his fanny pack as text scrolls across the bottom of the screen.

Don't worry, sis. I'll get us home. Somehow.

The tiny little eye peeps out approvingly, and the game controls become visible.

I take off running across the desert, getting a feel for the game. After bouncing off a few cacti, I figure out how to jump. After getting torn apart by coyotes, I figure out how to summon a black hole. After crumbling with dehydration from the noontime sun, I figure out how to slice open one of those offending cacti to pour water on my eyeball.

"What are you doing?"

I jump and accidentally hit the space bar, launching me off a cliff and into a canyon—and my doom.

"You made me die," I groan.

Devin pulls the laptop from my hands. "Hey. . ." he says, annoyed as heck, but trying to pretend he's not. Guess he meant it when he said he didn't want to be a cranky butthead anymore. "Ask for permission next time, OK?"

"That game—it's awesome," I gush. "I'm thinking about playing hooky today and finishing it. What happened to the beholder fam, anyway?"

"Technically, they're beholder-*kin*," he corrects me. "They're variants of the beholder race. I created them myself. But whatever. Who cares?" He snaps the screen shut and tucks the laptop into his armpit.

"Well, I like 'em!" I punch Captain Crankypants lightly on the arm and smile up at him. "Is this what you've been working on? With all the typing and grunting? Why didn't you make a design document for *that*?"

"I did, but it was stupid. I didn't even bother to turn it in." He shakes his head. "I should delete the whole game. Anyway, *whatever*. Speaking of school, are you ready? You *sure* you don't need a ride?"

"Nope. As a mature, dependable, and reliable citizen with a low carbon footprint, I plan on taking the bus. I even packed my own lunch."

"Oh, yeah? What'd you make?"

"Don't you worry about that," I say mysteriously. I definitely didn't want him to find out there was no lunch—I just wanted to sound responsible—so I start to slide off the couch and grab my bag.

"You sure you don't need a ride?"

"Yup, I'm sure. I don't need a thing. You sit here and look pretty, and I'll see Cry of the Beholder after school." I shoot him a couple of finger guns, then toss my backpack over my shoulder.

"No, you won't," he says flatly. "But I'll make you a snack when you get home, then we'll head out to CCC. I've got to fill out some paperwork."

Boo and boo.

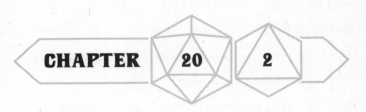

CHAPTER 20 2

"HEY!" HANNAH RUNS UP BEHIND ME ON MY WAY TO THE BUS ramp. She grabs my arm and pulls me away from the pressing crowd. "Look! I told Ms. Beecher I wasn't leaving until she graded it."

She shoves the paper so close to my face, I can't even see what I'm looking at. I can guess, though.

I snatch the math test out of her hand and look down at the giant purple 81%/B at the top of the page.

"I told her the red ink was kinda stressful," Hannah says. "Purple ink's friendlier. She agreed."

"Hannah, this is awesome!"

"Right? I asked her if she had a sticker or something she could put on it, but then she told me not to push it and get out of her classroom."

"Yes! Buffy shall not be exiled from the party!"

"Thanks to you." She drops her silly grin and gives me a squeeze. "For real, you're a good friend. I'd still be sitting there failing my face off if it wasn't for you."

"That's not true," I say. "You're smart. You just needed to believe it."

"OK, Tinker Bell." The goofy grin's back as she pats me on the head. "We'd better hope we make it to the bus on time."

Hannah skips off down the hall, swinging her test. She can act like she doesn't believe me, but I'm right. Some people don't know how cool they are.

I hustle to catch up to her, overshoot, and bounce off her back. She whirls around, pointing an interrogating finger in my face. "Hey, I forgot to ask. Are you still going to the Winter-Con thingy?"

And I was feeling so good a second ago. "I don't think so," I say, my heart sinking. "Devin backed out."

"Seriously?" She sticks out her tongue and rolls her eyes. "Ugh, but, whatever. I'm not gonna say a word. More Riley for me. Listen to this, I've got some news that'll turn that frown upside down."

"Oh yeah?"

"Mom said if I nailed this test, she'd take us all and pay our admission. You in?"

"Oh my God. Yes!" I practically shriek. A couple of Very Cool eighth graders snicker, but I'm sure I don't care.

"*Perfect.* Let's go tell Lucy! I'll call Jen as soon as I get home, if her mom hasn't locked her in the library or something until finals are over."

The whole bus ride home, Hannah and Lucy grill me about Winter-Con. I describe, in detail, each and every part of the event, from the comic-book signings to the tabletop games. "This year," I say, "Cat's making a room for gaming laptops, so we'll be able to try out a bunch of indie games. Evie said she was really excited about it."

"That's cool," Lucy says. "I've been looking for something new to play."

"Too bad Devin's being so stingy with his new game. You would love that one."

"Yeah?" Lucy's eyebrows raise with interest.

"I don't know." Hannah looks skeptical. "I'll bet the rulebook's the size a dictionary."

Lucy smacks her on the arm, then turns back to me. "What's it like?"

"I haven't played the whole thing yet, but it's awesome." I give them a rundown of the game so far, and Hannah nods in approval.

"When's it come out?" she asks.

"Half-past never?" I say, shaking my head at that ridiculous boy. "It'll be a miracle if I can wheedle him into letting me play past level one. He's determined to hide it away, wallowing in shame and misery."

"Too bad," Lucy says. "Because I would play the heck out of that thing."

Right?

I sit back in my seat. I bet a lot of people would. Then a teensy flicker of an idea tickles my brain. Maybe there *is* a way to show him that he's good enough for UCA—and young gamers everywhere, too, of course.

For the first time in weeks, I can't wait to get home.

▲　▼　▲　▼　▲

The second I walk in the door, Devin's already attempting to obliterate my plans. "Hey!" he says, grabbing his keys. "Go ahead and eat your snack real quick, then we can head over to CCC to fill out my paperwork."

Ooh, goody. Nothing I'd love better than to sit in a hard chair in a cold lobby and watch Devin fill out forms. Even if he were going somewhere cool, though, I'd still want to skip it. I've got things to do.

"Did you withdraw from UCA already?" I ask.

"Not yet. I withdrew from this term's classes, but I never quite got around to withdrawing completely, and now their office is closed for the holidays. I have to wait until after the first. It's a good thing CCC's offices are open this week."

There's got to be a reason he didn't fully withdraw. Like, maybe, deep down, he really wants to go back? I know I want him to, and not just for my own sake anymore.

"I wish it was over with," he mutters, then forces a smile. "Anyway, let's head out."

I put my fingers to my temples and massage them gently. "Do I have to? I've got a huge headache. All I want to do is lie down."

He's across the room in a flash, hand to my forehead. "You don't feel hot. You think you're coming down with something?"

"No. But I'm real tired. Maybe too much studying, you know. Finals and all."

"Maybe I should stay—"

"NO! I mean, no thanks. I'm just gonna sleep. You go ahead and take care of your school stuff."

He mulls it over for way too long. "All right, but don't go anywhere, OK? Keep the door locked and call me if you feel worse."

Of course, I won't.

He tucks me into bed, with a cool rag on my forehead and a warm cup of tea on my nightstand. I lie quietly until I hear the front door lock, then peep out the window and watch his truck pull away. I wait a few more minutes, cuddled up in bed, to make sure he didn't forget his wallet or anything.

Then I break into his room.

My tickle of an idea becomes a full-blown plan as I play. Cry of the Beholder is every bit as cool as I knew it would be. In the first three levels, I discover the mysterious threat that destroyed the beholder-kin's celestial home—a chaos kraken. It is an alien entity bent on spreading, well, chaos throughout the universe. It looks like a cross between a comet and a sea monster and thrives on disorder. Because this particular race of beholders has the ability to create and manifest realities, the kraken sees them as a threat to its disruption. Conner, the protagonist, is particularly dangerous to the kraken, due to his fondness for creating neat and orderly worlds. Worlds that tame the chaos, allowing no space for disorder and confusion.

If that's not Devin, I don't know what is. I swear if he were granted huge cosmic powers, he'd use them to put Mom and me in safety bubbles to keep all the world's chaos at bay.

Oh, and that little eyeball in the fanny pack? I'm pretty sure that's me.

The game is awesome and all, but I really think that by level three, he could have given me some powers. Plus, isn't he the one that thought a baby beholder in a jar was ridiculous? And the whole while he's got me in a fanny pack? *A fanny pack?!*

OK, it is a little funny.

I dig around in his Word files and find the game-design document. Yes, it's kind of spoilery, but I don't have time to make it through all the levels.

Devin could be home any moment and I don't have much time to execute my plan.

Winter-Con is on Saturday.

▲　▼　▲　▼　▲

The first time Cat answers, I hang up.

Dumb, I know, but I forgot what I was going to say and panicked. I'm still intimidated as heck by this chick, and apparently, the phone does not shield me from my tongue-tied admiration.

I wait a decent interval, so she won't know I'm the weirdo who hung up, then call again.

"The Natural Twenty," a husky voice says. "Cat speaking. What can I roll you for?"

I giggle because that pun will never stop being adorable, then blank again.

"Hello?"

"Hi."

Awkward pause while I search my mind for words.

"Can I help you?"

"No, but I think I can help you," I squeak out. It was supposed to sound cool and confident, like something Cat would say. It came out weird—precisely the type of thing I would say. It's all I can do not to hang up again.

There's another brief silence, then a throaty chuckle. "Oh, really?"

"Um, yeah."

"Go on. I'm intrigued."

Go on. OK, I can do that. "It's about Winter-Con."

"You want to buy tickets?"

"No. I mean, of course I do. I'm going to. But that's not why I called."

"OK, punkin'. Why *did* you call?"

I can't believe she hasn't hung up yet. She must think she's being pranked by a toddler who just discovered the phone. "So. Um. My brother made this game. . ."

"Mm-hm. That's cool."

"It is cool." What am I? A parrot?

"And?"

"I think you should put it in the gaming room Saturday."

"You want me to put your big brother's game in my event?" She sounds skeptically amused.

"Yeah, it's really good." I'm selling this horribly, and I know it. Why didn't I make note cards or write out a speech or something? This is a disaster.

"I'm sure it is, punkin'." Her voice is warm as she lets me down gently. "But I'm gonna have to take a pass. I already have a full roster—"

"Don't you want some local talent?!" I screech, anxiety clawing at my chest. Everything's riding on this plan. It's all I've got. I have to prove to Devin he can do this, that the time and distance *is* worth it, before it's too late. By the time the New Year rolls around, he's going to throw all his dreams away, pull out of UCA, and bury himself here.

With nothing to do in his spare time but take care of me.

Shudder.

I'm not letting this lady get off the phone until she agrees to at least *look* at his game. It's a matter of life and death. Well, life, anyway. I need my life back, and so does Devin.

If I can't convince her, how can I convince him?

"I'm sorry, but it's a no. I'm sure your brother's very nice—"

"He's not!" Adrenaline tinged with desperation crashes through me, swallowing up my nerves. My hands still shake as the torrent of words pours out, but my shyness has been replaced by the frantic need to convince her. "I mean, he is, but that's not why you need his game."

"Pumpkin . . ." she says, her voice low and soothing. "I love that you're such an awesome little sis. Your brother's lucky to have you in his corner, but I don't need any more games. How about let's drop it for now and I'll comp your Winter-Con ticket?"

The blood rushes to my cheeks as hot, angry tears sting my eyes. I am so, so sick of people blowing me off and telling me to "drop it." First Devin, then Mom, now Cat. This is too important to drop, and I'm done letting people ignore me.

"No. I will not drop it," I burst out. "You're not even listening to me. I'm trying to explain."

"Explain what, exactly?"

"Why you need this game."

"Why do I need this game?"

"You need it because it's good. Because it's fun. Because it's weird and strangely personal. Because . . . because . . ." What else? "Because I like it so much, I'm not even mad he made me a *baby beholder in a fanny pack*!"

"Wait, what?" she busts out laughing. I can't tell if it's at me or baby beholders in general, but either way, it's not cool.

"You heard me, ma'am!"

"Ma'am?" she says, still giggling. "I'm only twenty-eight."

"Then you are old enough to know quality content when you see it."

"All right, now, punkin.' Simmer down." She lets out a low shushing sound, and then chuckles *again*.

"No, not until you stop laughing at me. And I am not your punkin'. My name is Riley, and I will not simmer down," I assert proudly. "I am going to go to the computer, pull up my brother's ridiculously awesome game, and I'm going to send it to you, and you can't stop me because your email address is on your website."

"You got me there."

"That's right, I do." I point my finger at the phone, scowling. "I defy you not to enjoy this game."

"You defy me?"

"Yes. I defy you."

"OK, well, you do that."

"I will."

"Great." She sounds hugely entertained, but me? I can't tell if I'm about to throw up, cry, or keep on raging.

"It *is* great," I insist. "Just like Devin's game."

"Awesome. Send it over."

"Oh, you'd like that, wouldn't you?" I snarl, then freeze as my brain registers what was actually said. "What, really?" I say in a tiny voice.

"Don't get all meek on me now, pun—Riley," Cat says. "I want you to hang up that phone, march over to your computer, and send me that game, whether I like it or not. Any game that whips up that kind of fury is a game worth playing."

"For real?"

"For real, I've got be honest, though, you had me at baby beholder in a fanny pack."

So, of course, there is a slight snag. Devin's game is too ginormous to be emailed. I try seven times, but all I get is a lot of nope. Apparently, I can only send 10 megabytes of attachments. And apparently, Devin's game is a heckuva lot more than that.

Luckily, I have Google. I do a quick search: *How can I send a game that is too stinking big for email?* After scrolling through a dozen hits that make no sense, I land on an actually useful suggestion: *Upload it to a game-hosting site, like Discover or Cover, then send the link.*

I scroll a bit more on Google and then decide, OK, let's try it.

I run to the window, peep to make sure Devin's nowhere in sight, then scuttle back to the laptop. The website loads and welcomes me to Discover or Cover, which is written out in neon-green block letters, centered between two icons. The first is a picture of a magnifying glass held over a computer screen, while the second is a picture of a computer flattened by a rock.

I click on the how-to and read as fast as my little eyeballs will carry me. The deal is anybody can upload a game to the site and anybody around the world can play it. Then players rate the game on a scale of 1 to 5 magnifying glasses—1 is the suck, 5 is the awesome. After one week of being up, any game with an average of 3 magnifying glasses or higher is considered "discovered" and gets to stay. All the 0-, 1-, and 2-rated games get deleted—aka covered.

They strongly encourage you to send the link to everyone you've ever met or bumped into on the Internet because there's so many games in the newbie section, it's hard to get noticed—let alone played. That's fine by me. I only need it up long enough to show Cat and get played at Winter-Con. A week will do perfectly.

I create a log-in, read the Terms and Conditions, and upload the game.

Two minutes after I hit Send on my email to Cat, Devin comes home and parks his happy behind on the living-room sofa. For the rest of the night.

Blocking any hopes of secret access to the Almost Office computer.

I am in agony, and not just because Devin won't stop asking me how my headache is.

CHAPTER 20 3

AROUND ONE A.M., I POP OUT OF BED, HEAD TO THE ALMOST
Office, and fire up the computer. If, by some freak and unfortunate
chance, Devin wakes up and busts me, I plan on telling him I'm
googling herbal remedies for headaches.

I can't wait any longer. I have to check my email.

Fingers and toes crossed, breath held, I wait for the screen to load.

Yes!

Cat@Natural20.net has responded.

> Dear Riley,
>
> Give me a call tomorrow.
>
> I can't stop you because the number is on my website.
>
> But you already knew that, didn't you?
>
> —Cat

Grinning, I make my way back to bed.

▲　▼　▲　▼　▲

I take Cat up on her offer and call her the second I wake up.

"Riley, the store's not even open yet." Cat laughs.

Yeah, well, it's not like I'm guaranteed any privacy around this place lately. I've got to grab any chance I can get—and the only sure chance is while Devin's still sleeping. Besides, the wait was killing me.

"You said tomorrow," I remind her. "It's tomorrow."

"Well, looky here. So it is. Right there on the calendar—tomorrow."

"I don't like suspense," I whisper, more to myself than to her.

"Really? I love it, but everybody's different. OK, here's the deal: the game is rad."

"No way!" I shriek, then clap a hand over my mouth. After a quick listen to make sure the shower's still running, I lower my voice. "I mean, *I* know it is. But you think so too?"

"Oh, yeah. It's magically apocalyptic—just my jam. Gave it all five magnifying glasses, and that's not something I do lightly."

My grin hurts my mouth. "You're going to put it in Winter-Con?"

"Yup. Gonna square off a corner for 'local talent.' Heard that's what I needed. So, give me his details."

After I rattle off his name, age, and a little bit of a bio, she asks me about myself. "What's your deal? What are you into? You a computer geek too?"

"Not so much. I'm more of a role-playing nerd."

"Ooh, I likey. You got a group?"

Before I know it, I'm rattling off the entire history of my party. Cat listens attentively, interjecting "Awesome!" and "That's what I'm talking about" at all the right parts.

"Speaking of local talent," she says, when I finally stop to draw breath. "I'm thinking about adding a thirteen-and-under roleplaying table this year."

"Ooh, I'd love that!"

"Right? Kids don't want to play with someone they gotta call ma'am." She laughs. "You in?"

"I am so incredibly in. I can't wait to play."

"I'm not asking you to play, Riley. I'm asking you to DM."

My heart stops.

Did Cat just ask me to run a table at Winter-Con?

Me?

The girl who four months ago couldn't even make her own sandwich or find her own bus? This can't be real.

"Riley—you there?"

"I'm here." I may need an ambulance shortly, but I'm here.

"You can do it then, right?"

Can I? Talk in front strangers? Lead them? Make sure they have fun? There are so many thoughts in my brain, it makes me dizzy. I'm about to tell her no, tell her to ask Lucy instead, but then it occurs to me—that's exactly what Devin would expect me to do. Chicken out like a little coward.

Well, I won't.

I'm going to show him I can handle this. Then he'll see have to see that I'm OK. That I'm strong. That he can live his own life and follow his dreams, and so can I. We can be our own people and still love each other. It might even make us love each other more.

I gulp hard and hope my voice doesn't shake.

"Yes."

▲ ▽ ▲ ▽ ▲

Thursday afternoon marks a momentous occasion, because on Thursday afternoon, Devin lets me walk to Lucy's.

Yes. A whole ten yards.

By *myself.*

Without checking my backpack, planner, or homework first.

I've been showcasing all of my most responsible habits and manners, and it must be paying off. Or Devin meant it when he said he wasn't going to be such a butthead anymore. He's definitely been making an effort, which would be great if he wasn't so sad. He pretends he's not, but the forced smiles and fake humming almost make me miss the muttering.

I can't wait until Saturday. He still says he's not going to Winter-Con, but we'll see about that. I have my ways.

"You have to see this." Lucy yanks open the door before I even knock.

"Hello to you too."

"Hello, yourself." She takes off down the hall. "For real, I've got something to show you."

"OK . . ." I break into a jog to keep up.

Hannah is sitting cross-legged on the bed, with Lucy's laptop balanced across her knees. Lucy snatches it from her and points it at me.

"Hey! I was playing that!" Hannah pouts.

It takes a minute for my eyes to register what's on the screen. Then I see it: Cry of the Beholder.

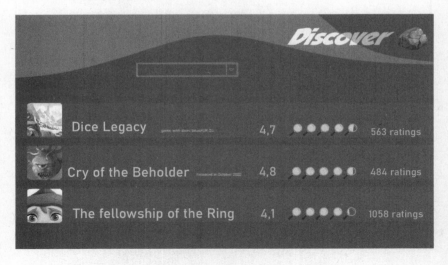

With 484 playthroughs, with an average of 4.8 magnifying glasses, an almost-perfect Discover rating.

"Oh my God. Oh my God." I sink onto the bed and stare at the screen. Devin is going to die. He is going to supernova in joy, die, and go to computer-geek heaven.

"It's this week's featured game." Lucy grins. "Look at the comments! People love it!"

Bruh, so cool.

Awesome. Weird, but awesome.

When's the sequel?

There's pages and pages of comments. I want to print them all and wallpaper Devin's room with them. Well, not the one where the jerk said it was the stupidest thing he'd ever seen, but the rest of them.

"Are you going to show him?" Lucy asks. "If that doesn't send him running back to California full of confidence and inspiration, I don't know what will."

"I'm definitely going to show him," I say. "But I think I'll wait for the big reveal at Winter-Con—make it, like, a *huge* surprise. Plus, he's a bit of a wild card lately. I don't want him to get all weird and take it down. I'll look like an idiot in front of Cat."

"That makes sense."

"You should show his teacher," Hannah says. "You know, the one that hurt his precious widdle feelings."

"You know . . . that's not a bad idea," I say. "I'll get up early Saturday and link it to her before we go. I'll bet they have faculty emails on their website."

"Solid plan." Lucy nods. "What about *you*? Are you ready for Saturday?"

"You know, I thought I'd be all cold sweats and barfing-my-brains-out nervous, but I'm not. I'm really, really excited. I think maybe I've got this."

▲　▼　▲　▼　▲

"Hey, welcome home!" Devin grabs his keys off the coffee table, then pulls an exhausted-looking Mom in for a hug. "I'm gonna pick up a pizza for dinner. Why don't you go take a nice hot bath? Wash off all the work."

"You're the best." She smiles up at him, holding his face in her hands. He looks even more exhausted than Mom, except he didn't work all day. He didn't really do much of anything at all, so there's no reason for those dark shadows under his eyes or the paleness in his cheeks. Mom's smile doesn't quite reach her eyes, but he doesn't seem to notice. He fake-grins back down at her, oblivious to her clenched jaw and searching gaze. I see it, though. She's worried about him, and it's gonna take a lot more than a hot bath to make her feel better.

She's got to be ready to give him a push by now. A nice, gentle, confidence-building one. I know she told me to drop it, but as Cat found out, I'm not really good at that. Besides, if my plan's going to work—*really* work—Mom and I need to be on the same team.

The second Devin's out the door, I pounce. "Hey, Mom?"

"Yeah?"

"We need to talk."

"Ooh." Mom shudders. "Are there four more anxiety-producing words in all the English language?"

Hm. Probably not. "Sorry. It's important."

Mom pulls me over to the couch. "What's up?"

"Um. OK." I take a deep breath. "I'm pretty sure you already know this, but Devin's not getting any happier. He's being nicer, yeah, but he's still bummed-out."

Mom bites her lip, nodding slightly. "I know, baby, and I know you're worried."

"Maybe," I say, "he needs a little encouragement."

"I'm encouraging," Mom crosses her arms defensively. "I've done nothing but encourage him since he got home."

"Oh, I know," I say quickly. "That's not what I meant. What I mean is maybe he needs some encouragement from neutral parties."

"Riley," Mom uncrosses her arms and leans forward. She grabs hold of my shoulders and looks deep into my eyes. "I love you, but I have no idea what you're talking about, so if you've got something to say, spit it out already."

It's a little rude, but way better than being blown off. "OK, well, here's the thing. I have a plan. A really, really good one." I spill all the details: Cry of the Beholder, my phone call with Cat, Devin's showcase at Winter-Con, my plan to trick him into coming to Winter-Con to see his triumph and get covered in true gamer glory. Mom's eyes widen as I pour out the story, and by the time I finish, there's a real, genuine grin covering her face.

"What do you think?" I ask, half-terrified she'll make me call it off.

"I think Devin is the luckiest big brother in the world." Tears fill her eyes, but the tightness in her jaw is gone. "It's just . . . are *you* going to be OK if he doesn't see it that way? Devin's a pretty private person, and while what you're doing is lovely, he might be angry you shared his work without asking."

"But he was never going to share," I say. "He was too insecure to even show his professor. I *had* to or else he'd never see how great he was."

"Hey." Mom takes my hand in hers. "I'm with you, and I think it's worth a shot. I just wanted to make sure you are prepared, just in case things don't go how you imagined them."

"But you do think it will work, right?"

"If it doesn't, nothing will," Mom says. "He's going to have to see how much *everybody* loves his work, not just his mom and sister. How can he quit after that? How can we let him? I'll shove him in his suitcase and drive him back myself."

The mental picture is hilarious, but I'm not ready to laugh. "And we're OK, too, aren't we? You know that you're a good mom and that I'm not an idiot and that I really can use the microwave, right?"

"I never thought you were an idiot."

"OK, maybe not. But you did think I was kind of a baby."

"*My* baby."

"Nice deflection." I roll my eyes.

"I don't think you're a baby," Mom says, squeezing my hand back. "You've grown so much in the past few months. You're more confident—mature, even. You ride the bus without complaining. You do the laundry. You help around the house. You listen to all my petty vents. You started a laundry-room D&D group, for Pete's sake. All while keeping your grades up."

"All without Devin," I remind her.

"Yeah," she says, her eyes glistening. "And you've also done a lot *for* Devin too. Don't think for a minute I don't see that."

"Pizza's here!" Devin bursts through the door, then stops abruptly as he spies Mom and me on the couch, deep in our feels. "Whoa, what's going on here?"

"Girl talk?" I offer.

"Yep, just a little girl talk." Mom pats my knee and shoots me a sly smile. "I'll grab some plates, and Riley, why don't you pick a movie?"

Once the pizza was eaten and the *Captain Marvel* credits had rolled, I head off to bed. "I'd better get some sleep. Winter-Con tomorrow, you know," I say. "You sure you don't want to go, Devin?" Figure I'll give it one more shot.

"Nah," he says, heartlessly shooting my shot down. "You go ahead. Have a good time."

"Oh, hey, Devin?" Mom says. "I know I told you I was off tomorrow, but I got called in. Keep your phone on, will you? Just in case Riley needs you. Hannah's mom's taking her, but just in case."

"Yeah, of course," he says.

"Good. We're all set then!" Mom blows me a kiss good night, accompanied by a sly wink.

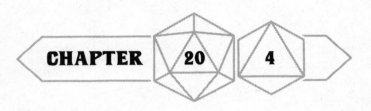

CHAPTER 20 4

"THIS. IS. AWESOME," LUCY WHISPERS.

The four of us squeeze into the Natural 20 and we are suddenly surrounded on all sides by dwarves, elves, superheroes, anime characters, and wall-to-wall comics.

The Natural 20 is a fantasy winter wonderland. An icy-blue frost dragon hangs from the ceiling, its silky wings billowing over the main room, while a large cut-out ice golem glowers at us from behind the cash register. The front counter is laced with snowflake garland and piled high with entry forms for the cosplay contest. To our left, a trio of artists wielding silver Sharpies sits behind a folding table scattered with comic books. Straight ahead, a frozen elemental statuette presides over

a packed table. They're already deep into the Icewind Dale campaign, oblivious to the crowds that press by them.

I peek past them toward the back. There are four more rooms in the building, usually reserved for casual game nights and parties. Today, though, one of them is packed with computers, with Devin's game up on the screen. Another one of those rooms has a table for me.

The crowd parts and Cat walks through. She's wearing white leather pants, a matching crop top, and ankle boots. A spiked silver crown rests on her short blond hair, and her skin is dusted with pale silver.

Coolest. Snow Queen. Ever.

"Hey!" I flag her down awkwardly. "I'm, um, Riley."

"Hi, um-Riley." She smiles at me. "I didn't realize we'd already met. You're the savvy shopper with the ranger friend."

"Present!" Hannah trills, raising her hand.

"And accounted for," Cat shoots her a finger gun, then turns back to me. "You'll start your game in about an hour or so, cool? It'll give you some time to hang out. But first, I want to show you something."

Once again, the crowd steps aside as she makes her way to the back of the store. We follow her down a hallway lined with movie posters and fantasy art, then hang a right. Long tables line the walls, and folding chairs pull up to computers. Cat points to three filled seats in the corner, and I gasp. Above the absorbed gamers, there's a beautifully lettered poster: "Cry of the Beholder by local developer Devin Henderson."

"Ooh," Jen says. "They are into it. Not that I blame them. Don't tell my mom, but I stayed up way too late last night playing. By the way, you're the baby, aren't you?" She looks me up and down. "Yeah, you're totally the baby."

"Shut up," I say, but I laugh. This is better than perfect. Not only are people playing it and loving it—there's a line. Time to get Devin down here.

"Where's your brother?" Cat asks, reading my mind. "I want to introduce him to everybody."

"Oh. Um. Running late?" I shrug. "Lucy, can I borrow your phone?"

She hands it over, and I scoot into the hallway, flattening myself against the wall.

Devin answers on the first ring.

"Is everything all right?" he asks the second he knows it's me.

I'm a little offended. I mean, why wouldn't everything be all right? But then I remember the purpose of my call. "No," I say weakly. "I'm sick."

"You're sick? Is it the headache again?"

"No. It's worse. I just threw up in the bathroom." I cough weakly, then realize that makes no sense if my ailment is vomiting.

Devin doesn't even notice. He's so racked with concern, I almost feel guilty. "Oh no, Riley," he says, all sympathy.

"Yeah, can you come get me? Hannah's mom won't be back for hours, and I feel really, *really* bad."

"I'll be there as soon as I can. Wait for me out front?"

"No, it's too cold out there. Cat said I could wait in the back."

"That's nice of her. I'll be right there. See you soon."

I hang up with a smug smile on my face. *That's right, my minion, hustle on down here. I'm not all you'll see.*

Devin makes it to the store in fifteen minutes flat. "Riley!" He pushes through the crowd, sending up a chorus of muttered hey-man's and watch-it-dude's. He reaches the corner of the game room where my friends and I are perched, watching gleefully as folks play his game. "Shouldn't you be sitting down?" He grabs my hand and pulls me toward the door.

Lucy, Hannah, and Jen start to giggle.

"Maybe you're the one who should sit down," Hannah says.

He freezes, dropping my hand and his jaw, and stares wide-eyed at the gamer over my shoulder. Well, his screen, actually.

"What the *heck* is *this*?" Devin hisses. His pale face turns all kinds of red, and his breath comes out in ragged bursts. He doesn't even try to fake a smile. "Riley, *what did you do?*"

I step back, swallowing hard. This wasn't how it was supposed to go at all. He's not supposed to be mad. Just surprised and happy. My stomach drops and I feel like I'm about to throw up for real.

Mom bursts through the crowd, saving me from having to answer right away. "Riley! Devin! Where is it? Where's the game? I have to see this!"

"Did somebody say Devin? I've been looking all over for that elusive weirdo." Suddenly, Cat is gliding toward us as well. She looks my brother up and down and grins. "You've got to be Devin. The resemblance is truly uncanny, beholder-boy."

She's not wrong. Not only is he wearing his signature T-shirt, ripped jeans, and Vans, but his eyes are bulging out so far, they're practically taking up his entire head.

And he did hiss at me . . .

"I'm sorry," Devin says, after shooting a *HOW COULD YOU?* glare my way and a *YOU HAVE BETRAYED ME!* glower Mom's way. "I'm a little confused."

Cat's eyes flick from me to Devin, then back to me. "Oh. I see what's going on here."

"Great, you can fill me in," Devin says. "Because I'm not one hundred percent sure I get it. Riley, you're not sick?"

I mumble something that is supposed to be a no as my friends move in closer around me and Lucy rests a hand on my back.

"You didn't tell your brother you called me, did you?" Cat asks.

I shake my head, not really feeling up to actual words.

"Did you tell him you put his game on Discover or Cover?"

"No."

Cat throws back her head and laughs, loud and long.

Devin, unfortunately, does not. "You *posted* my *game*? Without my *permission*? Why would you do that?" he shouts. "That's humiliating!"

A wave of side-eyes and straight-up stares washes over me, following his shout. Now, *that's* humiliating. I blush so hard my face hurts. So hard that it makes me mad.

"No, it's not," I holler right back. "What's *humiliating* is having nothing better to do than follow your twelve-year-old sister around. What's humiliating is slinking home to Florida with your tail between your legs, moping around the house all day because you *got a C in one class*. What's humiliating is giving up on your dreams because some teacher hurt your precious widdle feelings."

Jen snorts.

"What's *not* humiliating," I continue as I glare up at him, one hand on my hip, the other pointing a finger in his face, "is getting over five hundred hits on Discover or Cover, with a rating of . . . what was it again, girls?"

"Four point eight!" Lucy, Hannah, and Jen shout in unison.

"That's right. Four point eight. Definitely *not* humiliating. Neither is landing a featured spot at Winter-Con and a sign with your name on it." I quit waving my finger in his face and use it to point at the sign on the wall.

"Four point eight?" Devin whispers. The blood drains from his face, and his cheeks go from red-hot rage to pale, pasty surprise. He shoves his hands in his pockets, but not before I see that they're trembling.

"Yes. Four point eight, you brat." Mom grins, giving him a light shove. "And, yeah, I know I'm just some old lady who hasn't played a game since Oregon Trail, but even I know what a big deal that is."

"Speaking of a big deal, there's one more thing I didn't tell you." I take a breath, lift my chin, and say, "I sent the link to Dr. Duncan too."

"You *what*?" Devin's eyebrows fly up so high, they disappear beneath his overgrown bangs. His breath comes in ragged bursts, and his chest heaves beneath his loose T-shirt.

"I emailed her the link and told her to check it out. You know, her email is on the school website."

"And she couldn't stop you, right?" Cat grins at me slyly.

"Precisely." I nod. "She said she's going to take a look and email you later."

"I'm sure she loved it," Mom adds.

"What?!" Devin shrieks and whips his phone out his back pocket. His thumbs shake as he pulls up his email, and his eyes track wildly back and forth across the screen. I almost feel bad for him. *Almost.* But I know she's going to love it. I just know it. Even if she doesn't—what's she going to do? Argue with five hundred upvotes?

I cross my arms in front of me. "She email you already?"

Devin gives me a look, then holds the phone up, inches from my face.

> Hi, Devin!
>
> I hope all is well, and you're enjoying your time away. I was disappointed to see that you'd withdrawn from my class, but it looks like you've definitely been refilling the creative well. Your sis (cool kid, by the way) sent me Cry of the Beholder. Solid work. It's a new take on an iconic creature, and I like that I see YOU in it. Where were you hiding this away all semester? I'm interested to see what you do in our course on character development next term, should you return.
>
> Happy holidays!
>
> All good wishes,
>
> Dr. Duncan
>
> P.S. I do hope that you return.

I look past the phone to Devin and meet his eyes. And are those . . . *tears?*

"Come here," I say, pulling him out of the hallway. Nestled in a quiet corner between a *The Force Awakens* poster and a Chewbacca cutout, I throw my arms around him and give him a huge squeeze. "You can be mad at me all you want, but I'm glad everybody got to play your game."

"I am too," he says softly.

"Really?"

"Yeah. I'd never have been brave enough to post it, though." He scoffs and shakes his head. "Not after I got my precious widdle feelings hurt."

"Sorry. I shouldn't have said that."

"Nah, you were right. I was being a baby. But you—that was pretty gutsy." He cocks his head and looks at me curiously. "What'd you do? Cold-call Cat and beg her to take my game?"

"I *did not* beg," I say haughtily. "I simply told her how good it was."

"And she took it? Just like that?"

"Not really. She tried to hustle me off the phone at first, but I wasn't having it. I defied her not to like it and, in the end, she couldn't resist."

"That's awesome." He laughs, then sighs. "You really are growing up."

"OK, first of all, you sound forty when you say stuff like that," I say. "Second of all, you're right, I am. Which means you can go back to California. You *should* go back to California. I know I fought you hard on it, and I know I laid down some serious guilt trips, but you were right to go."

"I don't know. I still think—"

"What? That going away to college makes you like Dad?"

His eyes widen, then his gaze drops to the floor.

"It doesn't," I say, refusing to give him the chance to try to convince either of us otherwise. "You know it doesn't. You're a huge part of my life no matter where you are. He's not. Even if he lived in the apartment next door, he wouldn't be. But I'm OK with that because I've always had you, and I know I always will."

"You will. I promise."

"I know. I believe you. But I need you to trust me too. I need you to believe that I'm going to be OK—even when you're not there to cut the crust off my sandwiches. Which, um, by the way, I actually *like* the crust."

"For real?"

"For real. Shocker, I know." I punch him in the arm. "So, go. Get out of town. What do I need you for? You can't even make my sandwiches right. And don't get me started on your terrible mac and cheese . . ."

"Ouch." He laughs, then gives me a long, serious look. "You mean it? You think I should go back? But what about Mom?"

"Mom is fine." Mom steps into our hallway, hands on her hips. There's a Wonder Woman poster on the wall behind her, and the resemblance is uncanny. "Better than fine. Fabulous, even. You may not remember this, kid, but I changed your diapers. I drove you to your very first Winter-Con. I bought you your first computer, your first set of dice, and your first Final Fantasy game. I set up your Steam account and helped you track down the perfect wireless controller. More than all that, though, I raised you, and you're awesome. Can you trust me enough to take care of your sister when you're gone?"

"Of course, I'm sorry." Devin swallows hard. "I love you. You know that, right?"

"I do. But I need you to believe in me too," she says seriously. "You're awesome and all, but I'm not exactly helpless without you. I *can* handle my own business, you know? I might not handle it the way you or Valerie would, but I've raised awesome kids, so I must be doing *something* right."

"You are," Devin and I say in unison.

"Good. Then, Devin, you listen to me, and you listen good: You're taking your happy behind back to California in January. No take-backs. No more moping around my house. I don't want to see you until spring break."

"I get it, I get it." Laughing, Devin puts up his hands and steps away. "You can't wait for me to leave. Don't worry—I won't let the door hit me on the way out."

"About time," I say, grinning. Mom laughs and pulls me and Devin in for a three-way hug. I lean my cheek on her shoulder as Devin squeezes my arm. In that moment, I know we'll all be OK. Even when we're far apart.

"Riley?" The leather-clad snow queen sashays down the hall. "You ready? Your table's filling up fast."

"Ready for what?" Devin asks.

Untangling myself from the tight group hug, I wipe my eyes and comb my fingers through my hair. "Oh, I'm DMing a game in a minute."

"What?" His jaw drops, for, like, the thirtieth time today.

Mom pats his arm and gives him a smile. "I don't think you need to worry about Riley."

I follow Cat through the store, running through my campaign in my mind. I still can't believe I'm going to be a Winter-Con DM—that Cat asked me, of all people. A year ago, I would've been too scared to even join a game. But then again, a year ago, I wouldn't have done *anything* without Devin's help.

Who would have guessed he'd ever need mine?

So much has changed, but it's all for the good. Devin, Mom, and I, we're becoming the people we need to be, and I think that's the ultimate campaign.

"I brought your DM screen in," Lucy says as I settle into my seat at the head of the table.

"Your dice are right here." Jen smiles and drops them into my palm.

"We're playing with *boys*," Hannah whispers way too loudly, then gives me an exaggerated wink.

I look around the table, and it is packed. Some kids I recognize from school, like James, the boy with golden-brown skin, wavy hair, and a Zelda tee. He sits next to me in history, but we've never actually talked before. Pretty sure we will after this. He looks *really* excited to be here, bouncing around in his seat and grinning.

There's also Carmen, the tiny girl with the curly brown hair. She's in health class with me and Lucy, but she never says much. She smiles shyly at me from across the table.

The rest are new faces—all friendly, smiling, and eager to get started.

OK.

I guess I should get started then.

"So," I say, "does everybody have a character?"

"Please say no, please say no," Hannah chants, crossing her fingers.

Is she OK? "Why no?"

"Because then we can call Lucy's dad and make him bring us cupcakes."

"Oh," I say with a big grin. "I see."

A chorus of "What?" trickles around the table, and we're forced to explain our character-creation tradition.

"I don't have a character yet," Carmen says softly. "But don't worry about it, I'm just going to watch."

"Oh no, you're not," Jen says with a smile, and pulls out her dice.

"Yeah," Hannah pipes in. "We can totally speed-roll you a guy."

Lucy grabs the *Player's Handbook* out from under her chair and flips through to the Class page. "What do you think you'd like to be? You can be anything you want, you know."

The rest of the table leans in. Everybody loves a birthday party, and for the next few minutes we all work together to birth this half-elf bard of a baby.

I look up to see Devin in the doorway, watching. He looks happy.

Even better, he looks like himself.

"Hey, Devin?" I call, peeking over the edge of my DM screen. "You wanna pull up a chair?"

"Nah, I bumped into Evie a few minutes ago. I told her I'd meet her at the 'grown-up' table." He puts air-quotes around the word "grown-up," grinning slyly. "Besides, you've got this."

He's right. I do.

I take a deep breath and begin.

You stand at a crossroads, weighing your options beneath the pale moonlight.

To the right, the road is smooth. Well-marked signs point the way to the nearest inn, and not a pebble mars your path.

To the left, the road is treacherous. It is an uphill climb, overrun with brambles and littered with rocks and potholes. In the distance you see a glimmer of light, accompanied by the most beautiful music you have ever heard. Though the notes are soft, they fill you with excitement.

Which path do you choose?

ACKNOWLEDGMENTS

One of the best things about D&D is that it's never a solo endeavor. Campaigns are shaped and won by the party, with lots of fun and silliness along the way. Writing this book was a lot like that. Without the help and support of some magical folks, *Roll for Initiative* would never have happened.

To Lauren Galit, my agent, thank you for helping me to see what this book could be. Throughout all the drafts of this story, you were there to buff my intelligence with your feedback and insight. Your support and belief in my work over the years means more than you'll ever know.

To Britny Brooks, my editor, thank you for loving, understanding, and taking on my story. Your wisdom, enthusiasm, and epic nerdiness were exactly what this book needed to level up. This new adventure has been a joy and one that I will always treasure.

To Miriam Spitzer Franklin, thank you so much for your mentorship. Your belief in my early work, along with your guidance and advice, pushed me to grow as a writer while giving me the confidence to know I could.

To Caitlen Rubino-Bradway, thank you so much for your advice and support over the years. And thanks for lending your DM's eye to this early manuscript—you've helped me so much! To Amber Morris, my production editor, thank you for the care and skill in which you helped this book come together. To Rachelle Mandik, my copyeditor, thank you for your hard work and eagle eyes. It was so amazing to see the artistry and skill with which this book came together. Thanks to the stunning illustrations of Sara Gianassi and the brilliant design of Marissa Raybuck, *Roll for Initiative* has truly come to life. Thank you both for your talent and hard work.

Tommy! It happened! It really, really happened. You've been telling me it would, starting way back in the day when you gave me that little pink laptop. Thank you for being the amazing, supportive, brilliant, fun husband you are, and thanks for always believing in me. Looking forward to adventuring with you for many more years to come (also known as forever and ever).

Thank you to my wonderful children. To Dillan, for your D&D expertise and middle-grade-book love. To Isaac, for cheering me on through revisions and the tough times. To Elijah, for always believing that one day I'd have my own book. To Melanie, for reading over my shoulder and asking good questions. Love you all so much.

To Pat and Joe, the best parents a kid could have. You always encouraged me, no matter what I want to do, whether it be violin, guitar, photography, dance, voice, or theatre. You always gave me freedom to explore and be creative, and I appreciate it so much. To my siblings, Amy, Emily, and Jeremy, thank you for a magical childhood. No better dramatic training than a Gaskin Christmas play.

And to the students and staff of Woodville School, thank you all. Your creativity, intelligence, and bravery inspire me every day. Go, Mustangs!